Paul Leicester Ford, Benjamin Franklin

The Prefaces, Proverbs, and Poems of Benjamin Franklin

Originally Printed in Poor Richard's Almanacs for 1733-1758

Paul Leicester Ford, Benjamin Franklin

The Prefaces, Proverbs, and Poems of Benjamin Franklin
Originally Printed in Poor Richard's Almanacs for 1733-1758

ISBN/EAN: 9783337254872

Printed in Europe, USA, Canada, Australia, Japan

Cover: Foto ©Raphael Reischuk / pixelio.de

More available books at **www.hansebooks.com**

"*THE SAYINGS OF POOR RICHARD*"

THE

PREFACES, PROVERBS, AND POEMS

OF

BENJAMIN FRANKLIN

ORIGINALLY PRINTED IN

POOR RICHARD'S ALMANACS FOR 1733-1758

COLLECTED AND EDITED

BY

PAUL LEICESTER FORD

NEW YORK AND LONDON

G. P. PUTNAM'S SONS

The Knickerbocker Press

Poor Richard, 1733.

AN

Almanack

For the Year of Chrift

1733,

Being the Firft after LEAP YEAR.

And makes fince the Creation	Years
By the Account of the Eaftern *Greeks*	7241
By the Latin Church, when ☉ ent. ♈	6932
By the Computation of *W. W.*	5742
By the *Roman* Chronology	5682
By the *Jewifh* Rabbies.	5494

Wherein is contained

The Lunations, Eclipfes, Judgment of
the Weather, Spring Tides, Planets Motions &
mutual Afpects, Sun and Moon's Rifing and Setting, Length of Days, Time of High Water,
Fairs, Courts, and obfervable Days.

Fitted to the Latitude of Forty Degrees,
and a Meridian of Five Hours Weft from *London*,
but may without fenfible Error, ferve all the ad-
jacent Places, even from *Newfoundland* to *South-
Carolina*

By *RICHARD SAUNDERS*, Philom.

PHILADELPHIA:
Printed and fold by *B. FRANKLIN*, at the New-
Printing-Office near the Market

Note, This ALMANACK *us'd to contain but* 24 *Pages, and now has* 36 ; *yet the Price is very little advanc'd.*

Poor RICHARD improved:

BEING AN
ALMANACK
AND
EPHEMERIS
OF THE
MOTIONS of the SUN and MOON;
THE TRUE
PLACES and ASPECTS of the PLANETS;
THE
RISING and *SETTING* of the *SUN;*
AND THE
Rising, Setting *and* Southing *of the* Moon,
FOR THE
BISSEXTILE YEAR, 1748.

Containing also,

The Lunations, Conjunctions, Eclipses, Judgment of the Weather, Rising and Setting of the Planets, Length of Days and Nights, Fairs, Courts, Roads, &c. Together with useful Tables, chronological Observations, and entertaining Remarks.

Fitted to the Latitude of Forty Degrees, and a Meridian of near five Hours West from *London* ; but may, without sensible Error, serve all the NORTHERN COLONIES.

By *RICHARD SAUNDERS*, Philom.

PHILADELPHIA:
Printed and Sold by B. FRANKLIN.

INTRODUCTION.

A S one handles the little brown pamphlets,
so tattered, smoked, and soiled, which
constitute so large a proportion of American
colonial literature, it needs but small imagina-
tion to carry one back into the low-ceiled
kitchen, with its great broad fire-place, around
which the whole family nightly gathered,—
seated on settles whose high backs but ill shut
off the cold drafts that entered at doors, windows, and the chinks in the logs or clab-boards,
—their only light the fitful flame of the great
fore- and back-logs, eked out perhaps by a pine-
knot, or in more pretentious households by a
tallow-dip, suspended in its iron holder by a
hook in the mantel,—the mother and daughters
knitting, spinning, or skeining, with an eye on
the youngsters ; the sons making or mending
their farming tools, or cleaning their rifles and
traps ; while the grave and probably rheu-

matic sire studies the last printed sermon or theological tractate, newspaper, or political squib, "Death-bed Confession," or "Last Dying Speech," but most probably the weather predictions contained in the most valued of all publications—the Almanac,—and no doubt cogitates and worries over the impending ruin which the unfeeling philomath's prediction of "snow-blast" in July seems to entail upon him.

Few if any now living can appreciate how large a space this little pamphlet of a dozen leaves filled only one hundred years ago, and this importance increases as we trace it back to its first appearance in this country. To the present generation it is merely a cover for soap, patent medicine, or other quackery advertising, but in our colonial period it was the *vade mecum* of every household—a calendar, diary, meteorological bureau, jest-, recipe-, and indeed sometimes school-book; for, with the exception of the Bible, it was often the year's sole reading matter in many families, and a poor and shiftless one it was indeed, which, as the new year approached, had not the necessary sum, ranging from a penny to sixpence, to be exchanged for the annual issue. In every well-ordered kitchen a nail was driven in the chimney-breast, on which, as the old year waned, a

fresh almanac was hung. How eagerly must
all have read it for the first time ! How important were its weather predictions and statistical
matter ! How amusing its jokes and anecdotes,
which, served up anew year after year, were
greeted by no chestnut bell, and never became
old or stale. But if the humor was perennial,
not so the almanac ! Slowly as the season ad-
vanced it lost its first youthful freshness, became brown and thumbed, then ragged, till
when the trees commenced to shed their leaves
the almanac proved itself no bad imitator, and
its successor found no rival to contest its right
to the hook.

If we examine an almanac of the last century,
we are struck with the paucity of reading matter which sufficed to cause it to be read to pieces.
A title-page, which generally served as a table
of contents, and was often ornamented with
some frightful wood-cut, was usually followed
by an "Address to the Courteous Reader."
Then came the calendar, each month occupy-
ing a page, including, among other useful facts,
a weather prediction for each day or so, and
there was no hedging either. "High Wind,"
"Northwest Wind," "Raw and Chilly," "Frost,"
and "Snow-blast" are set down at random by
the philomaths with as much confidence and
certainty as if they were reporting yesterday's

weather, instead of predicting for six months
later. If the calendar failed to fill the page, the
matter was eked out by filling in the spaces at
the top or bottom with rhymes to the month
they chanced to be with, or with short anecdotes, mostly of a comic nature. If any pages
were left over from the calendar, they were
filled with extracts from books, by information
concerning the courts, the post-roads, facts in
history, or all combined.

We should hardly think the compiling of
such a work would entitle one to a high place
in the world of literature, but in "the good old
days of yore," a different value was set on
these productions, and so we find such time-
honored names as Chauncy, Sewall, Danforth,
Mather, and Dudley figuring on the title-page
as the compiler, or, as they were then almost
invariably styled, as the "philomath," or lover
of learning. To their readers, who still believed in witchcraft, governing stars, and horo-
scopes, the composition of an almanac savored
of magic, sorcery, if not illicit communion with
departed spirits, and the authors were therefore to them most awe-inspiring beings; and
probably the guild was not above adding to this
belief, as is shadowed in a poem of Philip Fre-
neau, written in the last century when the "art"
was first beginning to show signs of decay:

While others dwell on mean affairs,
Their Kings, their councils, and their Wars,
Philaster roves among the stars.

In melancholy silence he
Travels alone and cannot see
An equal for his company.

He tells us when the sun will rise
Points out fair days, or clouded skies ;—
No matter if he sometimes lies.

An annual Almanac to frame
And publish with pretended name
Is all his labour, all his aim.

   *   *   *   *   *   *

Thus nature waiting at his call,
His book, in vogue with great and small,
Is sought, admir'd, and read by all.

How happy thus on earth to stay
The planets keeping him in pay—
And when 't is time to post away

Old Saturn will the bait prepare,
And hook him up from toil and care
To make new calculations there.

But if the almanac and its compiler were of
great importance to the public, they were
equally so to the printer. Enjoying such a
popularity, the sales of the little pamphlet were
almost the only certain financial venture of the
year, and lucky was the printer who had secured the copy of a well-known and esteemed

philomath. To-day the bulk of these seem to differ little in accuracy or interest, but in the times when these were bought and read there were fashions and fads in almanacs, and while some flourished and brought money to both compiler and printer, others dragged along for a few years and finally disappeared.

Perhaps nothing better illustrates the place once held in American literature by these ephemera than the annals of American printing. A collection of the first issues of the early American presses established in the various towns would, with hardly an exception, consist of these little waifs. When, over two hundred and fifty years ago, Stephen Daye set up the first printing-office in this country, the first volume he printed was the almanac of "William Peirce, Mariner." When William Bradford, "after great Charge and Trouble," had "brought the great Art and Mystery of Printing" into the city of Philadelphia, Samuel Atkin's "Kalendarium Pennsilvaniense" was the first issue of his press. When the year's product of the three Philadelphia presses numbered but thirteen books, seven were almanacs, and the two of the six issues of the New York presses for this same year were of this character.

Such was the status of the almanac when, in the "first year of the reign of our well-be-

loved king, George II." and "of our Lord 1728,"
the youthful firm of " B. Franklin and H.
Meredith " set up the "New Printing Office
near the Market." However small and humble
the new venture opened, it had to have an almanac, and so the annual copy was engaged
from Thomas Godfrey, a Philadelphia scientist
of no mean note in those days, and contem-
porary inventor with Hadley of the quadrant.
For three years they published this with apparent satisfaction to all concerned, when a
match-making woman, in the person of Mrs.
Godfrey, enacted the Discordia, and introduced
the fatal apple. Franklin had rented the upper
part of his shop to the Godfreys, boarding with
them, and being of the weaker sex, Mrs. Godfrey naturally planned a match between the
seemingly prosperous young printer and a
marriageable relation. She made " opportunities of bringing us often together, till a serious
courtship on my part ensu'd, the girl being in
herself very deserving. The old folks encouraged me by continual invitations to supper, and
by leaving us alone together, till at length it
was time to explain." The prudent printer,
who in his almanac afterwards advised one to
" ne'er take a wife till thou hast a house (and a
fire) to put her in," "let her know that I [he]
expected as much money with their daughter

as would pay off my remaining debt for the printing house, which I believe was not then above a hundred pounds. She brought me word they had no such sum to spare ; I said they might mortgage their house in the loan-office. The answer to this, after some days, was, that they did not approve . . . and, there-fore, I was forbidden the house, and the daugh-ter shut up. . . . Mrs. Godfrey brought me afterward some more favorable accounts of their disposition, and would have drawn me on again ; but I declared absolutely my resolution to have nothing more to do with that family. This was resented by the Godfreys ; we differed, and they removed.''

Neither the loss of his lady-love nor tenants seem seriously to have inconvenienced the philosophic young printer, but one result of this courtship involved graver consequences to him. The Godfreys not merely ceased to be his tenants, but the philomath carried his yearly calculations to Andrew Bradford, Franklin's rival in the printing business, and near the end of the year 1732 the latter found himself in the lurch for the copy for his annual issue.

With the natural adaptability of the born Yankee, Franklin met this difficulty by com-piling his own almanac. Knowing, however, that the name of ''B. Franklin, printer,'' could hardly pass for a man of sufficient years and learning to be one of the philomathic brotherhood, he borrowed as a pen-name that of "Richard Saunders," the origi··· ·l of which belonged to an English "Chyrurgeon" of the eighteenth century, who for many years compiled a popular almanac entitled "The Apollo Anglicanus," which attained such a reputation that it was still published as late as 1781, though now quite forgot for its better-known western imitator. From another eighteenth-century English almanac entitled "Poor Robin," was probably derived the title of "Poor Richard," which so hit popular fancy; and under these borrowed plumes the almanac appeared.

The yearly issue was usually published as early as October of the preceding year, but the first intimation the city of brotherly love had of the new venture was, from the causes already mentioned, derived from the columns of *The Pennsylvania Gazette* of December 19, 1732, and was as follows :

"Just Published, for 1733 :

POOR RICHARD : An ALMANACK containing the Lunations, Eclipses, Planets Motions and Aspects, Weather, Sun and Moon's rising and setting, Highwater, &c. besides many pleasant and witty Verses, Jests and Sayings, Author's Motive of Writing, Prediction of the Death of his Friend Mr. *Titan* Leeds, Moon no Cuckold, Batchelor's Folly, Parson's Wine and Baker's Pudding, Short Visits, Kings and Bears, New Fashions,

Game for Kisses, Katherine's Love, Different Sentiments, Signs of a Tempest, Death a Fisherman, Con-
jugal Debate, Men and Melons, *H.* the Prodigal,
Breakfast in Bed, Oyster Lawsuit, &c. By RICHARD
SAUNDERS, Philomat. Printed and sold by *B. Franklin*, Price 3*s.* 6*d.* per Dozen. Of whom also may be had
Sheet Almanacks at 2*s.* 6*d.*"

It was not the custom of the time to advertise
to any extent. Most publishers of almanacs
thought they had done enough for their own
and the public's benefit when they had
announced through the press that "On Mon-
day next will be published, Leeds' Almanack
for ——" or "Now selling by the printer Jerman's Almanack for ——." It is easy to believe
then that this advertisement was of a nature to
attract notice, and make the public buy the
new almanac. Indeed it is the only explanation I have found for the almost instantaneous
large sale it met with. And sell it did—only a
trifle over two weeks after its first publication,
and in spite of the prejudicial fact that "A few
of the first that were printed had the Months of
September and October transposed," Franklin
announced in *The Pennsylvania Gazette* of January 4, 1733, that on "Saturday next will be
published for 1733 : The Second Edition of Poor
Richard"; and but a week later through the
same medium he advertised the publication of
a "Third Impression." Having discovered the
efficacy of advertising, Franklin was not back-

ward in using it for the next issue. In his
paper as early as November 8, 1733, the public
eye was informed, with nearly a whole column,
as below :

Just publish'd for 1734.

POOR RICHARD : An ALMANACK containing the
Lunations, Eclipses, Planets Motions and Aspects,
Weather, Sun and Moon's Rising and Setting, Highwater, &c. Besides many Pleasant and Witty Verses,
Jests and Notable Sayings. Thanks to the Publick for
his last Year's Encouragement. Of His Wife's good
Humour. Of His Prediction concerning the Day, Hour,
and Minute of *Titan Leeds's* Death. Mr. Leeds's Character. Remarks upon the Almanack published for 1734
in Leeds's Name. Gelding Time. Good Women, Stars
and Angels. Poor Dick's Litany. What Death is. What
spoils the Teeth. The Travellers Improvement. Blind
Fortune. Wedlock Lawyers, Preachers and Tomtit's
Eggs. Robin bit. How to perswade. Lawyer's Will,
Bucephalus and his Master. Crowing Hen. S——l the
Smith, and J——b the Tapster. The Teacher. Heirs
and Widows. John's Wit. The Dutch Maxim. Verses
by Mrs. Bridget Saunders, in Answer to the December
Verses of last Year. Short Dialogue between a Lawyer
and his Client, &c. By *Richard Saunders* Philom.
Philadelphia, Printed and sold by *B. Franklin*, Price
3s. 6d. per Doz.
To all, whom it may concern to know R. S.
I'm not High-Church, nor Low-Church, nor Tory, nor
  Whig,
No flatt'ring young Coxcomb, nor formal old Prig ;
Not eternally talking nor silently queint,
No profligate sinner, nor pragmatical Saint,
I'm not vain of my Judgment, nor pinn'd on a Sleeve,
Nor implicitly any Thing can I believe.
To sift Truth from all Rubbish, I do what I can,
And, God knows, If I err—I'm a fallible man.
I can laugh at a Jest, if not crack'd out of Time,
And excuse a Mistake, tho' not flatter a Crime.
Any faults of my Friends I wou'd scorn to expose,
And detest private Scandal, tho' cast on my Foes.
I put none to the Blush, on whatever Pretence,
For immodesty shocks both good Breeding and Sense.
No Man's Person I hate, tho' his Conduct I blame,

I can censure a Vice, without stabbing a Name.
To amend—not Reproach—is the Bent of my Mind,
A Reproof is half lost, when ill Nature is join'd.
Where Merit appears, tho' in Rags, I respect it,
And plead Virtue's Cause, shou'd the whole World reject it.
Cool Reason I bow to, wheresoever 't is found,
And rejoice when sound learning with Favour is crown'd.
To no Party a Slave, in no squabbles I join,
Nor damn the Opinion, that differs from mine.
Evil tongues I contemn, no Blasphemies I sing ;
I dote on my Country and am Liege to my King.
Tho' length of Days I desire, yet with my last Breath,
I 'm in hopes to betray no mean dreadings of Death :
And as to the Path, after Death to be trod,
I rely on the Will of a MERCIFUL GOD.

R. SAUNDERS.

Another cause for the large sale of the early
issues was without question due to the con-
troversies with his brother philomaths, which
Franklin originated by his jocose remarks upon
them in the prefaces of Poor Richard. With
delicious humor and satire, Mr. Saunders in
different issues gravely predicts the death of
one of his rivals, Titan Leeds, and the reconciliation of a second, John Jerman, to the
Catholic Church. Neither of these gentlemen,
though able to predict weather twelve months
in advance, could draw from the stars Franklin's purpose, and so they fell into his trap, and
in the prefaces to their respective issues they
replied to him with anger and "strong" words.
Leeds called him a "Fool and a Lyar" and "a
conceited scribbler," which Jerman echoed in
no minor key by stating that Franklin's predic-

tion was "altogether false and untrue," and that he was "one of Baal's false prophets." This was just what Franklin expected, and he used his opportunity to the utmost. With wit and humor he fanned the flame of controversy, to which his rivals replied with bad language and adjectives. He made every reader of Leeds and Jerman hear of and wish to see Poor Richard, and, once seen, it was a very clod-pate who could not discriminate between texts, one of which has been translated into a dozen languages, while the other has barely survived on the shelves of the antiquary.

But if this unusual advertising created a large sale of the early issues, its continuous success was due to a third cause. In his Autobiography Franklin tells us that "observing it was generally read, scarce any neighborhood in the province being without it, I consider'd it as a proper vehicle for conveying instruction among the common people, who bought scarcely any other books ; I therefore filled all the little spaces between the remarkable days in the calendar with proverbial sentences, chiefly such as inculcated industry and frugality as the means of procuring wealth, and thereby securing virtue ; it being more difficult for a man in want to act always honestly, as, to use here one of these proverbs, *it is hard for an empty sack to stand*

upright." It is these proverbs which made
Poor Richard the popular almanac of the
period. The religious schisms, the privations
of emigration, and the hard and dreary colonial
life had tinged our forefathers with a serious-
ness that produced practically no humor, and
the wise and witty sayings of Poor Richard
stand out as almost the sole production of this
kind in our colonial period. Certainly, though
written for the common people, they are the
only ones worth reading to-day, and it is not
strange that what, in a garbled and abbreviated
form, has achieved such a reputation, that to-
day it is as well known in Europe as in America,
and which is still constantly reprinted, should
in the colorless life of our frontier settlements
have enjoyed a popularity sufficient to keep the
presses busy printing the ten thousand copies
annually needed to supply the readers, who
extended as far north as Rhode Island, and
to the southward as far as the Carolinas. Indeed it is, so far as I am aware, the first literary
production of this country which to any extent
broke through the colony boundaries which at
that time so thoroughly localized thought and
people.

It is hardly necessary to state that Franklin
did not originate all the "Sayings of Poor
Richard." He himself tells us that they were

"the wisdom of many ages and nations." Any one familiar with Bacon, Rochefoucauld, and Rabelais, as well as others, will recognize old friends in some of these sayings, while a study of the collections of Proverbs, made in the early part of the last century by Ray and Palmer, will reveal the probable source from which Poor Richard pilfered. Yet with but few exceptions these maxims and aphorisms had been filtered through Franklin's brain, and were tinged with that mother wit which so strongly and individually marks so much that he said and wrote.

But for these exceptions, Poor Richard was like all his contemporaries. Here was the same comparatively poor printing, the same great economy of paper, not merely in margins, but in printing on every available blank which occurred. Here are anecdotes and poems so coarse that only a knowledge of eighteenth-century literature can save one from marvelling that the sheets containing them could gain admission into a decent household. But to the age that read Swift, Richardson, and Smollett, 't was no shame to read Poor Richard, and his coarseness at least was tinctured with genuine wit, and not merely coarse for coarseness sake. Here are the same dry though then important facts and tables concerning the sessions of the

different courts, post-roads, mails, and friends
meetings.   Here are the occasional " Tables of
Interest at Six per Cent," " Table of Coins,"
" Historical Chronology," " Act of Parliament,"
" Method of Inoculating for the Small Pox,"
" Receipt for making Dauphiny Soup, which in
Turkey is call Touble," and other matter of
such " gone-nothingness " as not to be worth
reprinting.   And here are the doggerel rhymes
which are bad enough to merit notice.

In his Autobiography, Franklin tells us that
by the saving ridicule of his father he " escaped
being a poet and most probably a bad one."
Certainly the poems of Poor Richard support
the truth of the latter part of this statement, if
not the former.   It is true that Mr. Saunders
tells us in one of his prefaces that " I need not
tell thee that many of them [the verses] are of
my own Making.   If thou hast any Judgement
in Poetry, thou wilt easily discern the Workman from the Bungler.   I know as well as thee,
that I am no *Poet* born and it is a Trade I never
learnt, nor indeed could learn.   If I make
Verses, 't is in Spight—Of Nature and my Stars
I write.—Why then should I give my Readers
bad Lines of my own, when *good Ones* of other
Peoples are so plentiful ? "   Perhaps then Poor
Richard should not be made responsible for all
these poems, but I have been able to identify

but one or two pieces as from other pens, and suspect that they must most of them be referred to one which had so little poetic feeling that it could write of it as a "trade" to be "learnt."

Such was the almanac which made Richard Saunders, yclept Poor Richard, a distinct individual to our colonial ancestors and gained him a reputation possessed by few even of our then governors and leading men. In 1746, by the death of that "Ornament and Head of our Profession, Mr. Jacob Taylor, who for upwards of forty years (with some few Intermissions only) supply'd the good people of this and the neighboring Colonies with the most accurate Calculations that have hitherto appear'd in America" (and who indeed was said to have assisted in the preparation of Poor Richard), the most serious rival of this latter was removed. This made an opening Franklin was too shrewd not to seize, and he announced that "since my Friend *Taylor* is no more, whose Ephemerides so long and agreeably serv'd and entertained these Provinces, I have taken the liberty to imitate his well-known Method, of giving two pages to each Month," and accordingly the title-page of the issue for 1748, was not only termed "Poor Richard Improved" (under which title it was subsequently printed), but announced to the public that "This Almanack us'd to contain but

24 Pages, and now has 36 ; yet the Price is very
little advanc'd." The almanac throve under its
new form, and such was the edition printed of
the issue for 1750, that Franklin sent a copy to
his "Honored Mother," as early as October
16th of the preceding year, with the statement
that "we print them early, because we send
them to many places far distant." By Franklin's accounts we know that in the last fourteen
years in which he was connected with the
almanac, the total sales were 141,257 copies,
amounting in the colonial currency to the sum
of £2213. 0. 8.

For twenty-five years Franklin compiled and
printed this almanac, (though it was continued
till near the end of the last century), and in the
last issue edited by him, being for the year 1758,
he contributed a preface to which almost the
entire knowledge of Poor Richard by the world
is due. It was in effect a skimming of the
cream from the twenty-four previous issues,
being a selection of aphorisims, rhymes, and
jokes run into a continuous piece, which was
described by Franklin as follows : "These
proverbs. . . I assembled and form'd into a connected discourse prefix'd to the Almanack of
1757 [sic] as the harangue of a wise old man to
the people attending an auction. The bringing
all these scatter'd counsels thus into a focus,

enabled them to make greater impression. The piece, being universally approved, was copied in all the newspapers of the Continent; reprinted in Britain on a broadside, to be stuck up in houses; two translations were made of it in French, and great numbers bought by the clergy and gentry, to distribute gratis among their poor parishioners and tenants."

It is this preface which has given the name of Poor Richard currency in alien races and a quotable quality to this day. It has been printed and reprinted again and again. In every size, from a "pot duodecimo" up to "imperial folio"; in thousands for the plow-boy, and in limited and privately printed editions at the expense of noblemen; for the "penny-horrible" hawker, and for the bibliomaniac; for the "Society for Preserving Property against Republicans and Levellers," and for the "Association for Improving the Condition of the Poor"; and under the titles of "Father Abraham's Speech," "The Way to Wealth," and "La Science du Bonhomme Richard," it has proved itself one of the most popular American writings. Seventy editions of it have been printed in English, fifty-six in French, eleven in German, and nine in Italian. It has been translated into Spanish, Danish, Swedish, Welsh, Polish, Gaelic, Russian, Bohemian,

Dutch, Catalan, Chinese, Modern Greek, and Phonetic writing. It has been printed at least four hundred times, and is to-day as popular as ever.

But for this re-hash, the rarity of the original issues would have caused Richard Saunders and his almanacs to be quite unknown. The few remaining copies of the original publications are bibliographical rarities which are eagerly sought for and command prices which are prohibitive to the ordinary reader. Of the two hundred thousand copies which a low estimate gives as the number printed while Franklin wrote the almanac, but a mere fraction are left us. After a search extending over several years, the editor can represent the entire number known to him with two units, and an examination of these would entail visits to New York, Philadelphia, and Washington—a task hitherto undertaken by no editor of Franklin.

Yet these originals do not deserve the fate that has been awarded to so much of our colonial literature. No publication which had a great popularity at any period of the world's history deserves entire forgetfulness. If only classed with the archæology of literature, they should still be read and remembered, so that we may better appreciate the thoughts, feelings, and interests of our by-gone generations. But the editor believes that Poor Richard has higher claims to public notice than for this reason. To collect and edit these pieces, so as for the first time to give them to the public in a form and dress that will permit of reading, has been to him a labor of love. Beyond the monthly calendars he has pruned as little as the nature of this reprint and the space at his command would allow of. Little which he believes Franklin wrote has been omitted, and so perhaps some of the volume may seem of but slight interest. If so, merely consider them as foils to the other parts, and blame not the Poor Richard who wrote :

" Bad commentators spoil the best of books,
So God sends meat (they say) the Devil Cooks "—

PAUL LEICESTER FORD.

BROOKLYN, N. Y.,
Dec. 16 1889.

POOR RICHARD FOR 1733.

PREFACE.

Courteous Reader,

I might in this place attempt to gain thy favour by declaring that I write Almanacks with no other view than that of the publick good, but in this I should not be sincere; and men are now a-days too wise to be deceiv'd by pretences, how specious soever. The plain truth of the matter is, I am excessive poor, and my wife, good woman, is, I tell her, excessive proud; she cannot bear, she says, to sit spinning in her shift of tow, while I do nothing but gaze at the stars; and has threatned more than once to burn all my books and rattling-traps, (as she calls my instruments,) if I do not make some profitable use of them for the good of my family. The printer has offer'd me some considerable share of the profits, and I have thus began to comply with my dame's desire.

Indeed, this motive would have had force enough to have made me publish an Almanack many years since, had it not been overpowered by my regard for my good friend and fellow-student, Mr. *Titan Leeds*, whose interest I was extreamly unwilling to hurt. But this obstacle (I am far from speaking it with pleasure,) is soon to be removed, since inexorable death, who was never known to respect merit, has already prepared the mortal dart, the fatal sister has already extended her destroying shears, and that ingenious man must soon be taken from us. He dies, by my calculation, made at his request, on Oct. 17, 1733, 3 ho., 29 m., P.M., at the very instant of the ☌ of ☉ and ☿. By his own calculation he will survive till the 26th of the same month. This small difference between us we have disputed whenever we have met these nine years past ; but at length he is inclinable to agree with my judgment. Which of us is most exact, a little time will now determine. As, therefore, these Provinces may not longer expect to see any of his performances after this year, I think myself free to take up the task, and request a share of publick encouragement, which I am the more apt to hope for on this account, that the buyer of my Almanack

may consider himself not only as purchasing an
useful utensil, but as performing an act of
charity to his poor

Friend and servant,

R. SAUNDERS.*

♄ Saturn diseas'd with age, and left for dead ;
Chang'd all his gold to be involv'd in lead.
♃ Jove, Juno leaves, and loves to take his range ;
From whom man learns to love, and loves to change.
♂ is disarmed, and to ♀ gone,
Where Vulcan's anvil must be struck upon.
That ☽ Luna 's horn'd, it cannot well be said,
Since I ne'er heard that she was married.

* Titan Leeds, in his "American Almanack" for 1734,
thus replies :
"Kind Reader, Perhaps it may be expected that I
should say something concerning an Almanack printed
for the Year 1733, Said to be writ by Poor Richard or
Richard Saunders, who for want of other matter was
pleased to tell his Readers, that he had calculated my
Nativity, and from thence predicts my Death to be the
17th of October, 1733. At 22 min. past 3 a-Clock in the Afternoon, and that these Provinces may not expect to see
any more of his (*Titan Leeds*) Performances, and this
precise Predicter, who predicts to a Minute, proposes to
succeed me in Writing of Almanacks ; but notwithstanding his false Prediction, I have by the Mercy of God
lived to write a Diary for the Year 1734, and to publish
the Folly and Ignorance of this presumptuous Author.
Nay, he adds another gross Falsehood in his said Almanack,viz—*That by my own Calculation, I shall survive until
the 26th of the said Month,* (October) which is as untrue
as the former, for I do not pretend to that Knowledge,
altho' he has usurpt the Knowledge of the Almighty
herein, and manifested himself a Fool and a Lyar.   And
by the mercy of God I have lived to survive this conceited
Scriblers Day and Minute whereon he has predicted
my Death ; and as I have supplyed my Country with
Almanacks for three seven Years by past, to general
Satisfaction, so perhaps I may live to write when his
Performances are Dead.   *Thus much from your annual
Friend, Titan Leeds. October* 18, 1733, 3. *ho.* 33 *min. P.M.*"

JANUARY.

More nice than wise.

Old batchelor would have a wife that 's wise,
   Fair, rich, and young, a maiden for his bed ;
Not proud, nor churlish, but of faultless size,
   A country houswife in the city bred.
      He 's a nice fool, and long in vain hath staid ;
      He should bespeak her, there 's none ready made.

Never spare the parson's wine, nor the baker's pudding.

Visits should be short, like a winter's day,
Lest you 're too troublesome, hasten away.

A house without woman and firelight, is like a body without soul or sprite.

Kings and bears often worry their keepers.

FEBRUARY.

N. N. of B——s county, pray don't be angry with poor Richard.

Each age of men new fashions doth invent ;
   Things which are old, young men do not esteem :
What pleas'd our fathers, doth not us content ;
   What flourished then, we out of fashion deem :
      And that 's the reason, as I understand,
      Why Prodigus did sell his father's land.

Light purse, heavy heart.

He 's a fool that makes his doctor his heir.

Ne'er take a wife till thou hast a house (and a fire) to put her in.

He 's gone, and forgot nothing but to say farewell to
his creditors.

Love well, whip well.

MARCH.

My love and I for kisses play'd,
   She would keep stakes, I was content,
But when I won, she would be paid,
   This made me ask her what she meant :
      Quoth she, since you are in this wrangling vein
      Here take your kisses, give me mine again.

Let my respected friend J. G.
Accept this humble verse of me,
Viz : Ingenious, learned, envy'd youth,
Go on as thou 'st began ;
Even thy enemies take pride,
That thou 'rt their countryman.

Hunger never saw bad bread.

APRIL.

Kind Katherine to her husband kiss'd these words,
  " Mine own sweet Will, how dearly I love thee ! "
If true (quoth Will) the world no such affords.
  And that its true I durst his warrant be :
     For ne'er heard I of woman good or ill,
     But always loved best, her own sweet Will.

Great talkers, little doers.

A rich rogue is like a fat hog, who never does good till
as dead as a log.

Relation without friendship, friendship without power, power without will, will without effect, effect without profit, and profit without virtue, are not worth a f * * * *.

MAY.

Mirth pleaseth some, to others 't is offence,
Some commend plain conceit, some profound sense ;
Some wish a witty jest, some dislike that,
And most would have themselves they know not what.
Then he that would please all, and himself too,
Takes more in hand than he is like to do.

The favour of the great is no inheritance.

Fools make feasts, and wise men eat them.

Beware of the young doctor and the old barber.

He has chang'd his one ey'd horse for a blind one.

The poor have little, beggars none ; the rich too much, enough, not one.

Eat to live, and not live to eat.

JUNE.

" Observe the daily circle of the sun,
    And the short year of each revolving moon :
    By them thou shalt foresee the following day,
    Nor shall a starry night thy hopes betray.
    When first the moon appears, if then she shrouds
    Her silver crescent, tip'd with sable clouds,
    Conclude she bodes a tempest on the main,
    And brews for fields impetuous floods of rain."

After three days men grow weary of a wench, a guest, and weather rainy.

To lengthen thy life, lessen thy meals.

The proof of gold is fire; the proof of woman, gold; the proof of man, a woman.

After feasts made, the maker scratches his head.

JULY.

" Ev'n while the reaper fills his greedy hands,
And binds the golden sheafs in brittle bands,
Oft have I seen a sudden storm arise
From all the warring winds that sweep the skies :
And oft whole sheets descend of slucy rain,
Suck'd by the spungy clouds from off the main ;
The lofty skies at once come pouring down,
The promis'd crop and golden labors drown."

Many estates are spent in the getting,
Since women for tea forsook spinning and knitting.

He that lieth down with dogs, shall rise up with fleas.

A fat kitchen, a lean will.

Distrust and caution are the parents of security.

Tongue double, brings trouble.

AUGUST.

" For us thro' twelve bright signs Apollo guides
The year, and earth in sev'ral climes divides.
Five girdles bind the skies, the torrid zone
Glows with the passing and repassing sun.
Far on the right and left, th' extreams of heav'n,
To frosts, and snows, and bitter blasts are giv'n.
Betwixt the midst and these, the gods assign'd
Two habitable seats for humane kind."

Take counsel in wine, but resolve afterwards in water.

He that drinks fast, pays slow.

Great famine when wolves eat wolves.

A good wife lost, is God's gift lost.

A taught horse, and a woman to teach, and teachers practising what they preach.

He is ill clothed that is bare of virtue.

SEPTEMBER.

Death is a fisherman, the world we see
His fish-pond is, and we the fishes be ;
His net some general sickness ; howe'er he
Is not so kind as other fishers be ;
For if they take one of the smaller fry,
They throw him in again, he shall not die :
But death is sure to kill all he can get,
And all is fish with him that comes to net.

Men and melons are hard to know.

He 's the best physician that knows the worthlessness of the most medicines.

Beware of meat twice boil'd, and an old foe reconcil'd.

A fine genius in his own country, is like gold in the mine.

There is no little enemy.

The heart of the fool is in his mouth, but the mouth of the wise man is in his heart.

OCTOBER.

Time was my spouse and I could not agree,
Striving about superiority :
The text which saith that man and wife are one,
Was the chief argument we stood upon :
She held, they both one woman should become ;
I held they should be man, and both but one.
Thus we contended daily, but the strife
Could not be ended, till both were one wife.

The old man has given all to his son.

O fool! to undress thy self before thou art going to bed.

Cheese and salt meat should be sparingly eat.

Doors and walls are fools paper.

Anoint a villain and he'll stab you, stab him, and he'll anoint you.

Keep your mouth wet, feet dry.

He has lost his boots, but sav'd his spurs.

NOVEMBER.

My neighbour H——y by his pleasing tongue,
Hath won a girl that's rich, wise, fair, and young;
The match (he saith) is half concluded, he
Indeed is wondrous willing; but not she,
And reason good, for he has run thro' all
Almost the story of the prodigal;
Yet swears he never with the hogs did dine;
That's true, for none would trust him with their swine.

Where bread is wanting, all's to be sold.

There is neither honour nor gain got in dealing with a vil-lain.

The fool hath made a vow, I guess,
Never to let the fire have peace.

Snowy winter, a plentiful harvest.

Nothing more like a fool, than a drunken man.

DECEMBER.

She that will eat her breakfast in her bed,
And spend the morn in dressing of her head,
And sit at dinner like a maiden bride,

And talk of nothing all day but of pride;
' God in his mercy may do much to save her,
But what a case is he in that shall have her.

God works wonders now and then;
Behold! a lawyer, an honest man.

He that lives carnally, won't live eternally.

Innocence is its own defence.

Time eateth all things, could old poets say,
The times are chang'd, our times *drink* all away.

Never mind it, she 'l be sober after the holidays.

THE BENEFIT OF GOING TO LAW.

Dedicated to the Countess of K—t and H-n-r-d-n.

Two beggars travelling along,
    One blind, the other lame.
Pick'd up an oyster on the way,
    To which they both laid claim :
The matter rose so high, that they
    Resolv'd to go to law,
As often richer fools have done,
    Who quarrel for a straw.
A lawyer took it straight in hand,
    Who knew his business was
To mind nor one nor t'other side,
    But make the best o' th' cause,
As always in the law 's the case ;
    So he his judgment gave,
And lawyer-like he thus resolv'd
    What each of them should have ;
        Blind plaintif, lame defendant, share
        The friendly laws impartial care,
        A shell for him, a shell for thee,
        The middle is the *lawyer's fee*.

POOR RICHARD FOR 1734.

PREFACE.

Courteous Reader.

Your kind and charitable assistance last year, in purchasing so large an impression of my Almanacks, has made my circumstances much more easy in the world, and requires my grateful acknowledgement. My wife has been enabled to get a pot of her own, and is no longer obliged to borrow one from a neighbour; nor have we ever since been without something of our own to put in it. She has also got a pair of shoes, two new shifts, and a new warm petticoat; and for my part I have bought a secondhand coat, so good that I am not now ashamed to go to town or be seen there. These things have render'd her temper so much more pacifick than it us'd to be, that I may say, I have slept more and more quietly within this last year, than in the three foregoing years put together. Accept my hearty thanks therefor, and my sincere wishes for your health and prosperity.

In the preface to my last Almanack, I foretold the death of my dear old friend and fellow-student, the learned and ingenious Mr. Titan Leeds, which was to be the 17th of October, 1733, 3 h., 29 m., P.M., at the very instant of the of ☉ and ☿. By his own calculation, he was to survive till the 26th of the same month, and expire in the time of the eclipse, near 11 o'clock, A.M. At which of these times he died, or whether he be really yet dead, I cannot at this present writing positively assure my readers; for as much as a disorder in my own family demanded my presence, and would not permit me, as I had intended, to be with him in his last moments, to receive his last embrace, to close his eyes, and do the duty of a friend in performing the last offices to the departed. Therefore it is that I cannot positively affirm whether he be dead or not; for the stars only show to the skilful what will happen in the natural and universal chain of causes and effects; but 't is well known, that the events which would otherwise certainly happen, at certain times, in the course of nature, are sometimes set aside or postpon'd, for wise and good reasons, by the immediate particular disposition of Providence;

which particular dispositions the stars can by
no means discover or foreshow. There is, however, (and I cannot speak it without sorrow,)
there is the strongest probability that my dear
friend is no more ; for there appears in his
name, as I am assured, an Almanack for the
year 1734, in which I am treated in a very gross
and unhandsome manner, in which I am called
a false predicter, an ignorant, a conceited scribbler, a fool, and a lyar. Mr. Leeds was too well
bred to use any man so indecently and so scur-
rilously, and moreover his esteem and affection
for me was extraordinary: so that it is to be
feared that pamphlet may be only a contrivance
of somebody or other, who hopes, perhaps, to
sell two or three years' Almanacks still, by the
sole force and virtue of Mr. Leeds' name. But,
certainly, to put words into the mouth of a gentleman and a man of letters against his friend,
which the meanest and most scandalous of the
people might be ashamed to utter even in a
drunken quarrel, is an unpardonable injury to
his memory, and an imposition upon the publick.

Mr. Leeds was not only profoundly skilful in
the useful science he profess'd, but he was a
man of exemplary sobriety, a most sincere
friend, and an exact performer of his word.
These valuable qualifications, with many others,

so much endeared him to me, that although it should be so, that, contrary to all probability, contrary to my prediction and his own, he might possibly be yet alive, yet my loss of honour, as a prognosticator, cannot afford me so much mortification as his life, health, and safety, would give me joy and satisfaction.

I am,

Courteous and kind reader,

Your poor friend and servant,

R. SAUNDERS.*

October 30, 1733.

Here I sit naked, like some fairy elf ;
My seat a pumkin ; I grudge no man's pelf,
Though I 've no bread nor cheese upon my shelf.
    I 'll tell thee, gratis, when it safe is
To purge, to bleed, or cut thy cattle, or—thy self.

Good women are like stars in darkest night,
Their virtuous actions shining as a light
To guide their ignorant sex, which oft times fall,
And falling oft, turn diabolical.

* In "The American Almanack" for 1735, Mr. Leeds once more replied to Poor Richard's joking in these words : "Corteous and Kind Reader. My Almanack being in its usual Method, needs no Explanation ; but perhaps it may be expected by some that I shall say something concerning *Poor Richard*, or otherwise *Richard Saunders's* Almanack, which I suppose was printed in the Year 1733, for the ensuing Year 1734, wherein he useth me with such good Manners, I can hardly find what to say to him, without it is to advise him not to be too proud because by his Prædicting my Death, and his writing an Almanack (I suppose at his Wifes Request)

Good women, sure, are angels on the earth :
Of those good angels we have had a dearth ;
And therefore all you men that have good wives,
Respect their virtues equal with your lives.

JANUARY.

From a cross neighbour, and a sullen wife,
A pointless needle, and a broken knife ;
From suretyship, and from an empty purse,
A smoaky chimney, and jolting horse ;
From a dull razor, and an aking head ;
From a bad conscience, and a buggy bed,
A blow upon the elbow and the knee ;
From each of these, good L—d, deliver me.

You cannot pluck roses without fear of thorns
Nor enjoy a fair wife without danger of horns.

Without justice courage is weak.

Many dishes, many diseases.
Many medicines, few cures.

Where carcasses are, eagles will gather,
And where good laws are, much people flock thither.

Would you live with ease, do what you ought, and not
what you please.

Better slip with foot than tongue.

as he himself says, she has got a Pot of her own and not
longer obliged to borrow one from a neighbour, she has
got also two new Shifts, a pair of new Shoes and a new
warm Petticoat ; and for his own part he had bought a
second-hand Coat so good that he is not ashamed to go
to Town, or to be seen there, (Parturiant Montes!) But
if Falshood and Inginuity be so rewarded, What may he
expect if ever he be in a capacity to publish that that is
either Just or according to Art? Therefore I shall say
little more about it than, as a Friend, to advise he will
never take upon him to prædict or ascribe any Persons
Death, till he has learned to do it better than he did
before."

FEBRUARY.

What death is, dost thou ask me ?
Till dead I do not know.
Come to me when thou hear'st I 'm dead ;
Then what 't is I shall show.
To die 's to cease to be, it seems ;
So learned Seneca did think ;
But we 've philosophers of modern date,
Who say 't is death to cease to drink.

Hot things, sharp things, sweet things, cold things, all rot the teeth,
And make them look like old things.

Blame-all and praise-all are two block heads.

Be temperate in wine, in eating, girls, and sloth, or the gout will seize you and plague you both.

MARCH.

Some of our sparks to London town do go,
Fashions to see, and learn the world to know ;
Who at return have nought but these to show,
New wig above, and new disease below.
Thus the jack-ass, a traveller once would be,
And roam'd abroad new fashions for to see,
But home returned, fashions he had none,
Only his main and tail were larger grown.

What pains our justice takes his faults to hide,
With half that pains sure he might cure 'em quite.

In success be moderate.

Take this remark from Richard, poor and lame,
Whate'er 's begun in anger, ends in shame.

What one relishes, nourishes.

No man e'er was glorious, who was not laborious.

APRIL.

When Fortune fell asleep, and Hate did blind her,
Art, Fortune lost, and Ignorance did find her.
Since when, dull Ignorance with Fortune's store,
Hath been inrich'd, and Art hath still been poor.
Poets say Fortune 's blind, and cannot see,
But certainly they must deceived be ;
Else could it not most commonly fall out,
That fools should have, and wise men go without.

All things are easy to industry,
All things difficult to sloth.

If you ride a horse, sit close and tight,
If you ride a man, sit easy and light.

A new truth is a truth, an old error is an error,
Tho' Clodpate won't allow either.

Don't think to hunt two hares with one dog.

Fools multiply folly.

Beauty and folly are old companions.

Hope of gain lessens pain.

MAY.

Wedlock, as old men note, hath likened been,
Unto a public crowd or common rout ;
Where those that are without would fain get in,
And those that are within, would fain get out.
Grief often treads upon the heels of pleasure,
Marry'd in haste, we oft repent at leisure ;
Some by experience find these words missplaced,
Marry'd at leisure, they repent in haste.

Where there 's marriage without love, there will be love without marriage.

Lawyers, preachers, and tomtit's eggs, there are more of them hatched than come to perfection.

Be neither silly nor cunning, but wise,

Neither a fortress nor a m * * * * * * * * d will hold out long after they begin to parley.

Who pleasure gives, shall joy receive.

Be not sick too late, nor well too soon.

JUNE.

When Robin now three days had married been,
    And all his friends and neighbours gave him joy,
This question of his wife he asked then,
    Why till her marriage day she proved so coy?
Indeed said he, 't was well thou didst not yield,
    For doubtless then my purpose was to leave thee :
O, sir, I once before was so beguil'd,
    And was resolved the next should not deceive me.

All things are cheap to the saving, dear to the wasteful.

Would you persuade, speak of interest, not of reason.

Some men grow mad by studying much to know,
But who grows mad by studying good to grow.

Happy 's the woing that 's not long a doing.

Jack Little sow'd little, and little he 'll reap.

JULY.

A lawyer being sick, and extream ill,
Was moved by his friends to make his will,
Which soon he did, gave all the wealth he had,
To frantic persons, lunatick and mad.
And to his friends this reason did reveal,
(That they might see with equity he 'd deal,)
From madmen's hands I did my wealth receive,
Therefore that wealth to madmen's hands I leave.

There have been as great souls unknown to fame as any of the most famous.

Do good to thy friend to keep him, to thy enemy to gain him.

A good man is seldom uneasy, an ill one never easie.

Teach your child to hold his tongue, he 'll learn fast enough to speak.

Don't value a man for the quality he is of, but for the qualities he possesses.

Bucephalus, the horse of Alexander, hath as lasting fame as his master.

AUGUST.

Some envious (speaking in their own renown,)
Say that my book was not exactly done :
They wrong me ; yet, like feasts, I 'd have my books
Rather be pleasing to the guests than cooks.
Ill thrives that hapless family that shows
A cock that 's silent, and a hen that crows :
I know not which lives more unnatural lives,
Obeying husbands, or commanding wives.

Sam's religion is like a Cheder cheese, 't is made of the milk of one-and-twenty parishes.

Grief for a dead wife, and a troublesome guest, continues to the threshold, and there is at rest,
But I mean such wives as are none of the best.

As charms are nonsense, nonsense is a charm.

He that cannot obey, cannot command.

An innocent plowman is more worthy than a vicious prince.

SEPTEMBER.

S——l the smith hath lately sworn and said,
That no disease shall make him keep his bed ;
His reason is, I now begin to smell it,

He wants more rum, and must be forc'd to sell it.
Nor less meant J——h, when that vow he made,
Than to give o'er his cousening tapster's trade ;
Who, check'd for short and frothy measure, swore
He never would from thenceforth fill pot more.

He that is rich need not live sparingly, and he that can live sparingly need not be rich.

If you would be reveng'd of your enemy, govern yourself.

A wicked hero will turn his back to an innocent coward.

Laws like to cobwebs, catch small flies,
Great ones break through before your eyes.

An egg to-day is better than a hen to morrow.

Drink water, put the money in your pocket, and leave the dry-bellyach in the punch-bowl.

Strange, that he who lives by shifts, can seldom shift himself.

OCTOBER.

Altho' thy teacher act not as he preaches,
Yet ne'erthcless, if good, do what he teaches ;
Good counsel, failing men may give, for why,
He that 's aground knows where the shoal doth lie.
My old friend Berryman oft, when alive,
Taught others thrift, himself could never thrive :
Thus like the whetstone, many men are wont
To sharpen others while themselves are blunt.

The magistrate should obey the laws, the people should obey the magistrate.

When 't is fair, be sure take your great coat with you.

He does not possess wealth, it possesses him.

Necessity has no law ; I know some attorneys of the same.

Onions can make ev'n heirs and widows weep.

As sore places meet most rubs, proud folks meet most affronts.

NOVEMBER.

Dorothy would with John be married ;
Dorothy's wise, I trow :
But John by no means Dorothy will wed ;
John 's the wiser of the two.
Those are my verses which Tom reads ;
That is very well known,
But in reading he makes them nonsense,
Then they are his own.

The thrifty maxim of the wary Dutch, is to save all the money they can touch.

He that waits upon fortune, is never sure of a dinner.

A learned blockhead is a greater blockhead than an ignorant one.

Marry your son when you will, but your daughter when you can.

Avarice and happiness never saw each other, how then should they become acquainted.

DECEMBER.

By Mrs. Bridget Saunders, my Dutchess, in answer to the December verses of last year.

He that for the sake of drink neglects his trade,
And spends each night in taverns till 't is late,
And rises when the sun is four hours high,
And ne'er regards his starving family,
God in his mercy may do much to save him,
But, woe to the poor wife, whose lot it is to have him.

Famine, plague, war, and an unnumbered throng of
guilt-avenging ills, to man belongs.

Is 't not enough plagues, wars, and famine, rise to
lash our crimes, but must our wives be wise?

He that knows nothing of it, may by chance be a
prophet, while the wisest that is may happen to miss.

If you would have guests merry with cheer, be so yourself, or so at least appear.

Reader, farewell! all happiness attend thee;
May each new-year better and richer find thee.

OF THE ECLIPSES, 1734.

There will be but two : The first, April 22, 18
min. after 5 in the morning; the second, October 15, 36 min. past 1 in the afternoon. Both
of the Sun ; and both, like Mrs. ——s's Modesty,
and old neighbour Scrape-all's money, invisible.
Or like a certain storekeeper late of —— county,
not to be seen in these parts.

Since the Eclipses take up so little space, I
have room to comply with the new fashion, and
propose a mathematical question to the sons of
art, which, perhaps, is not more difficult to
solve, nor of less use when solved, than some
of those that have been proposed by the ingenious M. G-——y.

It is this :

A certain rich man had 100 orchards, in each
orchard was 100 apple-trees, under each apple-
tree was 100 hogsties, in each hogstic was 100

sows, and each sow had 100 pigs. Question, How many sow-pigs were there among them?

Note, the answer to this question won't be accepted without the solution.

Felix quem faciunt aliena pericula cautum.

To such a height th' expence of COURTS is gone,
That poor men are redress'd —— till they 're undone.
William, your cause is good, give me my fee, and I 'll
   defend it.

But, alas! William is cast, the verdict goes against him. Give me another fee, and I 'll move the court in arrest of judgement. Then sentence is confirmed. T' other fee and I 'll bring a writ of error. But judgement is again confirmed, and Will condemned to pay costs. What shall we do now, Master, says William, Why, since it can't be helpt, there 's no more to be said; pay the knave his money, and I 'm satisfied.

Of disposition they 're most sweet,
Their clients always kindly greet;
And tho' at bar they rip old sores,
And brawl and scold like drunken w * * * * *,
Their angers in a moment pass
Away at night over a glass;
Nay, often laugh at the occasion,
Of their premeditated passion.
  O may you prosper as you treat us,
  Until the d——l sign your quietus.

POOR RICHARD FOR 1735.

PREFACE.

COURTEOUS READER,

This is the third time of my appearing in print, hitherto very much to my own satisfaction, and I have reason to hope, to the satisfaction of the publick also ; for the public is generous, and has been very charitable and good to me. I should be ungrateful then, if I did not take every opportunity of expressing my gratitude ; for *ingratum si dixeris omnia dixeris.* I therefore return the publick my most humble and hearty thanks.

Whatever may be the musick of the spheres, how great soever the harmony of the stars, 't is certain there is no harmony among the star-gazers ; but they are perpetually growling and snarling at one another like strange curs, or

like some men at their wives. I had resolved
to keep the peace on my own part, and affront
none of them ; and I shall persist in that resolution. But having receiv'd much abuse from
Titan Leeds deceas'd, (Titan Leeds when living
would not have used me so :) I say, having receiv'd much abuse from the ghost of Titan
Leeds, who pretends to be still living, and to
write Almanacks in spight of me and my predictions, I cannot help saying, that tho' I take
it patiently, I take it very unkindly. And
whatever he may pretend, 't is undoubtedly
true that he is really defunct and dead. First,
because the stars are seldom disappointed,
never but in the case of wise men, *sapiens
dominabitur astris*, and they foreshadowed his
death at the time I predicted it. Secondly,
't was requisite and necessary he should die
punctually at that time for the honor of astrology, the art professed both by him and his
father before him. Thirdly, 't is plain to every
one that reads his two last Almanacks, (for
1734 and '35,) that they are not written with
that life his performances use to be written
with ; the wit is low and flat ; the little hints
dull and spiritless ; nothing smart in them but
Hudibras's verses against astrology at the heads
of the months in the last, which no astrologer
but a *dead one* would have inserted, and no man

living would or could write such stuff as the
rest. But lastly, I shall convince him from his
own words that he is dead ; (*ex ore suo condem-
natus est,*) for in his preface to his Almanack
for 1734, he says : "Saunders adds another
gross falsehood in his Almanack, viz., that by
my own calculation, I shall survive until the
26th of the said month, October, 1733, which is
as untrue as the former." Now if it be as
Leeds says, untrue and a gross falsehood, that
he survived till the 26th of October, 1733, then
it is certainly true that he died before that time ;
and if he died before that time, he is dead now
to all intents and purposes, any thing he may
say to the contrary notwithstanding. And at
what time before the 26th is it so likely he
should die, as at the time by me predicted, viz.,
the 17th of October aforesaid? But if some
people will walk and be troublesome after
death, it may perhaps be borne with a little,
because it cannot well be avoided, unless one
would be at the pains and expence of laying
them in the *Red Sea ;* however, they should
not presume too much upon the liberty allowed
them. I know confinement must needs be
mighty irksome to the free spirit of an astronomer, and I am too compassionate to proceed
suddenly to extremities with it ; nevertheless,
tho' I resolve with reluctance, I shall not long

defer, if it does not speedily learn to treat its living friends with better manners.

I am,

Courteous reader,

Your obliged friend and servant,

R. SAUNDERS.

October 30, 1734.

———

Sold by the Printer hereof,

LARGE QUARTO BIBLES OF GOOD PRINT, Small Bibles, Testaments, Psalters, Primers, Account Books, demi-royal and small Paper, Ink, Ink-powder, Dutch Quills, Wafers, New Version of Psalms, Barclay's Apology, Beavan's Primitive Christianity, *Vade Mecum*, Aristotle's Works, with several other diverting and entertaining Histories. Also, all sorts of Blanks in the most Authentick Forms, and correctly printed.

JANUARY.

The two or three necessaries.

Two or three frolicks abroad in sweet May,
Two or three civil things said by the way,
Two or three languishes, two or three sighs,
Two or three *bless me's* and *let me die's !*
Two or three squeezes, and two or three tow-zes,
With two or three hundred pound spent at their houses,
Can never fail cuckolding two or three spouses.

Bad commentators spoil the best of books,
So God sends meat, (they say,) the devil cooks.

3

Approve not of him who commends all you say.

By diligence and patience, the mouse bit in two the cable.

Full of courtesie, full of craft.

Look before, or you 'll find yourself behind.

FEBRUARY.

Among the vain pretenders of the town,
Hibham of late is wondrous noted grown ;
Hibham scarce reads, and is not worth a groat,
Yet with some high-flown words and a fine coat,
He struts, and talks of books, and of estate,
And learned J——s he calls his intimate.
The mob admire ! thus mighty impudence,
Supplies the want of learning, wealth, and sense.

A little house well fill'd, a little field well till'd, and a little wife well will'd, are great riches.

Old maids lead apes there, where the old batchelors are turn'd to apes.

Some are weatherwise, some are otherwise.

MARCH.

There 's many men forget their proper station,
And still are meddling with the administration
Of government ; that 's wrong and this is right,
And such a law is out of reason quite ;
Thus, spending too much thought on state affairs,
The business is neglected, which is theirs.
So some fond traveller gazing at the stars,
Slips in next ditch, and gets a dirty a * * *.

Dyrro lynn y ddoeth e fydd.

The poor man must walk to get meat for his stomach, the rich man to get a stomach to his meat.

He that goes far to marry, will either deceive or be deceived.

Eyes and priests bear no jests.

APRIL.

William, because his wife was something ill,
Uncertain in her health, indifferent still,
He turn'd her out of doors without reply :
I ask'd if he that act could justify.
In sickness and in health, says he, I am bound
To keep her ; when she's worse or better found,
I 'll take her in again ; and now you 'll see,
She 'll quickly either mend or end, says he.

The family of fools is ancient.

Necessity never made a good bargain.

If pride leads the van, beggary brings up the rear.

There 's many witty men whose brains can't fill their bellies.

Weighty questions ask for deliberate answers.

MAY.

There 's nought so silly, sure, as vanity,
Itself its chiefest end does still destroy ;
To be commended still its brains are racking,
But who will give it what it 's always taking ?
Thou 'rt fair 't is true ; and witty, too, I know it ;
And well bred, Sally, for thy manners show it ;
But whilst thou mak'st self-praise thy only care,
Thou 'rt neither witty, nor well bred, nor fair.

Be slow in chusing a friend, slower in changing.

Old Hob was lately married in the night,
What needed day, his fair young wife was light.

Pain wastes the body ; pleasures the understanding.

The cunning man steals a horse, the wise man lets him alone.

When ♂ and ♀ in conjunction lie,
Then, maids, whate'er is ask'd of you, deny.

JUNE.

When will the miser's chest be full enough ?
When will he cease his bags to cram and stuff?
All day he labours, and all night contrives,
Providing as if he 'd an hundred lives.
While endless care cuts short the common span ;
So have I seen with dropsy swol'n, a man,
Drink and drink more, and still unsatisfied,
Drink till drink drown'd him, yet he thirsty dy'd.

A ship under sail and a big-bellied woman, are the handsomest two things that can be seen common.

Keep thy shop, and thy shop will keep thee.

The king's cheese is half wasted in parings ; but no matter, 't is made of the peoples milk.

Nothing but money, is sweeter than honey.

JULY.

On Louis the XIV. of France.

Louis ('t is true, I own to you)
Paid learned men for writing,
And valiant men for fighting ;
Himself could neither write nor fight,
Nor make his people happy ;
Yet fools will prate, and call him great,
Shame on their noddles sappy.

Of learned fools, I have seen ten times ten ; of unlearned wise men, I have seen a hundred.

Three may keep a secret, if two of them are dead.

Poverty wants some things, luxury many things, avarice all things.

A lie stands on one leg, truth on two.

What 's given shines, what 's receiv'd is rusty.

Sloth and silence are a fool's virtues.

AUGUST.

Sam had the worst wife that a man could have,
Proud, lazy sot, could neither get nor save ;
Eternal scold she was, and what is worse,
The d——l burn thee, was her common curse.
Forbear, quoth Sam, that fruitless curse, so common,
He 'll not hurt me, who 've married his kins-woman.

There 's small revenge in words, but words may be greatly revenged.

Great wits jump, says the poet, and hit his head against the post.

A man is never so ridiculous by those qualities that are his own, as by those that he affects to have.

Deny self for self's sake.

SEPTEMBER.

Blind are the sons of men, few of the kind,
Know their chief interest, or knowing, mind ;
Most, far from following what they know is best,
Trifle in earnest, but mind that in jest.
So Hal, the fiddle tunes harmoniously,
While all is discord in 's Œconomy.

Tim, moderate fare and abstinence much prizes in publick, but in private gormandizes.

Ever since follies have pleased, fools have been able to divert.

It is better to take many injuries, than to give one.

Opportunity is the great bawd.

OCTOBER.

Little half wits are wondrous pert, we find,
Scoffing and jeering on whole womankind,
All false, all whores, all this, and that, and t' other,
Not one exception left, ev'n for their mother.
But men of wisdom and experience know, ·
That there 's no greater happiness below,
Than a good wife affords ; and such there 's many,
For every man has one the best of any.

Early to bed and early to rise, makes a man healthy, wealthy, and wise.

To be humble to superiors is duty, to equals courtesy, to inferiors nobleness.

Here comes the orator, with his flood of words, and his drop of reason.

NOVEMBER.

The lying habit is in some so strong,
To truth they know not how to bend their tongue ;
And tho' sometimes their ends truth best would answer,
Yet lies come uppermost, do what they can, sir,
Mendacio delights in telling news,
And that it may be such, himself doth use
To make it ; but he now no longer need ;
Let him tell truth, it will be news indeed.

Sal laughs at every thing you say. Why ? Because she has fine teeth.

If what most men admire, they would despise.
'T would look as if mankind were growing wise.

The sun never repents of the good he does, nor does he ever demand a recompence.

An old young man will be a young old man.

DECEMBER.

'T is not the face with a delightful air,
A rosy cheek, and lovely flowing hair ;
Nor sparkling eyes to best advantage set,
Nor all the members rang'd in alphabet,
Sweet in proportion as the lovely dies,
Which brings th' etherial bow before our eyes,
That can with wisdom approbation find,
Like pious morals and an honest mind,
By virtue's living laws from every vice refin'd.

Are you angry that others disappoint you ? remember you cannot depend upon yourself.

One mend-fault is worth two find-faults, but one find-fault is better than two make-faults.

Reader, I wish thee health, wealth, happiness, and may kind heaven thy year's industry bless.

THE ECLIPSES.

I shall not say much of the signification of the Eclipses this year, for in truth they do not signifie much ; only I may observe by the way, that the first eclipse of the Moon being celebrated in ♎ Libra or the Ballance, foreshews a failure of justice, where people judge in their own cases. But in the following year, 1736, there will be six Eclipses, four of the Sun, and two of the Moon, which two Eclipses of the Moon will be both total, and portend great revolutions in Europe, particularly in Germany, and some great and surprising events relating to these northern colonies, of which I purpose to speak at large in my next.

THE COURTS.

When Popery in Britain sway'd, I 've read,
The lawyers fear'd they should be d * * * 'd when dead,
Because they had no saint to hand their prayers,
And in Heaven's court take care of their affairs.
Therefore consulting, Evanus they sent
To Rome with a huge purse, on this intent,
That to the holy Father making known
Their woful case, he might appoint them one.
Being arriv'd, he offered his complaint
In language smooth, and humbly begs a saint :
For why, says he, when others on Heaven would call,
Physicians, seamen, scholars, tradesmen, all
Have their own saints, we lawyers none at all.
  The pope was puzzled, never puzzled worse,
For with pleas'd eyes he saw the proffered purse,
But ne'er in all his knowledge or his reading,
He 'd met with one good man that practis'd pleading ;
Who then should be the saint? he could not tell.
At length the thing was thus concluded well.
Within our city, says his holiness,
There is one church fill'd with the images
Of all the saints, with whom the wall 's surrounded,
Blindfold Evanus, lead him three times round it,
Then let him feel, (but give me first the purse ;)
And take the first he finds, for better or worse.

Round went Evanus, till he came where stood
St. Michael with the Devil under 's foot ;
And groping round, he seized old Satan's head,
This be our saint, he cries : Amen, the father said.
But when they open'd poor Evanus' eyes,
Alack ! he sunk with shame and with surprize.

Says ♄ to ♂ Brother, when shall I see
Penn's people scraping acquaintance with thee ?
Says ♂ , only ♃ knows ; but this I can tell,
They neglect me for Hermes, they love him too well.
O, if that be the case, says ♄ , ne'er fear,
If they 're tender of Hermes, and holding him so dear,
They 'll solicit thy help e'er I 've finish'd my round,
Using ♂ Hermes' foes to deter or confound.

POOR RICHARD FOR 1736.

PREFACE.

Loving Readers,

Your kind acceptance of my former labours has encouraged me to continue writing, tho' the general approbation you have been so good as to favour me with, has excited the envy of some, and drawn upon me the malice of others. These ill-willers of mine, despited at the great reputation I gain'd by exactly predicting another man's death, have endeavoured to deprive me of it all at once in the most effectual manner, by reporting that I myself was never alive. *They say, in short, that there is no such a man as I am ;* and have spread this notion so thoroughly in the country, that I have been frequently told it to my face by those that don't know me. This is not civil treatment, to endeavour to deprive me of my very being, and reduce me to a non-entity in the opinion of the publick. But so long as I know myself to walk about, eat, drink and sleep, I am satisfied *that there is really such a man as I am*, whatever they may say to the contrary. And the world may be satisfied likewise, for if there was no such man as I am, how is it possible I should *appear pubickly* to hundreds of people, as I have done for several years past, in print? I need not, indeed, have taken any notice of so idle a report, if it had not been for the sake of my printer, to whom my enemies are pleased to ascribe my productions; and who it seems is as unwillingly to father my offspring as I am to lose the credit of it. Therefore, to clear him entirely, as well as to vindicate my own honour, I make this publick and serious declaration, which I desire may be believed, to wit : *That what I have written heretofore, and do now write, neither was, nor is written by any other man or men, person or persons, whatsoever.* Those who are not satisfied with this, must needs be very unreasonable.

My performance for this year follows; it submits itself, kind reader, to thy censure, but hopes (for) thy candor, to forgive its faults. It devotes itself entirely to thy service, and will serve thee faithfully. And if it has the good fortune to please its master, 't is gratification enough for the labour of

poor
R. SAUNDERS.

Presumptuous man ! the reason would'st thou find
Why formed so weak, so little, and so blind ?
First, if thou canst, the harder reason guess,
Why formed no weaker, blinder, and no less?
Ask of thy mother earth, why oaks are made
Taller or stronger than the weeds they shade ?
Or ask of yonder argent fields above,
Why Jove's sattelites are less than Jove ?

JANUARY.

Some have learn't many tricks of sly evasion,
Instead of truth they use equivocation,
And eke it out with mental reservation,
Which, to good men, is an abomination.
Our smith of late most wonderfully swore,
That whilst he breathed he would drink no more,
But since, I know his meaning, for I think,
He meant he would not breathe whilst he did drink.

He is no clown that drives the plow, but he that doth
clownish things.

If you know how to spend less than you get, you have
the philosopher's-stone.

The good pay-master is lord of another man's purse.

Fish and visitors smell in three days.

FEBRUARY.

Sam's wife provok'd him once ; he broke her crown,
The surgeon's bill amounted to five pounds ;
This blow (she brags) has cost my husband dear,
He 'll ne'er strike more, Sam chanc'd to overhear.
Therefore, before his wife the bill he pays,
And to the surgeon in her hearing says :
Doctor, you charge five pound, here e'en take ten,
My wife may chance to want your help again.

He that has neither fools nor beggars among his kindred, is the son of thunder-gust.

Diligence is the mother of good luck.

Do not do that which you would not have known.

MARCH.

Whate'er 's desired, knowledge, fame, or pelf,
Not one will change his neighbour with himself;
The learn'd are happy nature to explore,
The fool is happy that he knows no more.
The rich are happy in the plenty given ;
The poor contents him with the care of heaven.
Thus does some comfort ev'ry state attend,
And pride 's bestowed on all, a common friend.

Never praise your cider or horse.

Wealth is not his that has it, but his that enjoys it.

'T is easy to see, hard to foresee.

In a discreet man's mouth a publick thing is private.

APRIL.

By nought is man from beast distinguished,
More than by knowledge in his learned head,
Then youth improve thy time, but cautious see
That what thou learnest somehow useful be ;
Each day improving, Solon waxed old ;
For time he knew was better far than gold :
Fortune might give him gold which would decay,
But fortune cannot give him—yesterday.

Let thy maid-servant be faithful, strong, and homely.

Keep flax from fire, youth from gaming.

Bargaining has neither friends nor relations.

Admiration is the daughter of ignorance.

There 's more old drunkards, than old doctors.

MAY.

Lalus who loves to hear himself discourse,
Keeps talking still as if he frantick were,
And tho' himself might no where hear a worse,
Yet he no other but himself will hear.
Stop not his mouth, if he be troublesome,
But stop his ears, and then the man is dumb.

Here comes Courage! that seized the lion absent, and ran away from the present mouse.

He that takes a wife takes care.

Nor eye in a letter, nor hand in a purse, nor ear in the secret of another.

He that buys by the penny, maintains not only himself, but other people.

JUNE.

Things that are bitter, bitterer than gall,
Physicians say are always physical :
Now women's tongues if into powder beaten,
May in a potion or a pill be eaten,
And as there 's nought more bitter, I do muse,
That women's tongues in physick they ne'er use.
Myself and others who lead restless lives,
Would spare that bitter member of our wives.

He that can have patience can have what he will.

Now I have a sheep and a cow, every body bids me good-morrow.

God helps them that help themselves.

Why does the blind man's wife paint herself?

JULY.

Who can charge Ebrio with a thirst for wealth?
See, he consumes his money, time, and health

In drunken frolicks, which will all confound,
Neglects his farm, forgets to till his ground ;
His stock grows less that might be kept with ease ;
In nought but guts and debts he finds increase ;
In town reels as if he 'd shove down each wall,
Yet walls must stand, poor soul, or *he* must fall.

None preaches better than the ant, and she says nothing.

The absent are never without fault, nor the present without excuse.

Gifts burst rocks.

If wind blows on you through a hole,
Make your will and take care of your soul.

The rotten apple spoils his companion.

AUGUST.

The tongue was once a servant of the heart,
And what it gave she freely did impart ;
But, now hypocrisy is grown so strong,
The heart 's become a servant to the tongue.
Virtue we praise, but practice not her good,
(Athenian-like) we act not what we know,
As many men do talk of *Robin Hood*,
Who never did shoot arrow in his bow.

Don't throw stones at your neighbors', if your own windows are glass.

The excellency of hogs is—fatness, of men—virtue.

Good wives and good plantations are made by good husbands.

He that sells upon trust, loses many friends, and always wants money.

SEPTEMBER.

Briscap, thou 'st little judgement in thy head
More than to dress thee, drink and go to bed ;
Yet thou shalt have the wall and the way lead,
Since logick wills that simple things preceed.
 Walking and meeting one not long ago,
 I ask'd who 't was, he said, he did not know,
 I said, I know thee ; so said he, I you ;
 But he that knows himself I never knew.

Lovers, travellers, and poets, will give money to be heard.

He that speaks much, is much mistaken.

Creditors have better memories than debtors.

Forewarn'd, forearm'd.

OCTOBER.

Whymsical *Will* once fancy'd he was ill,
The Doctor call'd, who thus examin'd *Will ;*
How is your appetite ? O, as to that
I eat quite heartily, you see I 'm fat ;
How is your sleep anights ? 'T is sound and good ;
I eat, drink, sleep, as well as e'er I cou'd.
Will, says the doctor, clapping on his hat,
I 'll give you something shall remove all that.

Three things are men most likely to be cheated in, a horse, a wig, and a wife.

He that lives well is learned enough.

Poverty, poetry, and new titles of honour, make men ridiculous.

He that scatters thorns, let him not go barefoot.

There 's none deceived but he that trusts.

NOVEMBER.

When you are sick, what you like best is to be chosen for a medicine in the first place; what experience tells you is best, to be chosen in the second place; what reason (i. e. Theory,) says is best, is to be chosen in the last place. But if you can get Dr. *Inclination*, Dr. *Experience*, and Dr. *Reason* to hold a consultation together, they will give you the best advice that can be taken.

God heals and the doctor takes the fee.

If you desire many things, many things will seem but a few.

Mary's mouth costs her nothing, for she never opens it but at others expence.

Receive before you write, but write before you pay.

I saw few die of hunger, of eating—100,000.

DECEMBER.

☉ nearer the earth in winter than in summer, 15046 miles, (his lownes and short appearauce making winter cold, (● nearer in her *Perigon* than Apogem, 69512: ♄ nearer 49868 miles: ♃ nearer 38613 miles: ♂ nearer 80608 miles: ♀ nearer 6209 miles: ☿ nearer 181427 miles. And yet ☿ is never distant from the ☉ a whole sign, nor ♋ two. You 'll never find a ✳ ☉ ☿, nor a ♊ ☉ ♀.

Maids of America, *who gave you bad teeth ?*
Answer. Hot soupings and frozen apples.
5

Marry your daughter and eat fresh fish betimes.

He that would live in peace and at ease,
Must not speak all he knows, nor judge all he sees.
                                                    Adieu.

*In my last year's Almanack, I mentioned that
the visible Eclipses of this year, 1736, portended
some great and surprising events relating to
these* NORTHERN COLONIES, *of which I proposed
this year to speak at large.   But as those events
are not to happen immediately this year, I chuse
rather, upon second thought, to defer farther
mention of them, till the publication of my Almanack for that year in which they are to
happen.   However, that the reader may not be
entirely disappointed, here follow, for his present amusement, a few*

ENIGMATICAL PROPHECIES,

*Which they that do not understand, cannot well
explain.*

1. Before the middle of this year, a wind at N.
East will arise, during which the *water of the
sea* and rivers will be in such a manner raised,
that great part of the towns of *Boston, New-
port, New-York, Philadelphia*, the low lands
of *Maryland* and *Virginia*, and the town of
Charleston in *South Carolina* will be *under
water*.   Happy will it be for the sugar and salt,
standing in the cellars of those places, if there
be tight roofs and ceilings overhead; otherwise

without being a Conjurer, a man may easily
foretel that such commodities will receive
damage.

2. About the middle of the year, great number
of vessels fully laden, will be taken out of the
ports aforesaid, by a power with which we are
not now at war, and whose forces shall not be
descried or seen, either coming or going. But
in the end this may not be disadvantageous to
those places.

3. However, not long after, a visible Army of
20,000 *Musketeers* will land, some in Virginia
and Maryland, and some in the lower counties
on both sides of Delaware, who will over-run
the country, and sorely annoy the inhabitants :
But the air in this climate will agree with them
so ill towards winter, that they will die in the
beginning of cold weather like rotten sheep,
and by Christmas the inhabitants will get the
better of them.

Note,—*In my next Almanack these Enigmatical Prophecies will be explained.*

> For gratitude there 's none exceed 'em,
> (Their clients know this when they bleed 'em,)
> Since they who give most for their laws,
> Have most returned, and carry th' Cause.
> All know, except an arrant Tory,
> That Right and Wrong 's meer Ceremony,
> It is enough that the law jargon,
> Gives the best bidder the best bargain.

POOR RICHARD FOR 1737.

PREFACE.

COURTEOUS AND KIND READER,

This is the fifth time I have appeared in publick, chalking out the future year for my honest countrymen, and foretelling what shall, and what may, and what may not come to pass; in which I have the pleasure to find that I have given general satisfaction. Indeed, among the multitude of our astrological predictions, 't is no wonder if some few fail; for, without any defect in the art itself, 't is well known that a small error, a single wrong figure overseen in a calculation, may occasion great mistakes: But, however, we Almanack-makers may *miss it* in other things, I believe it will generally be allowed *that we always hit the day of the month*, and that I suppose is esteem'd one of the most useful things in an Almanack.

As to the weather, if I was to fall into the method my brother J——n sometimes uses, and tell you, *Snow here, or in New-England,—Rain here, or in South Carolina,—Cold to the northward,—Warm to the southward*, and the like, whatever errors I might commit, I should be something more secure of not being detected in them : But I consider it will be of no service to any body to know what weather it is 1000 miles off, and therefore I always set down positively what weather my reader will have, be he where he will at the time. We modestly desire only the favourable allowance of *a day or two before, and a day or two after* the precise day against which the weather is set ;—and if it does not come to pass accordingly, let the fault be laid upon the printer, who, 't is very like, may have transposed or misplac'd it, perhaps for the conveniency of putting in his holidays : and since, in spight of all I can say, people will give him great part of the credit of making my Almanacks, 't is but reasonable he should take some share of the blame.

I must not here omit to thank the publick for the gracious and kind encouragement they have hitherto given me :—But if the generous purchaser of my labours could see how often his *Fi'pence* helps to light up the comfortable fire, line the pot, fill the cup and make glad the heart of a poor man, and an honest good old woman, he would not think his money ill laid out, though the Almanack of his friend and servant,

R. SAUNDERS,

were one half blank paper.

HINTS TO THOSE THAT WOULD BE RICH.

The use of money is all the advantage there is in having money.

For 6£ a year you may have use of 100£, if you are a man of known prudence and honesty.

He that spends a groat a-day idly, spends idly above 6£ a year, which is the price of using 100£.

He that wastes idly a groat's worth of his time per day, one day with another, wastes the privilege of using 100£ each day.

He that idly loses 5s. worth of time, loses 5s., and might as prudently throw 5s. into the river.

He that loses 5s. not only loses that sum, but all the other advantage that might be made by turning it in dealing, which, by the time a young man becomes old, amounts to a comfortable bag of money.

Again, He that sells upon credit, asks a price for what he sells equivalent to the principal and interest of his money for the time he is like to be kept out of it ;— therefore,

He that buys upon credit pays interest for what he buys,

And he that pays ready money, might let that money out to use ; so that

He that possesses any thing he has bought, pays interest for the use of it.

Consider then, when you are tempted to buy any unnecessary household stuff, or any superfluous thing, whether you will be willing to pay *interest, and interest upon interest* for it as long as you live, and more if it grows worse by using.

Yet, in buying goods, 't is best to pay ready money, because,

He that sells upon credit, expects to lose 5 *per cent.* by bad debts ; therefore he charges on all he sells upon credit, an advance that shall make up that deficiency.

Those who pay for what they buy upon credit, pay their share of this advance.

He that pays ready money, escapes, or may escape, that charge.

A penny saved is two pence clear. A pin a-day is a groat a-year. Save and have.

Every little makes a mickle.

JANUARY.

God offer'd to the Jews salvation,
And 't was refus'd by half the nation :
Thus (tho' 't is life's great preservation),
Many oppose *innoculation.*
We 're told by one of the black robe,
The devil innoculated Job :
Suppose 't is true, what he does tell ;
Pray, neighbours, *did not Job do well ?*

The master-piece of man, is to live to the purpose.

He that steals the old man's supper do's him no wrong.

FEBRUARY.

The *Thracian* infant, entering into life,
Both parents mourn for, both receive with grief,
The Thracian infant snatched by Death away,
Both parents to the grave with joy convey.

This *Greece* and *Rome* you with derision view,
This is meer *Thracian* ignorance to you ;
But if you weigh the custom you despise,
This *Thracian* ignorance may teach the wise.

A countryman between two lawyers, is like a fish between two cats.

He that can take rest is greater than he that can take cities.

The miser's cheese is wholesomest.

MARCH.

Doris a widow past her prime,
  Her spouse long dead, her wailing doubles ;
Her real griefs increase by time ;
  What might abate, improves her troubles.
Those pangs her prudent hopes supprest,
  Impatient now she cannot smother,
How should the helpless woman rest ?
  One 's gone ;—nor can she get another.

Love and Lordship hate companions.

The nearest way to come at glory, is to do that for conscience which we do for glory.

There is much money given to be laught at, though the purchasers don't know it ; witness A's fine horse, and B's fine house.

APRIL.

A nymph and a swain to *Apollo* once prayed,
The swain had been jilted, the nymph been betray'd ;
They came for to try if his oracle knew,
E'er a nymph that was chaste, or a swain that was true.
Apollo stood mute, and had like t' have been pos'd,
At length he thus sagely the question disclos'd ;

He alone may be true in whom none will confide,
And the nymph may be chaste that has never been try'd.

He that can compose himself, is wiser than he that composes books.

Poor Dick eats like a well man, and drinks like a sick.

After crosses and losses, men grow humbler and wiser.

Love, cough, and a smoke, can't well be hid.

MAY.

Rich *Gripe* does all his thoughts and cunning bend,
T' increase that wealth he wants the soul to spend,
Poor *Shifter* does his whole contrivance set,
To spend that wealth he wants the sense to get.
How happy would appear to each his fate,
Had *Gripe* his humour, or he *Gripe's* estate ?
Kind *fate* and *fortune*, blend 'em if you can,
And of two *wretches* make one happy man.

Well done is better than well said.

Fine linnen, girls and gold so bright.
Chuse not to take by candle light.

He that can travel well a-foot, keeps a good horse.

There are no ugly loves, nor handsome prisons.

No better relation than a prudent and faithful friend.

JUNE.

Boy, bring a bowl of china here,
Fill it with water cool and clear ;
Decanter with Jamaica ripe,
And spoon of silver, clean and bright,
Sugar twice-fin'd in pieces cut,
Knife, sieve, and glass in order put,
Bring forth the fragrant fruit, and then
We 're happy till the clock strikes ten.

A traveller should have a hog's nose, deer's legs, and an ass's back.

At the working man's house hunger looks in, but dares not enter.

A good lawyer, a bad neighbour.

JULY.

Impudent *Jack*, who now lives by his shifts,
Borrowing of driblets, boldly begging gifts,
For twenty shillings lent him t'other day,
(By one who ne'er expected he would pay.)
On his friend's paper fain a note wou'd write ;
His friend, as needless, did refuse it quite ;
Paper was scarce, and 't was too hard, it 's true,
To part with cash, and lose his paper too.

Certainlie these things agree, the priest, the lawyer, and death, all three ;
Death takes both the weak and the strong,
The lawyer takes from both right and wrong,
And the priest from the living and dead has his fee.

The worst wheel of the cart makes the most noise.

AUGUST.

On his death bed poor Lubin lies ;
 His spouse is in despair ;
With frequent sobs, and mutual cries
 They both express their care.
A diff 'rent cause, says parson *Sly*,
 The same effect may give,
Poor *Lubin* fears that he shall die ;
 His wife—that he may live.

Don't misinform your doctor nor your lawyer.

 never saw an oft-transplanted tree,
Nor yet an oft-removed family,
That throve so well as those that settled be.

SEPTEMBER.

To-morrow you 'll reform, you always cry;
In what far country does this morrow lie,
That 't is so mighty long ere it arrive?
Beyond the *Indies* does this morrow live?
'T is so far-fetched, this morrow, that I fear
'T will be both very old, and very dear.
To-morrow I 'll reform, the fool does say;
To-day itself 's too late ;—the *wise* did yesterday.

Let the letter stay for the post, and not the post for the letter.

Three good meals a day is bad living.

'T is better leave for an enemy at one's death, than beg of a friend in one's life.

To whom thy secret thou dost tell,
To him thy freedom thou dost sell.

OCTOBER.

On T. T. who destroyed his Landlord's fine wood.

Indulgent nature to each kind bestows,
A secret instinct to discern its foes :
The goose, a silly bird, avoids the fox ;
Lambs fly from wolves ; and sailors steer from rocks ;
A rogue the gallows, as his fate, foresees,
And bears the like antipathy to trees.

If you 'd have a servant that you like, serve yourself.

He that pursues two hares at once, does not catch one and lets t' other go.

If you want a neat wife, chuse her on a Saturday.

If you have time, don't wait for time.

NOVEMBER.

You say you 'll spend five hundred pound,
 The world and men to know,
And take a tour all Europe round,
 Improving as you go.
Dear *Sam*, in search of other's sense,
 Discover not your own ;
But wisely double the expence,
 That you may pass unknown.

Tell a miser he 's rich, and a woman she 's old, you 'll get no money of one, nor kindness of t' other.

Don't go to the doctor with every distemper, nor to the lawyer with every quarrel, nor to the pot for every thirst.

DECEMBER.

Women are books, and men the readers be,
Who sometimes in those books erratas see ;
Yet oft the reader 's raptured with each line,
Fair print and paper, fraught with sense divine ;
Tho' some, neglectful, seldom care to read,
And faithful wives no more than bibles heed.
Are women books? says Hodge, then would mine were
An Almanack, to change her every year.

The creditors are a superstitious sect, great observers of set days and times.

The noblest question in the world is, *What good may I do in it?*

Nec sibi, sed toto, genitum se credere mundo.*

Nothing so popular as goodness.

* To believe himself born, not for himself, but for the whole world.- LUCAN, " Pharsalia."

In my last I published some *Enigmatical Prophecies*, which I did not expect any one would take for serious predictions. The explanation I promised follows, *viz :*

1. The water of the sea and rivers is raised in vapours by the sun, is form'd into clouds in the air, and thence descends in rain. Now when there is rain overhead (which frequently happens when the wind is at N.E.) the cities and places on the earth below, are certainly *under water.*

2. The power with which *we were not then at war*, but which, it was said, would take many full laden vessels out of our ports before the end of the year, is the WIND, whose forces also *are not descried either coming or going.*

3. The army which it was said would *land* in *Virginia, Maryland*, and the *lower counties* on *Delaware*, were not *Musketeers*, with guns on their shoulders as some expected ; but their namesakes, in pronunciation, tho' truly spelt *Moschitos*, arm'd only with a sharp sting. Every one knows they are fish before they fly, being bred in the water ; and therefore may properly be said *to land* before they become generally troublesome.

A WONDERFUL PROPHECY.

For January, 1737, which consists entirely of odd figures.

E'er of this odd odd year one month has roll'd,
What wonders, reader, shall the world behold !

Four kings with mighty force shall *Albion's* isle
Infest with wars and tumults for a-while;
Then some shall unexpected treasures gain,
While some mourn o'er an empty purse in vain:
And many a Christian's heart shall ake for fear,
When they the dreadful sound of trump shall hear.
Dead bones shall then be tumbled up and down,
In every city and in every town.

POOR RICHARD FOR 1738.

PREFACE BY MISTRESS SAUNDERS.

DEAR READERS,

My good man set out last week for Potowmack, to visit an old stargazer of his acquaintance, and to see about a little place for us to settle and end our days on. He left a copy of his Almanack seal'd up, and bid me send it to the press. I suspected something, and therefor, as soon as he was gone, I open'd it, to see if he had not been flinging some of his old skitts at me. Just as I thought, so it was. And truly (for want of something else to say, I suppose,) he had put into his preface, that his wife Bridget was this, and that, and t' other. What a peasecods! cannot I have a little fault or two, but all the country must see it in print! They have already been told, at one time that I am proud, another time that I am loud, and that I have

got a new petticoat, and abundance of that kind
of stuff; and now forsooth! all the world must
know, that *poor Dick's* wife has lately taken a
fancy to drink a little tea now and then. A
mighty matter truly, to make a song of!   'T is
true I had a little tea of a present from the
Printer last year; and what, must a-body throw
it away? In short, I thought the preface was
not worth a-printing, and so I fairly scratch'd it
all out, and I believe you 'll like our Almanack
never the worse for it.

Upon looking over the months, I see he has
put in abundance of foul weather this year;
and therefor I have scattered here and there,
where I could find room, some *fair, pleasant,
sunshiny,* &c., for the good women to dry their
clothes in. If it does not come to pass according to my desire, I have shown my goodwill,
however; and I hope they 'll take it in good part.

I had a design to make some other correc-
tions; and particularly to change some of the
verses that I don't very well like; but I have
just now unluckily broke my spectacles; which
obliges me to give it you as it is, and conclude
Your loving friend,
BRIDGET SAUNDERS.

You will excuse me, dear readers, that I
afford you no eclipses of the moon this year.

The truth is, I do not find they do you any good.

When there is one you are apt in observing it to expose yourselves too much and too long to the night air, whereby great numbers of you catch cold. Which was the case last year, to my very great concern. However, if you will promise to take more care of yourselves, you shall have a fine one to stare at the year after next.

JANUARY.

Dick's wife was sick, and pos'd the doctors' skill,
Who differ'd how to cure th' inveterate ill.
Purging the one prescribed. No, quoth another,
That will do neither good nor harm, my brother,
Bleeding 's the only way; 't was quick reply'd,
That 's certain death ; but e'en let *Dick* decide.
" *I 'se no great skill*," quo' Richard, " *by the Rood,*
But I think bleeding 's like to do most good."

There are three faithful friends—an old wife, an old dog, and ready money.

Great talkers should be crop'd, for they have no need of ears.

If you would have your shoes last, put no nails in 'em.

Who has deceiv'd thee so oft as thyself?

FEBRUARY.

In Christendom we all are *christians* now,
And thus I answer, if you ask me how ;
Where with *Christ's rules* our lives will not comply,
We bend it like a rule of lead, say I ;
Making it thus comply with what we be,

6

And only thus our lives with th' rule agree.
But from our fathers we 've the name perchance,
So as our king is called the king of France.

Is there anything men take more pains about than to make themselves unhappy?

Nothing brings more pain than too much pleasure; nothing more bondage than too much liberty, (or libertinism).

Read much, but not too many books.

MARCH.

Jack's wife was born in *Wiltshire*, brought up in *Cumberland*, led much of her life in *Bedfordshire*, sent her husband into *Huntingtonshire* in order to send him into *Buckinghamshire*. But he took courage in *Hartfordshire*, and carried her into *Staffordshire*, or else he might have lived and died in Shrewsbury.

He that would have a short Lent, let him borrow money to be repaid at Easter.

Write with the learned, pronounce with the vulgar.

Fly pleasures, and they 'll follow you.

APRIL.

The Old Gentry.

That all from Adam first begun,
 Since none but *Whiston* doubts,
And that his son, and his son's son
 Were ploughmen, clowns and louts;

Here lies the only difference now,
  Some shot off late, some soon ;
Your sires i' th' morning left the plow,
  And ours i' th' afternoon.

Cæsar did not merit the triumphal car more than he that conquers himself.

Hast thou virtue ?—acquire also the graces and beauties of virtue.

Buy what thou hast no need of, and e'er long thou shalt sell thy necessaries.

If thou hast wit and learning, add to it wisdom and modesty.

MAY.

A Frugal Thought.

In an acre of land are 43,560 square feet.
In 100 acres are 4,356,000 square feet ;
Twenty pounds will buy 100 acres of the proprietor,
In £20 are 4,800 pence ; by which divide the
Number of feet in 100 acres ; and you will find
That one penny will buy 907 square feet ; or
A lot of 30 feet square—*Save your pence.*

You may be more happy than princes, if you will be more virtuous.

If you would not be forgotten, as soon as you are dead and rotten, either write things worth reading, or do things worth the writing.

Sell not virtue to purchase wealth, nor liberty to purchase power.

JUNE.

Epitaph on a talkative Old Maid.

Beneath this silent stone is laid,
A noisy, antiquated maid,
Who, from her cradle talk'd till death,
And ne'er before was out of breath.

Whither she 's gone we cannot tell;
For if she talks not, she 's in ——— !
If she 's in ———, she 's there unblest
Because she hates a place of rest.

Let thy vices die before thee.

Keep your eyes wide open before marriage, half shut afterwards.

The ancients tell us what is best; but we must learn of the moderns what is fittest.

JULY.

One month a lawyer, thou the next will be
A grave physician, and the third a priest:
Chuse quickly one profession of the three,
Marry'd to her thou yet may'st court the rest.
Resolve at once; deliberate no more;
Leap in, and stand not shiv'ring on the shore.
On any one amiss thou can'st not fall;
Thou 'lt end in nothing, if thou grasps at all.

Since I cannot govern my own tongue tho' within my own teeth, how can I hope to govern the tongues of others?

'T is less discredit to abridge petty charges, than to stoop to petty gettings.

Since thou art not sure of a minute, throw not away an hour.

AUGUST.

While faster than his costive brain indites,
Philo's quick hand in flowing nonsense writes,
His case appears to me like honest *Teague's*,
When he was run away with by his legs.
Phœbus, give Philo o'er himself command;
Quicken his senses, or restrain his hand;
Let him be kept from paper, pen and ink;
So he may cease to write and learn to think.

If you do what you should not, you must hear what you would not.

Defer not thy well doing ; be not like St. George, who is always a-horseback, and never rides on.

Wish not so much to live long, as to live well.

SEPTEMBER.

These lines may be read backward or forward.

Joy, Mirth, Triumph, I do defie :
Destroy me death fain would I die :
Forlorn am I, love is exil'd,
Scorn smiles thereat ; hope is beguil'd,
    Men banish'd bliss, in woe must dwell,
    Then joy, mirth, triumph, all farewell.

As we must account for every idle word, so we must for every idle silence.

I have never seen the Philosopher's stone that turns lead into gold, but I have known the pursuit of it turn a man's gold into lead.

Never intreat a servant to dwell with thee.

OCTOBER.

A doubtful meaning.

The female kind is counted ill :
And is indeed : the contrary ;—
No man can find : that hurt they will :
But every where : shew charity :
To nobody ; malicious still ;
In word or deed : believe you me.

Time is an herb that cures all diseases.

Reading makes a full man—meditation a profound man—discourse a clear man.

If any man flatters me, I 'll flatter him again, though he were my best friend.

NOVEMBER.

A monster in a course of vice grown old,
Leaves to his gaping heir his ill gain'd gold;
The preacher fee'd, strait are his virtues shown;
And render'd lasting by the sculptur'd stone.
If on the stone or sermon we rely,
Pity a worth like his, should ever die!
If credit to his real life we give,
Pity a wretch like him, should ever live.

Wish a miser long life, and you wish him no good.

None but the well-bred man knows how to confess a fault, or acknowledge himself in an error.

Drive thy business;—let not that drive thee.

There is much difference between imitating a good man, and counterfeiting him.

DECEMBER.

The wise man says, *it is a wise man's part*
To keep his tongue close prisoner in his heart.
If he then be a fool whose thought denies
There is a God, how desp'rately unwise,
How much more fool is he, whose language shall
Proclaim in public, *there 's no God at all:*
What then are they, nay fools in what degree,
Whose actions shall maintain 't?—*Such fools are we.*

Wink at small faults—remember thou hast great ones.

Eat to please thyself, but dress to please others.

Search others for their virtues, thyself for thy vices.

Never spare the parson's wine, nor baker's pudding.

Each year one vicious habit rooted out,
In time might make the worst man good throughout.

Ready money for OLD RAGS may be had of the printer
hereof; by whom is made and sold very good
LAMPBLACK.

POOR RICHARD FOR 1739.

PREFACE.

KIND READER,

Encouraged by thy former generosity, I once more present thee with an almanack, which is the 7th of my publication. While thou art putting pence in my pocket, and furnishing my cottage with necessaries, *Poor Dick* is not unmindful to do something for thy benefit. The stars are watch'd as narrowly as old *Bess* watch'd her daughter that thou may'st be acquainted with their motions, and told a tale of their influences and effects, which may do thee more good than a dream of last year's snow.

Ignorant men wonder how we astrologers foretell the weather so exactly unless we deal with the old black devil. Alas! 't is as easy as ————————. For instance; The stargazer peeps at the heavens thro' a long glass: He sees perhaps TAURUS or the great bull, in a mighty chase, stamping on the floor of his house, swinging his tail about, stretching out his neck, and opening wide his mouth. 'T is natural from these appearances to judge that this furious bull is puffing, blowing and roaring. Distance being considered and time allow'd for all this to come down,—there you have wind and thunder.—He spies perhaps *Virgo* (or the virgin) she turns her head round as it were to see if anybody observ'd her; then crouching down gently, with her hands on her knees, she looks wistfully for a while right forward. He judges rightly what she 's about: and having calculated the distance and allow'd time for its falling, finds that next spring we shall have a fine *April* shower. What can be more natural and easy than this?—I might instance the like in many other particulars; but this may be sufficient to prevent our being taken for conjurors.—O, the wonderful knowledge to be found in the stars!—Even the smallest things are written there, if you had but skill to read. When my brother *J—m—n* erected a scheme to know which was best for his sick horse, to sup a new-laid egg, or a little broth, he found that the stars gave their verdict for broth,—and the horse having sup'd his broth; ————————— Now, what do you think became of that horse?—You shall know in my next.

Besides the usual things expected in an almanack, I hope the profess'd teachers of mankind
will excuse my scattering here and there some
instructive hints in matters of morality and religion.—And be not thou disturbed, O grave
and sober reader, if among the many serious
sentences of my book, thou findest me trifling
now and then and talking idly.—In all the
dishes I have hitherto cooked for thee, there
is solid meat enough for thy money. There are
scraps from the table of wisdom, that will if
well digested yield strong nourishment to thy
mind. But squeamish stomachs cannot eat
without pickles ; which 't is true are good for
nothing else, but they provoke an appetite.
The vain youth that reads my almanack for
the sake of an idle joke, will perhaps meet
with a serious reflection, that he may ever
after be the better for.

Some people observing the great yearly demand for my almanack, imagine I must by this
time have become rich, and consequently ought
to call myself *Poor Dick* no longer. But, the
case is this, when I first begun to publish, the
printer made a fair agreement with me for my
copies, by virtue of which he runs away with
the greatest part of the profits. However, much
good may 't do him ;—I do not grudge it him ;
he is a man I have a great regard for, and wish

his profit ten times greater than it is.   For I am,
dear reader, his, as well as thy

Affectionate friend,

R. SAUNDERS.

Very good LAMPBLACK, made and sold by
the printer hereof.

JANUARY.

Giles Joll, as sleeping in his cart he lay,
Some pilfering villains stole his team away ;
Giles wakes and cries,—What 's here ? a dickens, what?
Why, how now ?—Am I Giles ? or am I not ?
If he, I 've lost six geldings, to my smart ;
If not, odds buddikins, I 've found a cart.

When death puts out our flame, the snuff will tell
If we are wax, or tallow by the smell.

At a great penny worth, pause a while.

As to his wife, *John* minds St. Paul, he 's one that hath
a wife, and is as if he 'd none.

Kings and bears often worry their keepers.

FEBRUARY.

Lord if our days be *few*, why do we spend,
And lavish them to such an evil end ?
Or why if they be *evil*, do we wrong
Ourselves and thee, in wishing them so long ?
Our days decrease, our evils still renew,
We make them *ill*, thou kindly mak'st them *few*.

If thou would'st live long, live well ; for folly and
wickedness shorten life.

Trust thyself, and another shall not betray thee.

MARCH.

Thus with kind words, squire Edward cheer'd his friend ;
Dear *Dick !* thou on my friendship may'st depend ;
I know thy fortune is but very scant ;
But, be assur'd, I 'll ne'er see *Dick* in want.
Dick 's soon confin'd,—his friend no doubt would free
   him :
His word he kept,—in want he ne'er would see him.

He that pays for work before it 's done, has but a pennyworth for two pence.

Historians relate, not so much what is done, as what
they would have believed.

O malster ! break that cheating peck ; 't is plain,
Whene'er you use it you 're a knave in Grain.

APRIL.

For 's country *Codrus* suffer'd by the sword,
And, by his death, his country's fame restor'd ;
Cæsar into his mother's bosom bare
Fire, sword, and all the ills of civil war :
Codrus confirm'd his country's wholesome laws ;
Cæsar in blood still justified his cause ;
Yet following kings ne'er 'dopted Codrus' name,
But *Cæsar*, still, and emperor 's the same.

Doll learning *propria quæ maribus* without book,
Like *nomen crescentis genitivo* doth look.

Grace thou thy house, and let not that grace thee.

Thou cans't not joke an enemy into a friend, but thou
may'st a friend into an enemy.

Eyes and Priests,—Bear no tests.

MAY.

Think bright *Florella*, when you see,
The constant changes of the year,

That nothing is from ruin free,
The gayest things must disappear.
Think of your beauties in their bloom,
The spring of sprightly youth improve ;
For cruel age, alas, will come,
And then 't will be too late to love.

He that falls in love with himself, will have no rivals.

Let thy child's first lesson be obedience, and the second will be what thou wilt.

Blessed is he that expects nothing, for he shall never be disappointed.

Rather go to bed supperless than run in debt for a breakfast.

JUNE.

On his late deafness.

Deaf, giddy, helpless, left alone,
To all my friends a burthen grown,
No more I hear a great church bell,
Than if it rung out for my knell :
At thunder now no more I start,
Than at the whispering of ———
Nay what 's incredible, alack !
I hardly hear my *Bridget's* clack.

Let thy discontents be secrets.

A man of knowledge like a rich soil, feeds
If not a world of corn, a world of weeds.

An infallible remedy for *toothache*, viz.—Wash the root of an aching tooth, in *Elder vinegar*, and let it dry half an hour in the sun ; after which it will never ache more.

JULY.

Says *George* to *William*—Neighbour, have a care,
Touch not that tree—'t is sacred to despair ;

Two wives I had, but, ah ! that joy is past !
Who breath'd upon those fatal boughs their last.
The best in all the row, without dispute,
Says *Will*—Would mine but bear such precious fruit !
When next you prune your orchard, save for me
(*I have a spouse*) one cyon of that tree.

A modern wit is one of *David's* fools.

No resolution of repenting hereafter, can be sincere.

Pollio who values nothing that 's within,
Buys books as men hunt beavers—for their skin.

Honour thy father and mother, i. e. Live so as to be an honour to them tho' they are dead.

AUGUST.

Ships sailing down Delaware bay this month, shall hear at ten leagues distance, a confused rattling noise, like a shower of hail upon a cake of ice. Don't be frighted good passengers ! the sailors can inform you, that it is nothing but lower county teeth in the ague. In a southerly wind you may hear it in Philadelphia.

Witness G. L. M. cum multis aliis.

If thou injurest conscience, it will have its revenge on thee.

Hear no ill of a friend, nor speak any of an enemy.

Pay what you owe, and you 'll know what is your own.

Be not niggardly of what costs thee nothing, as courtesy, counsel, and countenance.

Thirst after desert—not reward.

SEPTEMBER.

The sun now clear, serene the golden skies,
Where'er you go, fast the shadow flies ;
A cloud succeeds ; the sunshine now is o'er,
The fleeting phantom fled, is seen no more ;
With your bright day, its progress too does end :
See here, vain man ! the picture of thy friend.

Beware of him that is slow to anger : He is angry for something, and will not be pleased for nothing.

No longer virtuous, no longer free, is a maxim as true with regard to a private person as a commonwealth.

When man and woman die, as poets sung,
His heart 's the last part moves,—her last, the tongue.

OCTOBER.

What legions of fables and whimsical tales
Pass current for gospel where priestcraft prevails !
Our ancestors were thus most strangely deceiv'd,
What stories and nonsense for truth they believ'd.
But we their wise sons, who these fables reject,
Ev'n truth now-a-days, are too apt to suspect ;
From believing too much, the right faith we let fall ;
So now we believe,—'troth,—nothing at all.

Proclaim not all thou knowest, all thou owest, all thou hast, nor all thou can'st.

Let our fathers and grandfathers be valued for *their* goodness, ourselves for our own.

Industry need not wish.

Sin is not hurtful because it is forbidden, but it is forbidden because it is hurtful.

NOVEMBER.

Pinchall, possessing heaps of wealth,
Lives miserably poor ;

He says 't is to preserve his health,
    But means by it his store.
 Let *Freeman* but the world invite
    To dine on good cheer *gratis*,
Then he will gorge like half-starved wight
    And cram his *nunquam satis*.

Nor is a duty beneficial because it is commanded, but
it is commanded because it is beneficial.

A . . . they say has wit; for what?
For writing?———No,—for writing not.

George came to the crown without striking a blow,
Ah!—quoth the Pretender, would I could do so.

DECEMBER.

In travel, pilgrims oft do ask to know
What *miles* they 've gone, and what they have to go;
The way is tedious, and their limbs opprest,
And their desire is to be at rest.
In life's more tedious journey, man delays
T' enquire out the number of his days :
He cares, not he, how slow his hours spend,
The journey 's better than the journey's end.

O Lazy bones ! Dost thou think God would have given
thee arms and legs, if he had not design'd thou should'st
use them.

On the Law.—Nigh neighbour to the squire, poor Sam
    complain'd
Of frequent wrongs, but no amends he gain'd.
Each day his gates thrown down ; his fences broke,
And injur'd still the more, the more he spoke ;
At last, resolv'd his potent foe to awe,
A suit against him he began in law ;
Nine happy terms thro' all the forms he run,
Obtain'd his cause—had costs—and was *undone*.

A cure for poetry.—Seven wealthy towns contend for Homer dead,
Thro' which the living Homer beg'd his bread.

Great beauty, great strength, and great riches are really and truly of no great use ; a right heart exceeds all.

A TRUE PROGNOSTICATION FOR 1739.

COURTEOUS READER,

Having consider'd the infinite abuses arising from the false prognostications published among you, made under the shadow of a pot of drink, or, so, I have here calculated one of the most sure and unerring that ever was seen in black and white, as hereafter you 'll find. For doubtless it is a heinous, foul and crying sin, to deceive the poor gaping world, greedy of the knowledge of futurity as we Americans all are.

Take notice by the by, that having been at a great deal of pains in the calculation, if you don't believe every syllable, jot and tittle of it, you do me a great deal of wrong; for which either here or elsewhere, you may chance to be claw'd off with a vengeance.—A good cowskin, crabtree, or bull's pizzle may be plentifully bestow'd on your outward man. You may snuff up your noses as much as you please, 't is all one for that.

Well, however, come, smite your noses my little children ; pull out your best eyes, on wi' your barnacles, and carefully observe every scruple of what I 'm going to tell you.

Of the GOLDEN NUMBER.

The Golden number, *non est inventus*, I cannot find it this year by any calculation I have made. I must content myself with a number of copper. No matter, go on.

Of the ECLIPSES *this year*.

There are so many invisible eclipses this year, that I fear, not unjustly, our pockets will suffer inanition, be full empty, and our feeling at a loss.—During the first visible eclipse *Saturn* is retrograde: For which reason the crabs will go sidelong, and the ropemakers backward. The belly will wag before, and the ⸺ shall sit down first. *Mercury* will have his share in these affairs, and so confound the speech of the people, that when a *Pennsylvanian* would say PANTHER he shall say PAINTER.—When a New Yorker thinks to say THIS he shall say DISS, and the people in *New England* and *Cape May* will not be able to say COW for their lives, but will be forc'd to say KEOW by a certain involuntary twist in the root of their tongues. No *Connecticut man*, nor *Marylander* will be able to open his mouth this year, but SIR shall be the first or last syllable he pronounces, and

7

sometimes both.—Brutes shall speak in many places, and there will be above seven and twenty irregular verbs made this year, if Grammar don't interpose.—But who can help these misfortunes.

Of the DISEASES *this year.*

This year the stone-blind shall see but very little; the deaf shall hear but poorly; and the dumb sha'n't speak very plain. And it's much, if my Dame *Bridget* talks at all this year. Whole flocks, herds, and droves of sheep, swine and oxen, cocks and hens, ducks and drakes, geese and ganders shall go to pot; but the mortality will not be altogether so great among cats, dogs and horses. As to old age 't will be incurable this year, because of the years past. And towards the fall some people will be seiz'd with an unaccountable inclination to roast and eat their own ears: Should this be call'd madness, Doctors? I think not. But the worst disease of all will be a certain most horrid, dreadful, malignant, catching, perverse and odious malady, almost epidemical, insomuch that many shall run mad upon it; I quake for very fear when I think on 't; for I assure you very few will escape this disease; which is called by the learned Albromazar *Lacko'mony.*

Of the FRUITS *of the* EARTH.

I find that this will be a plentiful year of all manner of good things, to those who have enough; but the orange trees in *Greenland* will go near to fare the worse for the cold.— As to oats, they 'll be a great help to horses. I dare say there won't be much more bacon than swine. *Mercury* somewhat threatens our parsley beds, yet parsley will be to be had for money. Hemp will grow faster than the children of this age, and some will find there 's too much on 't. As for corn, fruit, cyder and turnips, there never was such plenty as will be now; if poor folks may have their wish.

Of the CONDITION *of some countries.*

I FORESEE an universal droughth this year thro' all the northern colonies. Hence there will be *dry* rice in *Carolina*, *dry* tobacco in *Virginia* and *Maryland*, *dry* bread in *Pennsylvania* and *New York;* and in *New England* *dry* fish and *dry* doctrine. *Dry* throats will be every where; but then how pleasant it will be to drink cool cyder! tho' some will tell you nothing is more contrary to thirst.—I believe it, and indeed, *contraria, contrariis curantur.*

R. SAUNDERS.

POOR RICHARD FOR 1740.

PREFACE.

October 7, 1739.

COURTEOUS READER,

You may remember that in my first Almanack, published for the year 1733, I predicted the death of my dear friend, *Titan Leeds*, Philomat, to happen that year on the 17th day of October, 3 h. 29 m. P. M. The good man, it seems, died accordingly. But W. B. and A. B. [*] have continued to publish Almanacks in his name ever since ; asserting for some years that he was still living ; At length when the truth could no longer be concealed from the world, they confess his death in their Almanack for 1739, but pretend that he died not till last year, and that before his departure he had furnished them with calculations for 7 years to come.—Ah, *my friends*, these are poor shifts and thin dis-

* William and Andrew Bradford, printers in New York and Philadelphia.

guises ; of which indeed I should have taken little or no notice, if you had not at the same time accused me as a false predictor ; an aspersion that the more affects me, as my whole livelyhood depends on a contrary character.

But to put this matter beyond dispute, I shall acquaint the world with a fact, as strange and surprising as it is true ; being as follows, viz.—

On the 4th instant, towards midnight as I sat in my little study writing this Preface, I fell fast asleep ; and continued in that condition for some time, without dreaming any thing, to my knowledge. On awaking, I found lying before me the following, viz.—

Dear Friend SAUNDERS,

My respect for you continues even in this separate state, and I am griev'd to see the aspersions thrown on you by the malevolence of avaricious publishers of Almanacks, who envy your success.—They say your prediction of my death in 1733 was false, and they pretend that I remained alive many years after. But I do hereby certify, that I did actually die at that time, precisely at the hour you mention'd, with a variation only of 5 min. 53 sec. which must be allow'd to be no great matter in such cases.— And I do further declare that I furnish'd them with no calculations of the planets motions, &c.

seven years after my death, as they are pleased to give out : so that the stuff they publish as an Almanack in my name is no more mine than 't is yours.

You will wonder perhaps, how this paper comes written on your table. You must know that no separate spirits are under any confinement till after the final settlement of all accounts. In the meantime we wander where we please, visit our old friends, observe their actions, enter sometimes into their imaginations, and give them hints waking or sleeping that may be of advantage to them. Finding you asleep, I enter'd your left nostril, ascended into your brain, found out where the ends of those nerves were fastened that move your right hand and fingers, by the help of which I am now writing unknown to you ; but when you open your eyes you will see that the hand written is mine, tho' wrote with yours.

The people of this infidel age, perhaps, will hardly believe this story. But you may give them these three signs by which they shall be convinced of the truth of it.—About the middle of June *next,* J. J - - - - n, *Philomat, shall be openly reconciled to the* Church of Rome, *and give all his goods and chattels to the chappel, being perverted by a certain* country school-master.—*On the 7th of* September *following my*

*old Friend W. B - - - - t shall be sober 9 hours,
to the astonishment of all his neighbours :—
And about the same time W. B. and A. B. will
publish another Almanack in my name, in
spight of truth and common sense.*

*As I can see much clearer into futurity, since
I got free from the dark prison of flesh, in
which I was continually molested and almost
blinded with fogs arising from tiff, and the
smoke of burnt drams ; I shall in kindness to
you, frequently give you information of things
to come, for the improvement of your Almanack : being, Dear Dick, Your Affectionate
Friend,*

T. LEEDS.

For my own part I am convinced that the
above letter is genuine. If the reader doubts of
it, let him carefully observe the three *signs ;*
and if they do not actually come to pass, believe
as he pleases.

I am his humble Friend,
R. SAUNDERS.

OF THE ECLIPSES FOR 1740.

There will be six Eclipses this year, &c. &c.
&c. Some of these Eclipses foreshow great grief
and many tears among the soft sex this year;
whether for the breaking of their crockery ware,

the loss of their loves, or in repentance for their sins, I shall not say : tho' I must own I think there will be a great deal of the latter in the case.—War we shall hear but too much of (for all christians have not yet learn'd to *love one another*), and, I doubt, of some ineffectual treaties of peace.   I pray Heav'n defend these Colonies from every enemy ; and give them bread enough, peace enough, money enough, and plenty of good cyder.

JANUARY.

My sickly spouse, with many a sigh
Once told me,—*Dicky*, I shall die :
I griev'd, but recollected strait,
'T was bootless to contend with fate :
So resignation to Heaven's will
Prepar'd me for succeeding ill ;
'T was well it did ; for on my life,
'T was Heav'n's will to spare my wife.

To bear other people's afflictions, every one has courage and enough to spare.

No wonder Tom grows fat, th' unwieldy sinner, makes his whole life but one continual dinner.

An empty bag cannot stand upright.

FEBRUARY.

While the good priest with eyes devoutly clos'd,
Left on the book the marriage fee expos'd,
The new made bridegroom his occasion spies,
And pleas'd, repockets up the shining prize ;

Yet not so safe, but Mr. *Surplice* views
The *frolic*, and demands his pilfer'd dues.
No, quoth the man, good Doctor, I 'll non suit y',
A plain default, I found you off your duty?
More carefully the holy book survey :
Your rule is, you should *watch* as well as *pray*.

Happy that Nation,—fortunate that age, whose history is not diverting.

What is a Butterfly?—at best he 's but a catterpillar drest.—The gaudy Fop 's his picture just.

None are deceived, but they that confide.

MARCH.

When *Pharoah's* sins provok'd th' Almighty's hand,
To pour his wrath upon the guilty land ;
A ten fold plague the great avenger shed,
The King offended, and the nation bled.
Hads't thou, unaided, *Feria*, but been sent,
Vial elect, for *Pharoah's* punishment.
Thro' what a various curse the wretch had run,
He more than Heaven's ten plagues had felt in one.

An open foe may prove a curse ;
But a pretended friend is worse.

A Wolf eats sheep but now and then,
Ten Thousands are devour'd by men.

Man's tongue is soft, and bone doth lack ;
Yet a stroke therewith may break a man's back.

APRIL.

Says Roger to his wife, my dear ;
The strangest piece of news I hear !
A *law*, 't is said, will quickly pass
To purge the matrimonial class ;

Cuckolds, if any such we have here,
Must to a man be thrown i' the river.
She smiling cry'd,—My dear, you seem
Surpriz'd ! *Pray han't you learn'd to swim ?*

Many a meal is lost for want of meat.

To all apparent beauties blind
Each blemish strikes an envious mind.

The poor have little,—beggars none ;
The rich too much—enough not one.

MAY.

A carrier every night and morn
Would see his horses eat their corn :
This sunk the hostler's vails, 't is true,
But then his horses had their due.
Were we so cautious in all cases,
Small gain would rise from greater places.

There are lazy minds as well as lazy bodies.

Tricks and trechery are the practice of fools that have
not wit enough to be honest.

Who says Jack is not generous ?—he is always fond
of giving, and cares not for receiving,——what ?—why,
advice.

JUNE.

How weak, how vain is human pride !
Dares man upon himself confide ?
The wretch who glories in his gain
Amasses heaps on heaps in vain.
Can those (when tortur'd by disease)
Cheer our sick heart, or purchase ease ?
Can those prolong one gasp of breath,
Or calm the troubled hour of death ?

The Man who with undaunted toils,
Sails unknown seas to unknown soils,
With various wonders feasts his sight :
What stranger wonders does he write ?

Fear not death ; for the sooner we die, the longer shall
we be immortal.

JULY.

The monarch of long regal line,
Was rais'd from dust as frail as mine :
Can he pour health into his veins,
Or cool the fever's restless pains ?—
Can he (worn down in nature's course)
New-brace his feeble nerves with force?
Can he (how vain is mortal pow'r !)
Stretch life beyond the destin'd hour ?

Those who in quarrels interpose,
Must often wipe a bloody nose.

Promises may get thee friends, but non-performance
will turn them into enemies.

In other men we faults can spy,
And blame the mote that dims their eye ;
Each little speck and blemish find ;
To our own stronger errors blind.

AUGUST.

The man of pure and simple heart
Thro' life disdains a double part,
He never needs the screen
His inward bosom to disguise.
In vain malicious tongues assail.
Let envy snarl, let slander rail,
From virtue's shield (secure from wound)
Their blunted venom'd shafts rebound.

When you speak to a man, look on his eyes ; when he speaks to thee, look on his mouth.

Jane, why those tears?—why droops your head ?
Is then your other husband dead ?
Or, doth a worse disgrace betide ?
Hath no one since his death apply'd ?

Observe all men ; thyself most.

SEPTEMBER.

We frequently misplace *esteem*
By judging men by what they seem.
With partial eyes we 're apt to see,
The man of noble pedigree.
To birth, wealth, power, we should allow
Precedence, and our lowest bow :
In that is due distinction shown ;
Esteem is Virtue's right alone.

Thou hadst better eat salt with the philosophers of *Greece, than sugar with the courtiers* of Italy.

Seek Virtue, and of that possest,
To Providence resign the rest.

Marry above thy match, and thou 'lt get a master.

Fear to do ill, and you need fear nought else.

OCTOBER.

What 's beauty ?—Call ye that your own,
A flow'r that fades as soon as blown !
Those eyes of so divine a ray,
What are they? Mould'ring, mortal clay,
Those features cast in heav'nly mould,
Shall, like my coarser earth, grow old ;
Like common grass, the fairest flow'r
Must feel the hoary season's power.

He makes a foe, who makes a jest.

Can grave and formal pass for wise
When men the solemn owl despise?

Some are justly laught at for keeping their money
foolishly, others for spending it idly: He is the greatest fool that lays it out in a purchase of repentance.

NOVEMBER.

Old *Socrates* was obstinately good,
Virtuous by force, by inclination lewd.
When secret movements drew his soul aside,
He quell'd his lust, and stemm'd the swelling tide ;
Sustain'd by reason still, unmov'd he stood,
And steady bore against th' opposing flood.
He durst correct what nature form'd amiss,
And forc'd unwilling virtue to be his.

Who knows a fool, must know his brother ;
For one will recommend another.

Avoid dishonest gain : no price,
Can recompence the pangs of vice.

When befriended, remember it :
When you befriend,—forget it.

Great souls with generous pity melt ;
Which coward tyrants never felt.

DECEMBER.

O blessed season ! lov'd by saints and sinners,
For long devotions, or for longer dinners ;
More grateful still to those who deal in books,
Now not with readers, but with pastry cooks :
Learn'd works, despis'd by those to merit blind,
By these well weigh'd, their certain value find.
Bless'd lot of paper, falsely called *waste*,
To bear those cates which authors seldom taste.

Employ thy time well, if thou meanest to gain leisure.

A flatterer never seems absurd :
The flatter'd always takes his word.

Lend money to an enemy, and thou 'lt gain him ; to a friend, and thou 'lt lose him.

Neither praise nor dispraise, till seven Christmasses be over.

COURTS.

I know you lawyers can, with ease,
Twist words and meanings as you please ;
That language, by your skill made pliant,
Will bend to favour every client ;
That 't is the fee directs the sense
To make out either side's pretence :
When you peruse the clearest case,
You see it with a double face,
For scepticism 's your profession ;
You hold there 's doubt in all expression.
  Hence is the Bar with fees supplied,
Hence eloquence takes either side.
Your hand would have but paltry gleaning,
Could every man express his meaning.
Who dares presume to pen a deed,
Unless you previously are fee'd ?
'T is drawn, and, *to augment the cost*,
In dull prolixity engrost :
And now we 're well secur'd by law,
Till the next brother find a flaw.

POOR RICHARD FOR 1741.

[PREFACE OMITTED.]

JANUARY.

Your homely face, Flippanta, you disguise
With patches, numerous as Argus' eyes :
I own that patching 's requisite for you :
For more we 're pleas'd, if less your face we view :
Yet I advise, if my advice you 'd ask,
Wear but one patch :——but be that patch a mask.

Enjoy the present hour, be mindful of the past ;
And neither fear nor wish the approaches of the last.

Learn of the skilful : He that teaches himself, hath a
fool for his master.

FEBRUARY.

The cringing train of pow'r survey ;
What creatures are so low as they !
With what obsequiousness they bend !
To what vile actions condescend !
Their rise is in their meanness built,
And flatt'ry is their smallest guilt.

Best is the tongue that feels the rein ;
He that talks much, talks in vain ;
We from the wordy torrent fly :
Who listens to the chattering Pye ?

III

Think Cato sees thee.

No wood without bark.

MARCH.

Enrag'd was Buckram, when his wife he beat,
That she 'd so often, lousy knave repeat.
At length he seized and drag'd her to the well,
I 'll cool thy tongue, or I 'll thy courage quell.
Ducking, thy case, poor Buckram, little mends;
She had her lesson at her fingers' ends.
Sows'd over head, her arms she raises high;
And cracking nails the want of tongue supply.

Monkeys, warm with envious spite,
Their most obliging friends will bite:
And fond to copy human ways,
Practice new mischiefs all their days.

Joke went out and brought home his fellow, and they
two began a quarrel.

APRIL.

Rash mortals, e'er you take a wife,
Contrive your pile to last for life:
On sense and worth your passion found,
By decency cemented round;
Let prudence with good-nature strive,
To keep esteem and love alive;
Then, come old age whene'er it will,
Your friendship shall continue still.

Let thy discontents be thy secrets;—if the world knows
them 't will despise thee and increase them.

E'er you remark another's sin,
Bid your own conscience look within.

Anger and folly walk cheek by jole; repentance treads
on both their heels.

MAY.

Fair decency, celestial maid,
Descend from Heav'n to beauty's aid :
Tho' beauty may beget desire,
'T is thou must fan the lover's fire :
For beauty, like supreme dominion,
Is but supported by opinion :
If decency bring no supplies,
Opinion falls and beauty dies.

Turn Turk, Tim, and renounce thy faith in words as well as actions : Is it worse to follow Mahomet than the Devil ?

Don't overload gratitude ; if you do, she 'll kick.

Be always ashamed to catch thyself idle.

JUNE.

When painful Colin in his grave was laid,
His mournful wife this lamentation made :
I 've lost, alas ! (poor wretch, what must I do ?)
The best of friends, and best of husbands too.
Thus of all joy and happiness bereft :
And with the charge of ten poor children left ;
A greater grief no woman sure can know.
Who (with ten children)—who will have me now ?

Where yet was ever found the mother,
Who 'd change her booby for another ?

At 20 years of age the will reigns ; at 30 the wit ; at 40 the judgment.

Christianity commands us to pass by injuries ; policy, to let them pass by us.

JULY.

Nature expects mankind should share
The duties of the publick care.
8

Who 's born for sloth? To some we find
The plough-share's annual toil assigned;
Some at the sounding anvil glow;
Some the swift gliding shuttle throw;
Some, studious of the wind and tide,
From pole to pole our commerce guide,

Lying rides upon debt's back.

They who have nothing to be troubled at, will be troubled at nothing.

Wife, from thy spouse each blemish hide,
More than from all the world beside :
Let DECENCY be all thy pride.

AUGUST.

Some (taught by industry) impart
With hands and feet the works of art;
While some, of genius more refined,
With head and tongues assist mankind;
Each aiming at one common end
Proves to the whole a needful friend.
Thus, born each other's useful aid,
By turns are obligations paid.

Nick's passions grow fat and hearty : his understanding looks consumptive !

If evils come not, then our fears are vain ;
And if they do, fear but augments the pain.

If you would keep your secret from an enemy, tell it not to a friend.

Rob not for burnt offerings.

SEPTEMBER.

The Monarch, when his table 's spread,
To th' farmer is oblig'd for bread ;

And when in all his glory drest,
Owes to the loom his royal vest ;
Do not the mason's toil and care
Protect him from th' inclement air?
Does not the cutler's art supply
The ornament that guards his thigh ?

Bess *brags she 's* a beauty, and can prove the same :
As how ? Why thus, sir, 't is her puppy's name.

Up, sluggard, and waste not life ; in the grave will be
sleeping enough.

Well done, is twice done.

Clearly spoken, Mr. Fogg ! You explain English by
Greek.

OCTOBER.

All these in duty, to the throne
Their common obligations own.
'T is he (his own and people's cause)
Protects their properties and laws :
Thus they their honest toil employ,
And with content the fruits enjoy,
In every rank, or great or small,
'T is INDUSTRY supports us all.

Formio bewails his sins with the same heart,
As friends do friends when they 're about to part.
Believe it, Formio will not entertain
One cheerful thought till they do meet again.

Honours change manners.

NOVEMBER.

Syl. dreamt that bury'd in his fellow clay,
Close by a common beggar's side he lay :

And, as so mean a neighbour shock'd his pride,
Thus, like a corpse of consequence, he cry'd;
Scoundrel, begone; and henceforth touch me not:
More manners learn; and, at a distance, rot.
How! scoundrel! in a hautier tone cry'd he;
Proud lump of dirt, I scorn thy words and thee:
Here all are equal; now thy case is mine;
This is my rotting place, and that is thine.

Jack eating rotten cheese, did say,
Like Samson I my thousands slay:
I vow, quoth Roger, so you do,
And with the self-same weapon too.

There are no fools so troublesome as those that have wit.

Quarrels never could last long,
If on one side only lay the wrong.

DECEMBER.

On a Bee, stifled in honey.

From flower to flower, with eager pains,
See the poor busy lab'rer fly!
When all that from her toil she gains,
Is, in the sweets she hoards, to die.
'T is thus, would man the truth believe,
With life's soft sweets, each fav'rite joy:
If we taste wisely, they relieve;
But if we plunge too deep, destroy.

Let no pleasure tempt thee, no profit allure thee, no ambition corrupt thee, no example sway thee, no persuasion move thee, to do any thing which thou knowest to be evil; so shalt thou always live jollily: for a good conscience is a continual Christmas. Adieu.

COURTS.

He that by injury is griev'd,
And goes to law to be relieved,
Is sillier than a sottish chouse,
Who, when a thief has robb'd his house,
Applies himself to cunning men
To help him to his goods again :
When, all he can expect to gain,
Is but to squander more in vain.
For lawyers, lest the Bear defendant,
And plaintiff Dog should make an end on 't,
Do stave and tail with writs of error,
Reverse of judgment and demurrer,
To let them breathe a-while, and then,
Cry *whoop*, and set them on again ;
Until, with subtil cobweb cheats,
In which, when once they are embrangl'd,
The more they stir the more they 're tangl'd
For while their purses can dispute,
There 's no end of th' immortal suit.

POOR RICHARD FOR 1742.

PREFACE.

COURTEOUS READER,

This is the ninth year of my endeavours to serve thee in the capacity of a calendar-writer. The encouragement I have met with must be ascribed in a great measure to your charity, excited by the open, honest declaration I made of my poverty at my first appearance. This my brother *Philomaths* could, without being conjurors, discover ; and *Poor Richard's* success has produced ye a *Poor Will,* and a *Poor Robin ;* and no doubt a *Poor John*, &c., will follow, and we shall all be, *in name,* what some folks say we are already *in fact,* a parcel of *poor almanacmakers.* During the course of these nine years, what buffetings have I not sustained ! The fraternity have been all in arms. Honest *Titan,* deceased, was raised, and made to abuse his old friend. Both authors and printers were angry. Hard names, and many were bestowed on me. *They denied me to be the author of my own works ;* declared there never was any such person ; asserted that I was dead sixty years ago ; prognosticated my death to happen within a twelvemonth ; with many other malicious inconsistencies, the effects of blind passion, envy at my success, and a vain hope of depriving me, dear reader, of thy wonted countenance and favor. *Who knows him ?* they cry ; *where does he live ?* But what is that to them ? If I delight in a private life, have they any right to drag me out of my retirement ? I have good reasons for concealing the place of my abode. It is time for an old man, as I am, to think of preparing for his great remove. The perpetual teasing of both neighbours and strangers to calculate nativities, give judgement on schemes, and erect figures, discover thieves, detect horse-stealers, describe the route of runaways and strayed cattle ; the crowd of visitors with a thousand trifling questions, *Will my ship return safe ? Will my mare win the race ? Will her next colt be a pacer ? When will my wife die ? Who shall be my husband ? and HOW LONG first ? When is the best time to cut hair, trim cocks, or sow salad ?* these and the

like impertinences I have now neither taste nor
leisure for. I have had enough of them. All
that these angry folks can say will never provoke me to tell them where I live ; I would eat
my nails first.

My last adversary is *J. J——n, Philomat*, who
declares and protests (in his preface, 1741) that
the *false prophecy put in my Almanac, concerning him, the year before, is altogether* false and
untrue, and *that I am one of Baal's false prophets.*
This *false, false prophecy* he speaks of related
to his reconciliation with the Church of Rome ;
which notwithstanding his declaring and pro-
testing, is, I fear, too true. Two things in his
elegiac verses confirm me in this suspicion.
He calls the first of November *All-Hallows
Day*. Reader, does it in the least savour of the
pure language of friends? But the plainest
thing is his adoration of saints, which he confesses to be his practice in these words, page 4,

> " When any trouble did me befall,
>   To my dear *Mary* then I would call."

Did he think the whole world so stupid as not
to take notice of this? So ignorant as not to
know that all Catholics pay the highest regard
to the *Virgin Mary?* Ah, friend *John*, we
must allow you to be a poet, but you are cer-

tainly no Protestant. I could heartily wish your religion were as good as your verses.

RICHARD SAUNDERS.*

JANUARY.

Foot, Horse and Waggons, now cross Rivers, dry,
And Ships unmov'd, the boistrous Winds defy,
In frozen Climes : when all conceal'd from Sight,
The pleasing Objects that to Verse invite ;
The Hills, the Dales, and the delightful Woods,
The flowry Plains, and Silver-streaming Floods,
By Snow disguis'd, in bright Confusion lie,
And with one dazling Waste fatigue the Eye.

Strange ! that a Man who has wit enough to write a Satyr ; should have folly enough to publish it.

He that hath a Trade, hath an Estate.

* In the preface of " The American Almanack " for 1743 John Jerman wrote :
" *To the* READERS, Here is presented to your View and Service an *Almanack* for the Year 1743 according to my yearly Method, so I hope it needs no Explanation. I have put down the Judgment of the Weather as usual, and as I find the Aspects and Positions of the Planets to signifie ; but no Man can be infallible therein, by reason of the many contrary Causes happening at or near the same Time, and the inconstancy of the Summer Showers and Gusts, being very often great Rain Hail and Thunder in one Place, and none at all in another Place within a few Miles distance. However, I think mine comes as near the Matter as any other if not nearer.
" The Reader may expect a Reply from me to *R——S——rs* alias *B—— F——ns* facetious Way of proving me *no Protestant.* I do hereby protest, that for *that* and such kind of Usage the *Printer* of that witty Performance shall not have the Benefit of my Almanack for this Year. To avoid further Contention, and judging it unnecessary to offer any Proofs to those of my Acquaintance that I am not a Papist, I shall with these few Lines conclude, and give place to what I think more agreeable to my Readers.

JOHN JERMAN."

Have you somewhat to do to-morrow ; do it to-day.

FEBRUARY.

James ne'er will be prefer'd ; he cannot bow
And cringe beneath a supercilious Brow ;
He cannot fawn, his stubborn Soul recoils
At Baseness, for his Blood too highly boils.
A Courtier must be supple, full of Guile,
Must learn to praise, to flatter, to revile
The Good, the Bad ; an Enemy, a Friend ;
To give false hopes, and on false Hopes depend.

No workman without tools,
Nor Lawyer without Fools,
Can live by their Rules.

The painful Preacher, like a candle bright,
Consumes himself in giving others Light.

Speak and speed : the close mouth catches no flies.

MARCH.

As honest *Hodge* the Farmer sow'd his Field,
Chear'd with the Hope of future Gain 't would yield,
Two upstart Jacks in Office, proud and vain,
Come riding by, and thus insult the Swain : ˙
You drudge and sweat, and labour here, Old Boy,
But we the Fruit of your hard Toil enjoy.
Belike you may, *quoth Hodge*, and but your Due,
For, Gentlemen, 't is HEMP I 'm sowing now.

Visit your Aunt, but not every Day ; and call at your Brother's, but not every night.

Bis dat, qui cito dat.*

Money and good Manners make the Gentleman.
Late Children, early Orphans.

* He who gives promptly, gives twice as much.

APRIL.

The Winter spent, *Joe* feels the Poet's Fire,
The Sun advances, and the Fogs retire :
The genial Spring unbinds the frozen Earth,
Dawns on the trees, and gives the Prim-rose Birth.
Loos'd from their Friendly Harbours, once again,
Our floating Forts assemble on the Main ;
The Voice of War the gallant Soldier wakes ;
And weeping *Cloe* parting Kisses takes.

Ben beats his Pate, and fancys wit will come ;
But he may knock, there 's nobody at home.

The good Spinner hath a large Shift.

Tom, vain 's your Pains ; They all will fail :
Ne'er was good Arrow made of a Sow's Tail.

MAY.

What knowing Judgment, or what piercing Eye,
Can MAN's mysterious Maze of Falsehood try ?
Intriguing MAN, of a suspicious Mind,
MAN only knows the Cunning of his Kind ;
With equal Wit can counter-work his Foes,
And Art with Art, and Fraud with Fraud oppose.
Then heed ye FAIR, e'er you their Cunning prove,
And think of Treach'ry, while they talk of LOVE.

Empty Freebooters, cover'd with Scorn :
They went out for Health, & came ragged and torn,
As the Ram went for Wool, and was sent back shorn.

Ill Customs & bad Advice are seldom forgotten.

He that sows thorns, should not go barefoot.

JUNE.

Sometimes a Man speaks Truth without Design,
As late it happen'd with a Friend of mine.

Two reverend Preachers talking, one declar'd,
That to preach twice each Sunday was full hard.
To you, perhaps (says t' other), *for I suppose,*
That all Men don't with the same Ease compose :
But I, desiring still my Flock to profit,
Preach twice each Sunday, and make nothing of it.

Reniego de grillos, aunque Jean d'aro.*

Men meet, mountains never.

When Knaves fall out, honest Men get their goods :
When Priests dispute, we come at the Truth.

JULY.

Man only from himself can suffer Wrong ;
His Reason fails as his Desires grow strong :
Hence, wanting Ballast, and too full of Sail,
He lies expos'd to every rising Gale.
From Youth to Age, for *Happiness* he 's bound ;
He splits on Rocks, or runs his Bark aground ;
Or, wide of Land, a desart Ocean views,
And, to the last, the flying Port pursues.

Kate would have Thomas, no one blame her can :
Tom won't have Kate, and who can blame the Man ?

A large train makes a light Purse.

Death takes no bribes.

One good Husband is worth two good Wives ; for the
scarcer things are the more they 're valued.

AUGUST.

The Busy-Man's Picture.

BUSINESS, thou Plague and Pleasure of my Life,
Thou charming Mistress, thou vexatious Wife ;

* Execrate fetters, notwithstanding Jean d'Arc.

Thou Enemy, thou Friend, to Joy, to Grief,
Thou bring'st me all, and bring'st me no Relief,
Thou bitter, sweet, thou pleasing, teazing Thing,
Thou Bee, that with thy Honey wears a Sting ;
Some Respite, prithee do, yet do not give,
I cannot with thee, nor without thee, live.

He that riseth late, must trot all day, and shall scarce overtake his business at night.

He that speaks ill of the Mare, will buy her.

You may drive a gift without a gimblet.

Eat few Suppers, and you 'll need few Medecines.

SEPTEMBER.

The Reverse.

Studious of Ease, and fond of humble Things,
Below the Smiles, below the Frowns of Kings :
Thanks to my Stars, I prize the Sweets of Life,
No sleepless Nights I count, no Days of Strife.
I rest, I wake, I drink, I sometimes love,
I read, I write, I settle, or I rove ;
Content to live, content to die unknown,
Lord of myself, accountable to none.

You will be careful, if you are wise ; How you touch men's Religion, or Credit, or Eyes.

After Fish,
Milk do not wish.

Heb Ddnw heb ddim, a Dnw, a digon.*

They who have nothing to trouble them, will be troubled at nothing.

* Without God without ought, God and enough.

OCTOBER.

On him true HAPPINESS shall wait
Who shunning noisy Pomp and State
Those *little* Blessings of the *Great*
       Consults the Golden Mean.
In prosp'rous Gales with Care he steers,
Nor adverse Winds, dejected, fears,
In ev'ry Turn of Fortune bears
       A Face and Mind serene.

Against Diseases here, the strongest Fence,
Is the defensive Virtue, Abstinence.

Fient de chien & marc d'argent,
Seront tout un au jour du jugement.*

If thou dost ill, the joy fades, not the pains ;
If well, the pain doth fade, the joy remains.

NOVEMBER.

Celia's rich Side-board seldom sees the Light,
Clean is her Kitchen, and her Spits are bright ;
Her Knives and Spoons, all rang'd in even Rows,
No Hands molest, nor Fingers discompose :
A curious Jack, hung up to please the Eye,
Forever still, whose Flyers never fly :
Her Plates unsully'd shining on the Shelf ;
For *Celia* dresses nothing, *but herself.*

To err is human, to repent divine ; to persist devilish.

Money & Man a mutual Friendship show :
Man makes false Money, Money makes Man so.

Industry pays Debts, Despair encreases them.

Bright as the day and as the morning fair,
Such Cloe is, & common as the air.

    / * Dog's dung and silver marks
    / Are all one at the day of judgement.

DECEMBER.

Among the Divines there has been much Debate,
Concerning the World in its ancient Estate ;
Some say 't was once good, but now is grown bad,
Some say 't is reform'd of the Faults it once had :
I say 't is the best World, this that we now live in,
Either to lend, or to spend, or to give in ;
But to borrow, to beg, or to get a Man's own,
It is the worst World that ever was known.

Here comes Glib-Tongue : who can out-flatter a Dedication ; and lie, like ten Epitaphs.

Hope and a Red-Rag, are Baits for Men and Mackerel.

With the old Almanack and the old Year,
Leave thy old Vices, tho' ever so dear.

Honest Men often go to Law for their Right ; when Wise Men would sit down with the Wrong, supposing the first Loss least. In some Countries, the Course of the Courts is so tedious, and the Expence so high, that the Remedy, *Justice*, is worse than *Injustice*, the Disease. In my Travels I once saw a Sign call'd *The Two Men at Law ;* One of them was painted on one Side, in a melancholy Posture, all in Rags, with this Scroll, *I have lost my Cause.* The other was drawn capering for Joy, on the other Side, with these Words, *I have gain'd my Suit ;* but he was stark naked.

RULES OF HEALTH AND LONG LIFE, AND TO PRESERVE FROM MALIGNANT FEVERS, AND SICKNESS IN GENERAL.

Eat and drink such an Exact Quantity as the Constitution of thy Body allows of, in reference to the Services of the Mind.

They that study much, ought not to eat so much as those that work hard, their Digestion being not so good.

The exact Quantity and Quality being found out, is to be kept to constantly.

Excess in all other Things whatever, as well as in Meat and Drink, is also to be avoided.

Youth, Age, and Sick require a different Quantity.

And so do those of contrary Complexions; for that which is too much for a flegmatick Man, is not sufficient for a Cholerick.

The Measure of Food ought to be (as much as possibly may be) exactly proportionate to the Quality and Condition of the Stomach, because the Stomach digests it.

That Quantity that is sufficient, the Stomach can perfectly concoct and digest, and it sufficeth the due Nourishment of the Body.

A greater Quantity of some things may be eaten than of others, some being of lighter Digestion than others.

The Difficulty lies, in finding out an exact Measure; but eat for Necessity, not Pleasure, for Lust knows not where Necessity ends.

Wouldst thou enjoy a long Life, a healthy Body, and a vigorous Mind, and be acquainted also with the wonderful works of God? labour in the first place to bring thy Appetite into Subjection to Reason.

RULES TO FIND OUT A FIT MEASURE OF MEAT AND DRINK.

If thou eatest so much as makes thee unfit for Study, or other Business, thou exceedest the due Measure.

If thou art dull and heavy after Meat, it's a sign thou hast exceeded the due Measure; for Meat and Drink ought to refresh the Body, and make it chearful, and not to dull and oppress it.

If thou findest these ill Symptoms, consider whether too much Meat, or too much Drink occasions it, or both, and abate by little and little, till thou findest the incouveniency removed.

Keep out of the Sight of Feasts and Banquets as much as may be; for 't is more difficult to refrain good Cheer, when it's present, than from the Desire of it when it is away; the like you may observe in the Objects of all the other Senses.

If a Man casually exceeds, let him fast the next Meal, and all may be well again, provided it be not too often done ; as if he exceed at Dinner, let him refrain a Supper, &c.

A temperate Diet frees from Diseases ; such are seldom ill, but if they are surprised with Sickness, they bear it better, and recover sooner; for most Distempers have their Original from Repletion.

Use now and then a little Exercise a quarter

9

of an Hour before Meals, as to swing a Weight, or swing your Arms about with a small Weight in each Hand ; to leap, or the like, for that stirs the Muscles of the Breast.

A temperate Diet arms the Body against all external Accidents ; so that they are not so easily [hurt] by Heat, Cold or Labour ; if they at any time should be prejudiced, they are more easily cured, either of Wounds, Dislocations or Bruises.

But when malignant Fevers are rife in the Country or City where thou dwelst, 't is adviseable to eat and drink more freely, by Way of Prevention ; for those are Diseases that are not caused by Repletion, and seldom attack Full-feeders.

A sober Diet makes a Man die without Pain ; it maintains the Senses in Vigour ; it mitigates the Violence of the Passions and Affections.

It preserves the Memory, it helps the Understanding, it allays the heat of Lust ; it brings a Man to a Consideration of his latter End ; it makes the Body a fit Tabernacle for the Lord to dwell in ; which makes us happy in this World, and eternally happy in the World to come, through Jesus Christ our Lord and Saviour.

POOR RICHARD FOR 1743.

PREFACE.

FRIENDLY READER,

BECAUSE I would have every Man make
Advantage of the Blessings of Providence, and
few are acquainted with the Method of making
Wine of the Grapes which grow wild in our
Woods, I do here present them with a few easy
Directions, drawn from some Years Experience,
which if they will follow, they may furnish
themselves with a wholesome sprightly Claret
which will keep for several Years, and is not inferior to that which passeth for *French* Claret.

Begin to gather Grapes from the 10th of *September* (the ripest first) to the last of *October*,
and having clear'd them of Spider webs, and
dead Leaves, put them into a large Molasses or

Rum-Hogshead ; after having washed it well, and knock'd one Head out, fix it upon the other Head, on a Stand, or Blocks in the Cellar, if you have any, if not, in the warmest Part of the House, about 2 Feet from the Ground ; as the Grapes sink, put up more, for 3 or 4 Days ; after which, get into the Hogshead bare-leg'd, and tread them down until the Juice works up about your Legs, which will be in less than half an Hour ; then get out, and turn the Bottom ones up, and tread them again, a Quarter of an Hour ; this will be sufficient to get out the good Juice ; more pressing wou'd burst the unripe Fruit, and give it an ill Taste. This done, cover the Hogshead close with a thick Blanket, and if you have no Cellar, and the Weather proves Cold, with two.

In this Manner you must let it take its first Ferment, for 4 or 5 Days it will work furiously ; when the Ferment abates, which you will know by its making less Noise, make a Spile-hole within six Inches of the Bottom, and twice a Day draw some in a Glass. When it looks as clear as Rock-water, draw it off into a clean, rather than new Cask, proportioning it to the Contents of the Hogshead or Wine * Vat ; that is, if the Hogshead holds twenty Bushels of Grapes,

---

* Vat *or* Fatt, *a Name for the Vessel, in which you tread the Grapes, and in which the* Must *takes its first Ferment.*

Stems and all, the Cask must at least, hold 20
Gallons, for they will yield a Gallon per Bushel.
Your Juice or Must * thus drawn from the Vat,
proceed to the second Ferment.

You must reserve in Jugs or Bottles, 1 Gallon
or 5 Quarts of the Must to every 20 Gallons you
have to work; which you will use according to
the following Directions.

Place your Cask, which must be chock full,
with the Bung up, and open twice every Day,
Morning and Night; feed your Cask with the
reserved Must; two Spoonfuls at a time will suf-
fice, cleaning the Bung after you feed it, with
your Finger or a Spoon, of the Grape-Stones and
other Filth which the Ferment will throw up;
you must continue feeding it thus until *Christmas*, when you may bung it up, and it will be
fit for Use, or to be rack'd into clean Casks
or Bottles, by *February*.

N. B. Gather the Grapes after the Dew is off,
and in all dry Seasons. Let not the Children
come at the Must, it will scour them severely.
If you make Wine for Sale, or to go beyond
Sea, one quarter Part must be distill'd, and the
Brandy put into the three Quarters remaining.
One Bushel of Grapes, heap Measure, as you

* Must *is a Name for the Juice of the Wine before it is
fermented, afterwards 't is called Wine.*

gather them from the Vine, will make at least a Gallon of Wine, if good, five Quarts.

Those Directions are not design'd for those who are skill'd in making Wine, but for those who have hitherto had no Acquaintance with that Art.

JANUARY.

On the Florida War.

From *Georgia* t' *Augustine* the General goes ;
From *Augustine* to *Georgia* comes our Foes ;
Hardy from *Charleston* to *St. Simons* hies,
Again from thence to *Charleston* back he flies.
Forth from *St. Simons* then the *Spaniards* creep ;
Say, Children, Is not this your Play, *Bo Peep ?*

How few there are who have courage enough to own their Faults, or resolution enough to mend them !

Men differ daily, about things which are subject to Sense, is it likely then they should agree about things invisible.

FEBRUARY.

Democritus, dear Droll, revisit Earth ;
And with our Follies glut thy heighten'd Mirth :
Sad *Heraclitus*, serious Wretch, return ;
In louder Grief, our greater Crimes to mourn
Between you both, I unconcern'd stand by :
Hurt, can I laugh ? and honest, need I cry.

Mark with what insolence and pride,
Blown Bufo takes his haughty stride ;
As if no toad was toad beside.

Ill Company is like a dog who dirts those most, that he loves best.

MARCH.

From bad Health, bad Conscience, & Parties dull Strife
From an insolent Friend, & a termagant Wife,
From the Kindred of such (on one Side or t' other)
Who most wisely delight in plaguing each other;
From the Wretch who can cant, while he Mischief
    designs,
From old rotten Mills, bank'd Meadows & Mines;
From Curses like these if kind Heav'n defends me,
I 'll never complain of the Fortune it sends me.
In prosperous fortunes be modest and wise,
The greatest may fall, and the lowest may rise:
But insolent People that fall in disgrace,
Are wretched and no body pities their Case.

Le sage entend à demi mot.*

Sorrow is dry.

APRIL.

A Parrot is for Prating priz'd,
But prattling Women are despis'd;
She who attacks another's Honour
Draws every living Thing upon her.
Think, Madam, when you stretch your Lungs,
That all your Neighbors too have Tongues;
One Slander fifty will beget;
The World with Interest pays the Debt.

The World is full of fools and faint hearts; and yet every one has courage enough to bear the misfortunes, and wisdom enough to manage the Affairs of his neighbour.

Beware, beware! he 'll cheat 'ithout scruple, who can without fear.

      * The wise understand half a word.

MAY.

The Snows are gone, and genial Spring once more
  New clothes the Meads with Grass, the Trees with
    Leaves;
And the proud Rivers that disdain'd a Shore
  Within their Banks now roll their lessen'd Waves.
Nature seems all renew'd, youthful and gay,
  Ev'n Luna doth her monthly Loss supply;
But Years and Hours that whirl our Time away,
  Describe our State, and tell us *we must die.*

The D——l wipes his B——ch with poor Folks Pride.

Content and Riches seldom meet together,
Riches take thou, contentment I had rather.

Speak with contempt of none, from slave to king,
The meanest Bee hath, and will use, a sting.

JUNE.

Every Man for himself, &c.

A Town fear'd a Siege, and held Consultation,
What was the best Method of Fortification:
A grave skilful Mason declar'd his Opinion,
That nothing but Stone could secure the Dominion.
A Carpenter said, Tho' that was well spoke
Yet he'd rather advise to defend it with Oak.
A Tanner much wiser than both these together,
Cry'd, *Try what you please, but nothing's like Leather.*

The church, the state, and the poor, are 3 daughters which we should maintain, but not portion off.

A achwyno heb achos; gwneler achos iddo.*

A little well-gotten will do us more good,
Than lordships and scepters by Rapine and Blood.

* A complainant without cause, give him cause to complain.

JULY.

Friend *Col* and I, both full of whim,
   To shun each other oft' agree ;
For I 'm not Beau enough for him ;
   And he 's too much a Beau for me.
Then let us from each other fly
   And Arm in-arm no more appear ;
That I may ne'er offend your Eye ;
   That you may ne'er offend my Ear.

Borgen macht sorgen.*

Let all Men know thee, but no man know thee thoroughly : Men freely ford that see the shallows.

'T is easy to frame a good bold resolution ;
But hard is the Task that concerns execution.

Cold & cunning come from the north :
but cunning sans wisdom is nothing worth.

AUGUST.

On buying a BIBLE.

'T is but a Folly to rejoice, or boast,
How small a Price thy well bought Purchase cost,
Until thy Death, thou shalt not fully know
Whether it was a Pennyworth or no ;
And, at that time, believe me 't will appear
Extreamly cheap, or else extreamly dear.

'T is vain to repine,
Tho' a learned Divine
Will die at nine.

A noddo duw, ry noddir.†

* Borrowing makes sorrowing.
† Should read *A noddo Duw, rhy nodder*—*i.e.*, Assurance hath he doubly sure, who by his God is kept secure.

Ah simple Man ! when a boy two precious jewels were given thee, Time and good Advice ; one thou hast lost, and the other thrown away.

No sunno i bûn
Na wnaid i ûn.*

SEPTEMBER.

Good Death, said a Woman, for once be so kind
To take me, and leave my dear Husband behind,
But when Death appear'd with a sour Grimace,
The Woman was dash'd at his thin hatchet Face ;
So she made him a Courts'y, and modestly sed,
If you come for my Husband, he lies there in Bed.

Dick told his spouse, he durst be bold to swear
Whate'er she prayed for, Heav'n would thwart her pray'r :
Indeed ! says Nell, 't is what I 'm pleas'd to hear ;
For now I 'll pray for your long life, my dear.

The sleeping Fox catches no poultry,   Up ! up !

OCTOBER.

A Musketo just starv'd, in a sorry Condition,
Pretended to be a most skilful Musician ;
He comes to a Bee-hive, and there he would stay
To teach the Bees Children to sing *Sol la fa.*
The Bees told him plainly the Way of their Nation,
Was breeding up Youth in some honest Vocation ;
Lest not bearing Labour, they should not be fed,
And then curse their Parents for being high bred.

If you 'd be wealthy, think of saving, more than of getting : The Indies have not made Spain rich, because her Outgoes equal her Incomes.

Tugend bestehet wen alles vergehet.†

* He who would when he could :
   Is not able when he would ?
† Virtue remains when all else is lost.

Came you from Court? for in your Mien
A self-important air is seen.

NOVEMBER.

A year of Wonders now behold!
Britons despising *Gallic* Gold!
A Year that stops the *Spanish* Plunders!
A Year that they must be Refunders!
· A Year that sets our Troops a marching!
A Year secures our Ships from Searching!
A Year that Charity's extended!
A Year that *Whig* and *Tory* 's blended!
Amazing Year! that we 're defended!

Hear what Jack Spaniard says,
Con todo el Munda Guerra
Y Paz con Ingalatierra.*

If you 'd have it done, Go : If not, send.

Many a long dispute among Divines may be thus
abridg'd, It is so : It is not so, It is so ; It is not so.

DECEMBER.

Inclement Winter rages o'er the Plains
Incrusts the Earth and binds the Floods in Chains.
Is the Globe mov'd? or does our Country roll,
In nearer Latitude to th' artic Pole?
The Fate of *Lapland* and its Cold we bear,
Yet want the Fur, the Sledge and harness'd Deer:
To punish Guilt, do angry Stars combine
Conjunct or Opposite, Quarrile or Trine?

Experience keeps a dear school, yet Fools will learn in
no other.

Felix quem faciunt aliena pericula cautum.†

---

* With all the world at war, there is peace in England.
† Happy is he that takes caution from others.

How many observe Christ's Birth-day! How few his Precepts! O! 't is easier to keep Holidays than Commandments.

Once on a Time it by Chance came to pass,
That a Man and his Son were leading an Ass.
Cries a Passenger, Neighbour, you 're shrewdly put to 't,
To lead an Ass empty, and trudge it on foot.
Nay, quoth the old Fellow, if Folk do so mind us
I 'll e'en climb the Ass, and Boy mount behind us:
But as they jogg'd on they were laugh't and hisse'd,
What, two booby Lubbers on one sorry Beast!
This is such a Figure as never was known;
'T is a Sign that the Ass is none of your own.
Then down gets the Boy, and walks by the Side,
Till another cries, What, you old Fool must you ride?
When you see the poor Child that 's weakly and young
Forc'd thro' thick and thin to trudge it along,
Then down gets the Father, and up gets the Son;
If this cannot please them we ne'er shall have done.
They had not gone far, but a Woman cries out,
O you young graceless Imp, you 'll be hang'd, no doubt!
Must you ride an Ass, and your Father that 's grey
E'en foot it, and pick out the best of his Way?
So now to please all they but one Trick lack,
And that was to carry the Ass a pick pack:
But when that was try'd, it appear'd such a Jest,
It occasioned more Laughter by half than the rest.
Thus he who 'd please all, and their Good liking gain,
Shows a deal Good Nature, but labours in vain.

A Person threatning to go to Law, was dissuaded from it by his Friend, who desired him to *consider*, for the Law was chargeable. I don't care, reply'd the other, I will not consider, I 'll go to Law. Right, said his Friend, for if you go to law, I am sure you don't consider.

A Farmer once made a Complaint to a Judge,
My Bull, if it please you, Sir, owing a Grudge,
Belike to one of your good Worship's Cattle,
Has slain him out-right in a mortal Battle :
I'm sorry at heart because of the Action,
And want to know how must be made Satisfaction.
Why, you must give me your Bull, that's plain
Says the Judge, or pay me the Price of the Slain.
But I have mistaken the Case, Sir, says *John*,
The dead Bull I talk of, & please you, 's my own :
And yours is the Beast that the Mischief has done.
The Judge soon replies with a serious Face :
Say you so ; then this Accident *alters the Case.*

POOR RICHARD FOR 1744.

PREFACE.

Courteous Reader,

This is the Twelfth Year that I have in this Way laboured for the Benefit —— Whom? —— of the Publick, if you 'll be so good-natured as to believe it; if not, e'en take the naked Truth, 't was for the Benefit of my own dear self; not forgetting in the mean time, our gracious Consort and Dutchess the peaceful, quiet, silent Lady *Bridget*. But whether my Labours have been of any Service to the Publick or not, the Publick I must acknowledge has been of Service to me; I have lived Comfortably by its Benevolent Encouragement; and I hope I shall always bear a grateful Sense of its continued Favour.

My Adversary *J . . n J . . . . . n* has indeed made an Attempt to *out-shine* me by pretending to penetrate *a Year deeper* into Futurity; and

142

giving his Readers *gratis* in his Almanack for
1743 an Eclipse of the Year 1744, to be beforehand with me : His Words are, " The first Day
"of *April* next Year 1744, there will be a
"GREAT ECLIPSE of the Sun ; it begins
"about an Hour before Sunset. It being in the
"Sign Aries, the House of Mars, and in the 7th,
"shows Heat, Difference and Animosities be-
"tween Persons of the highest Rank and
"Quality," &c. I am very glad, for the Sake
of * * * se Persons of Rank and Quality, that
there is ** *manner of Truth* in this Prediction :
They may, * * * * * please, live in Love and
Peace. And I * * * * * his Readers (they are
but few, indeed, and so the Matter 's the less)
not to give themselves any Trouble about observing this imaginary Great Eclipse ; for they
may stare till they 're blind without seeing the
least Sign of it. I might, on this Occasion,
return Mr. *J* - - - - - *n* the Name of *Baal's false
Prophet* he gave me some Years ago in his
Wrath, on Account of my Predicting his Reconciliation with the *Church of Rome*, (tho' he
seems now to have given up that Point) but I
think such Language * * * * * * * old Men and
Scholars unbecoming ; and * * * * * * * * * * the
Affair with the Buyers of his Almanack as well
as he can, who perhaps will not take it very
kindly, that he has done what in him lay (by

sending them out to gaze at an invisible Eclipse
on the first of *April*) to make *April Fools* of
them all. His old thread-bare Excuse which he
repeats Year after Year about the *Weather*,
"That no Man can be infallible therein, by
"Reason of the many contrary Causes happen-
"ing at or near the same time, and the Un-
"constancy of the Summer Showers and Gusts,"
&c. will hardly serve him in the Affair of
Eclipses ; and I know not where he 'll get
another.

I have made no Alteration in my usual
Method, except adding the Rising and Setting
of the Planets, and the Lunar Conjunctions.
Those who are so disposed, may thereby very
readily learn to know the Planets, and distinguish them from each other.

> *I am, dear Reader,*
>> *Thy obliged Friend,*
>>> R. SAUNDERS.

THE COUNTRY MAN.

Happy the Man whose Wish and Care
  A few paternal Acres bound,
Content to breathe his native Air,
    In his own Ground.

Whose Herds with Milk, whose Fields with **Bread,**
  Whose Flocks supply him with Attire,
Whose Trees in Summer yield him Shade,
    In Winter Fire.

Blest, who can unconcernedly find
  Hours, Days and Years slide soft away,
In Health of Body, Peace of Mind,
        Quiet by Day,

Sound Sleep by Night ; Study and Ease
  Together mixt ; Sweet Recreation ;
And Innocence which most does please
        With Meditation.

Thus let me live, unseen, unknown,
  Thus unlamented let me die,
Steal from the World, and not a Stone
        Tell where I lie.

JANUARY.

Biblis does Solitude admire,
  A wond'rous Lover of the Dark ;
Each Night puts out her Chamber Fire,
  And just keeps in a *single Spark ;*
'Till four she keeps herself alive,
  Warm'd by her Piety, no doubt :
Then, tir'd with kneeling, just at five,
  She sighs —— and lets that Spark *go out.*

He that drinks his Cyder alone, let him catch his Horse alone.

Who is strong? He that can conquer his bad Habits.

Who is rich? He that rejoices in his Portion.

FEBRUARY.

Our youthful Preacher see, intent on Fame ;
Warm to gain Souls ?—No, 't is to gain a Name.
Behold his Hands display'd, his Body rais'd ;
With what a Zeal he labours —— to be prais'd.
Touch'd with each Weakness which he does arraign,
  10

With Vanity he talks against the Vain ;
With Ostentation does to Meekness guide ;
Proud of his Periods form'd to strike at Pride.

He that has not got a Wife, is not yet a compleat Man.

MARCH.

Without Repentance none to Heav'n can go,
Yet what Repentance is few seem to know :
'T is not to cry out *Mercy*, or to sit
And droop, or to confess that thou hast fail'd ;
'T is to bewail the Sins thou didst commit,
And not commit those Sins thou hast bewail'd.
He that *bewails*, and not *forsakes* them too,
Confesses rather what he *means to do*.

What you would seem to be, be really.

If you 'd lose a troublesome Visitor, lend him money.

Tart Words make no Friends : spoonful of honey will catch more flies than Gallon of Vinegar.

APRIL.

With what a perfect World-revolving Power
Were first the unwieldy Planets launch'd along
Th' illimitable Void !   Thus to remain
Amid the Flux of many thousand Years,
That oft has swept the busy Race of Men,
And all their labour'd Monuments away :
Unresting, changeless, matchless, in their Course ;
To Night and Day, with the delightful Round
Of Seasons, faithful, not eccentric once :
So pois'd, and perfect is the vast Machine !

Make haste slowly.

Dine with little, sup with less :   Do better still ; sleep supperless.

Industry, Perseverance, & Frugality, make Fortune yield.

MAY.

Irus tho' wanting Gold and Lands,
Lives chearful, easy, and content ;
Corons, unbless'd, with twenty Hands
Employ'd to count his yearly Rent.
Sages in Wisdom ! tell me which
Of these you think possesses more !
One with his Poverty is rich,
And one with all his Wealth is poor.

I 'll warrant ye, goes before Rashness ; Who 'd-a-tho't comes sneaking after.

Prayers and Provender hinder no Journey.

JUNE.

Of all the Causes which conspire to blind
Man's erring Judgment, and misguide the Mind,
What the weak Head with strongest Biass rules,
Is *Pride*, that never-failing Vice of Fools.
Whatever Nature has in Worth deny'd,
She gives in large Recruits of needful Pride ;
For as in Bodies, thus in Souls we find
What wants in Blood & Spirits, swell'd with Wind.

Hear Reason, or she 'll make you feel her.

Give me yesterday's Bread, this Day's Flesh, and last Year's Cyder.

JULY.

All-conq'ring Heat, oh intermit thy Wrath !
And on my throbbing Temples potent thus
Beam not so hard ! Incessant still you flow,
And still another fervent Flood succeeds,
Pour'd on the Head profuse. In vain I sigh,

And restless turn, and look around for night ;
Night is far off ; and hotter Hours approach.
Who can endure ! - - - -

God heals, and the Doctor takes the Fees.

Sloth (like Rust) consumes faster than Labour wears :
the used Key is always bright.

Light Gains heavy Purses.

AUGUST.

Would men but follow what the Sex advise,
All things would prosper, all the World grow wise.
'T was by *Rebecca's* Aid that *Jacob* won
His Father's Blessing from an elder Son.
Abusive *Nabal* ow'd his forfeit Life
To the wise Conduct of a prudent Wife.
At *Hester's* Suit, the persecuting Sword
Was sheath'd, and *Israel* liv'd to bless the Lord.

Keep thou from the Opportunity, and God will keep
thee from the Sin.

Where there 's no Law, there 's no Bread.

As Pride increases, Fortune declines.

SEPTEMBER.

All other Goods by Fortune's Hand are giv'n,
A WIFE is the peculiar gift of Heav'n.
Vain Fortune's Favours, never at a Stay,
Like empty Shadows, pass, and glide away ;
One solid Comfort, our eternal Wife,
Abundantly supplies us all our Life :
This Blessing lasts (if those that try say true)
As long as Heart can wish—and longer too.

Drive thy Business, or it will drive thee.

A full Belly is the Mother of all Evil.

The same man cannot be both Friend and Flatterer.

He who multiplies Riches multiplies Cares.

An old man in a House is a good Sign.

OCTOBER.

Be Niggards of *Advice* on no Pretence ;
For the worst Avarice is that of Sense.
Yet 't is not all, your Counsel 's free and true ;
Blunt Truths more Mischief than nice Falshoods do.
Men must be taught as if you taught them not,
And Things unknown propos'd as Things forgot ;
Without *Good Breeding* Truth is disapprov'd
That only makes superior Sense belov'd.

Those who are fear'd, are hated.

The Things which hurt, instruct.

The Eye of a Master, will do more Work than his Hand.

A soft Tongue may strike hard.

NOVEMBER.

Sylvia while young, with ev'ry Grace adorn'd,
Each blooming Youth, and fondest Lover scorn'd :
In Years at length arriv'd at Fifty-nine,
She feels Love's Passion as her Charms decline :
——Thus Oaks a hundred Winters old
  Just as they now expire,
Turn Touchwood, doated, grey and old,
  And at each Spark take Fire.——

If you 'd be belov'd, make yourself amiable.

A true Friend is the best Possession.

Fear God, and your Enemies will fear you.

DECEMBER.

This World 's an Inn, all Travellers are we ;
And this World's Goods th' Accommodations be.
Our Life is nothing but a Winter's Day ;
Some only break their *Fast*, and so away.
Others stay Dinner, and depart full fed.
The deepest Age but *sups* and goes to bed.
He 's most in Debt that lingers out the Day ;
Who dies betimes has less and less to pay.

Epitaph on a Scolding Wife by her Husband. Here my poor Bridget's Corps doth lie, she is at rest,—and so am I.

COURTS.

Two trav'ling Beggars, (I 've forgot their name)
On Oister found to which they both laid Claim.
Warm the Dispute ! At length to Law they 'd go,
As richer Fools for Trifles often do.
The Cause two Petty foggers undertake,
Resolving right or wrong some Gain to make.
They jangle till the Court this Judgment gave,
Determining what every one should have.
  Blind Plaintiff, lame Defendant, share
  The friendly Law's impartial Care :
  A Shell for him, a Shell for thee ;
  The MIDDLE'S Bench and Lawyer's Fee.

POOR RICHARD FOR 1745.

PREFACE.

Courteous Reader,

For the Benefit of the Publick, and my own Profit, I have performed this my thirteenth annual Labour, which I hope will be as acceptable as the former.

The rising and setting of the Planets, and their Conjunctions with the Moon, I have continued; whereby those who are unacquainted with those heavenly Bodies, may soon learn to distinguish them from the fixed Stars, by observing the following directions.

All those glittering Stars, (except five) which we see in the Firmament of Heaven, are called fixed Stars, because they keep the Same Distance from one another, and from the Ecliptic; they rise and set at the same point of the Hori-

zon, and appear like so many lucid Points fixed
to the celestial Firmament. The other five have
a particular and different motion, for which
Reason they have not always the same Distance
from one another ; and therefore they have been
called wandering Stars or Planets, viz. *Saturn*
♄ , Jupiter ♃ , *Mars* ♂ , *Venus* ♀ , and Mercury
☿ , and these may be distinguished from the
fixed Stars by their not twinkling. The brightest of the five is *Venus*, which appears the
biggest ; and when this glorious Star appears,
and goes before the Sun, it is called *Phosphorus*,
or the Morning Star, and Hesperus, or the Even-
ing-Star, when it follows the Sun. Jupiter
appears almost as big as *Venus*, but not so
bright. *Mars* may be easily known from the
rest of the Planets, because it appears red like
a hot Iron or burning Coal, and twinkles a little. *Saturn*, in Appearance, is less than Mars,
and of a pale colour. *Mercury* is so near the
Sun that it is seldom seen.

Against the 6th Day of *January* you may see
♂ rise 10 35, which signifies the Planet *Mars*
rises 35 Minutes after 10 o'Clock at Night, when
that Planet may be seen to appear in the East.
Also against the 10th Day of January you will
find ♀ sets 7 13, which shows *Venus* sets 13
Minutes after 7 o'Clock at Night. If you look
towards the West that Evening, you may see

that beautiful Star till the Time of its setting. Again, on the 18th Day of the same Month, you will find ♄ rise 9 18, which shews that Saturn rises 18 Minutes after 9 at Night.

Or the Planets may be known by observing them at the time of their Conjunctions with the Moon, *viz*. against the 14 Day of January are inserted these characters ☌ ☽ ♄ , which shews there will be a Conjunction of the Moon *and Saturn* on that Day. If you look out about 5 o'Clock in the Morning, you will see Saturn very near the Moon. The like is to be observed at any other time by the rising and setting of the Planets, and their Conjunctions with the moon ; by which method they may be distinctly known from the fixed Stars.

I have nothing further to add at present, but my hearty Wishes for your Welfare, both temporal and spiritual, and Thanks for all your past Favours, being

Dear Reader,

Thy obliged Friend,

R. SAUNDERS.

Go, wond'rous creature ! mount where Science guides,
Go measure Earth, weigh air, and state the Tides ;
Shew by what Laws the wand'ring Planets stray,
Correct old Time, and teach the Sun his Way.
Go soar with Plato to th' empyreal Sphere,
To the *first* Good, *first* Perfect, and *first* Fair ;

Or tread the mazy Round his Follow'rs trod,
And, quitting Sense, called imitation *God*,
As Eastern Priests in giddy circles run
And turn their Heads to imitate the *Sun*.
Go teach Eternal Wisdom how to rule,—
Then drop into thyself, and be a Fool.

JANUARY.

I give and I devise (old Euclio said,
And sigh'd) " My Lands and Tenements to Ned "
Your money, Sir? My money, Sir! what, all?
" Why — if I must—(then wept) I give it *Paul* "
The Mannor, Sir? " The Mannor! hold, he cry'd ;
" Not that - - - I cannot part with that " - - - and dy'd.

Beware of little Expences, a small leak will sink a
great ship.

Wars bring scars.

A light purse is a heavy curse.

As often as we do good, we sacrifice.

Help, Hands ; For I have no Lands.

FEBRUARY.

Self Love but serves the virtuous Mind to wake,
As the small Pebble stirs the peaceful Lake ;
The Centre mov'd, a Circle strait succeeds,
Another still, and still another spreads,
Friend, Parent, Neighbour, first it will embrace,
His Country next, and next all human Race ;
Wide and more wide, th' o'erflowings of the Mind
Take every Creature in of every Kind.

It 's common for Men to give pretended Reasons instead of one real one.

MARCH.

Fame but from Death a Villian's Name can save,
As Justice tears his Body from the Grave ;
When what t'oblivion better were resign'd
Is luring on high to poison half Mankind.
All Fame is foreign but of *true Desert*,
Plays round the Head, but comes not to the Heart.
One *self-approving Hour* whole Years outweighs
Of stupid Starers and of loud Huzza's.

Vanity backbites more than Malice.

He 's a Fool that cannot conceal his Wisdom.

Great spenders are bad lenders.

All blood is alike ancient.

APRIL.

'T is not for Mortals always to be blest :
But him the least the dull and painful Hours
Of Life oppress, whom sober SENSE conducts,
And VIRTUE, thro' this Labyrinth we tread.
Virtue and Sense are one ; and, trust me, he
Who has not Virtue, is not truly wise.

You may talk too much on the best of subjects.

A Man without ceremony has need of great merit in
its place.

No gains without pains.

MAY.

Virtue, (for mere GOOD-NATURE, is a Fool)
Is Sense and Spirit, with HUMANITY ;
'T is sometimes angry, and its Frown confounds
'T is ev'n vindictive, but in Vengeance just.

Knaves fain would laugh at it ; some great ones dare;
But at his Heart, the most undaunted Son
Of Fortune dreads its name and awful charms.

Had I revenged wrong, I had not worn my skirts so long.

Graft good fruit all, or graft not at all.

JUNE.

Unhappy *Italy !* whose alter'd State
Has felt the worst Severity of Fate ;
Not that *Barbarian* Band her *Fasces* broke
And bow'd her haughty neck beneath her yoke ;
Nor that her Palaces to Earth are thrown,
Her Cities desart, and her Fields unsown ;
But that her ancient spirit is decay'd,
That sacred Wisdom from her Bounds is fled,
That there the Source of Science flows no more,
Whense its rich Streams supply'd the world before.

Idleness is the greatest Prodigality.

Old young and old long.

Punch coal, cut candle, and set brand on end, is neither good house-wife, nor good house-wife's friend.

JULY.

Hot from the Field, indulge not yet your Limbs
In wish'd Repose, nor court the fanning Gale,
Nor taste the Spring. Oh ! by the sacred Tears
Of Widows, Orphans, Mothers, Sisters, Sires,
Forbear ! . . . no other Pestilence has driven
Such myriads o'er th' irremedeable Deap.

He who buys had need have 100 Eyes, but one 's enough for him that sells the Stuff.

There are no fools so troublesome as those that have wit.

AUGUST.

Has God, thou fool ! work'd solely for thy Good,
Thy Joy, thy Pastime, thy Attire, thy Food ?
Who for thy Table feeds the wanton Fawn,
For him as kindly spread the flow'ry Lawn.
Is it for thee the Lark descends and sings ?
Joy tones his Voice, Joy elevates his Wings.
Is it for thee the Mock bird pours his Throat ?
Loves of his own, and Raptures, swell the note.

Many complain of their Memory, few of their Judgement.

One Man may be more cunning than another, but not more cunning than every body else.

SEPTEMBER.

The bounding steed you pompously bestride,
Shares with his Lord the Pleasure and the Pride.
Is thine alone the seed that strows the Plain ?
The Birds of Heav'n shall vindicate their Grain.
Thine the full Harvest of the golden Year ?
Part pays, and justly, the deserving Steer.
The Hog that plows not, nor obeys thy Call,
Lives on the Labours of this Lord of all.

To God we owe fear and love ; to our neighbours justice and character ; to our selves prudence and sobriety.

Fools make feasts and wise men eat them.

Light heel'd mothers make leaden-heel'd daughters.

OCTOBER.

For Forms of Government let Fools contest,
Whate'er is best administer'd is best ;
For Modes of Faith let graceless Zealots fight

His can't be wrong, whose Life is in the right :
All must be false, that thwart this one great End,
And all of God, that bless Mankind, or Mend.

The good or ill hap of a good or ill life, is the good or
ill choice of a good or ill wife.

'T is easier to prevent bad habits than to break them.

NOVEMBER.

Fair Summer 's gone, and Nature's Charms decay.
See gloomy Clouds obscure the cheerful Day !
Now hung with Pearls the dropping Trees appear,
Their faded Honours scatter'd here and there.
Behold the Groves that shine with silver Frost
Their Beauty wither'd, and their Verdure lost,
Sharp Boreas blows, and Nature feels Decay
Time conquers all and we must Time obey.

Every Man has assurance enough to boast of his hon-
esty--few of their Understanding.

Interest which blinds some People, enlightens others.

DECEMBER.

These Blessings, Reader, may Heav'n grant to thee ;
A faithful Friend, equal in Love's degree ;
Land fruitful, never conscious of the Curse,
A liberal Heart and never-failing Purse ;
A smiling Conscience, a contented mind ;
A temp'rate knowledge with true Wisdom join'd ;
A life as long as fair, and when expir'd,
A kindly Death, unfear'd as undesir'd.

An Ounce of wit that is bought Is worth a pound that
is taught.

He that resolves to mend hereafter, resolves not to
mend now.

COURTS.

The Christian Doctrine teaches to believe
Its every Christian's Duty, to forgive
Could we forgive as fast as Men offend
The LAWS slow Progresses would quickly end
Revenge of past Offences is the Cause
Why peaceful Minds consented to have Laws,
Yet Plaintiffs and Defendants much mistake
Their Cure, and their Diseases lasting make ;
For to be reconcil'd, and to comply
Would prove their cheap and shortest Remedy.

POOR RICHARD FOR 1746.

PREFACE.

Who is *Poor Richard?* People oft enquire,
Where lives? What is he?—never yet the nigher.
Somewhat to ease your Curiositie,
Take these slight Sketches of my Dame and me.
   Thanks to kind Readers and a careful Wife,
With plenty bless'd, I lead an easy Life ;
My business Writing ; less to drain the Mead,
Or crown the barren Hill with useful Shade ;
In the smooth Glebe to see the Plowshare worn,
And fill the Granary with needful Corn.
Press nectarous Cyder from my loaded Trees,
Print the sweet Butter, turn the Drying Cheese
Some Books we read, tho' few there are that hit
The happy Point where Wisdom joins with Wit ;
That set fair Virtue naked to our View,
And teach us what is *decent*, what is *true*.
The Friend sincere, and honest Man, with Joy
Treating or treated oft our Time employ.
Our Table next, Meals temperate ; and our Door
Op'ning spontaneous to the bashful Poor.
Free from the bitter Rage of Party Zeal,
All those we love who seek the publick Weal.

Nor blindly follow Superstitious Love,
Which cheats deluded Mankind o'er and o'er.
Not over righteous, quite beyond the Rule,
Conscience perplext by every canting Tool.
Nor yet when Folly hides the dubious Line,
When Good and Bad the blended Colours join ;
Rush indiscreetly down the dangerous Steep,
And plunge uncertain in the darksome Deep.
Cautious, if right ; if wrong resolv'd to part
The Inmate Snake that folds about the Heart.
Observe the *Mean*, the *Motive*, and the *End*,
Mending our selves, or striving still to mend.
Our Souls sincere, our Purpose fair and free,
Without Vain Glory or Hypocrisy :
Thankful if well ; if ill, we kiss the Rod ;
Resign with Hope, and put our Trust in God.

JANUARY.

Nothing exceeds in Ridicule, no doubt
A Fool *in* Fashion, but a Fool that 's *out ;*
His Passion for Absurdity 's so strong
He cannot bear a Rival in the Wrong.
Tho' wrong the Mode, comply ; more sense is shewn
In wearing others Follies than your own.
If what is out of Fashion most you prize
Methinks you should endeavour to be wise.

When the well 's dry, we know the worth of water.

He that whines for Glass without G
Take away L and that 's he.

FEBRUARY.

Man 's rich with little, were his Judgement true,
Nature is frugal, and her wants are few ;
Those few Wants answer'd bring sincere Delights,
II

But Fools creat themselves new Appetites.
Fancy and Pride seek Things at Vast Expence,
Which relish not to *Reason* nor to Sense
Like Cats in Air-pumps, to subsist we strive
On Joys to thin to keep the Soul alive.

A good Wife & Health, is a Man's best Wealth.

A quarrelsome Man has no good Neighbours.

MARCH.

O sacred Solitude ! divine Retreat !
Choice of the Prudent ! Envy of the Great !
By thy pure Stream, or in thy waving Shade,
We court fair Wisdom, that celestial Maid :
The genuine Offspring of her lov'd Embrace
(Strangers on Earth) are Innocence and Peace.
There blest with Health, with Business unperplext,
This Life we relish, and insure the next.

Wide will wear, but narrow will tear.

Silks and sattins put out the kitchen fire.

Vice knows she 's ugly, so puts on her Mask.

APRIL.

Zara resembles Ætna crown'd with snows,
Without she freezes, and within she glows ;
Twice e'er the Sun descends, with Zeal inspir'd
From the vain Converse of the World retir'd,
She reads the Psalms and Chapters of the Day,
In — — — some lewd Novel, new Romance, or Play,
Thus gloomy Zara, with a solemn Grace,
Deceives Mankind, and *hides* behind her *Face*.

It 's the esiest Thing in the World for a Man to decieve Himself.

Women & Wine
Game & Deceit
Make the Wealth small
And the Wants great

All Mankind are beholden to him that is kind to the Good.

MAY.

Pleasures are few, and fewer we enjoy ;
Pleasure like Quicksilver, is bright and *coy ;*
We try to grasp it with our utmost skill,
Still it eludes us, and it glitters still.
If seiz'd at last, compute your mighty Gains
What is it but rank Poison in your Veins.

A Plowman on his Legs is higher than a Gentleman on his Knees.

Virtue and Happiness are Mother and Daughter.

The generous Mind least regards Money and yet most feels the Want of it.

For one poor Man there are an hundred indigent.

JUNE.

What 's Man's Reward for all his Care and Toil?
But *One ;* a female Friends endearing Smile :
A tender Smile, our Sorrows only Balm,
And in Life's Tempest the sad Sailors calm.
How have I seen a gentle Nymph draw nigh,
Peace in her Air, Persuasion in her Eye ;
Victorious Tenderness, it all o'ercame,
Husbands look'd mild, and Savages grew tame.

Dost thou love Life ? Then do not squander Time ; for that 's the Stuff Life is made of.

Good Sense is a Thing all need, few have, and non think they want.

JULY.

Who taught the rapid Winds to fly so fast,
Or shakes the Centre with his Western Blast?
Who from the Skies can a whole Deluge pour?
Who Strikes thro' Nature, with the solemn Roar
Of dreadful *Thunder*, points it where to fall
And in fierce Lightning wraps the flying Ball?
Not he who trembles at the darted Fires,
Falls at the Sound, and in the Flash expires.

What's proper is becoming : See the Blacksmith with his white Silk Apron !

The Tongue is ever turning to the aching tooth.

Want of Care does us more damage than Want of Knowledge.

AUGUST.

Can Gold colour *Passion*, or make *Reason* shine,
Can we dig *Peace* or *Wisdom* from the mine?
Wisdom to Gold prefer, for 't is much less
To make our *fortune*, than our *Happiness*.
That Happiness which Great Ones often see,
With Rage and Wonder, in a low Degree,
Themselves unblest. The Poor are *only* poor
But what are they who *droop* amid their Store?

Take Courage Mortal ; Death can't banish thee out of the Universe.

The Sting of a Reproach is the Truth of it.

Do me the favour to deny me at once.

SEPTEMBER.

Can Wealth give Happiness? look round and see?
What gay Distress ! What splendid Misery !
Whatever Fortune lavishly can pour
The Mind annihilates, and calls for more.

Wealth is a Cheat, believe not what it says;
Greatly it promises, but never pays.
Misers may startle, but they shall be told,
That Wealth is Bankrupt, and *insolvent* Gold.

The most exquisite Folly is made of Wisdom spun too fine.

A life of leisure and a life of laziness are two things.

OCTOBER.

Some ladies are too beauteous to be wed,
For where 's the Man that 's worthy of their Bed?
If no Disease reduce her Pride before,
Lavinia will be ravisht at three score.
Then she submits to venture in the Dark,
And nothing, now, is wanting - - - - but her spark.

Mad Kings and mad Bulls are not to be held by treaties and packthread.

Changing Countries or Beds, cures neither a bad Manager, nor a Fever.

NOVEMBER.

There are, who, tossing on the Bed of *Vice,*
For Flattery's Opiate give the highest price;
Yet from the saving Hand of *Friendship* turn,
Her Med'cines dread, her generous offers Spurns.
Deserted *Greatness !* who but pities thee?
By Crowds encompass'd, thou no *Friend* canst see
Or should kind *Truth* invade thy tender Ear
We pity still, for thou no Truth can bear.

A true great Man will neither trample on a Worm nor sneak to an Emperor.

Ni ffyddra llaw dyn er gwneithr da idd ei hûn.*

* Our hand has no stain if it work to our gain.

DECEMBER.

What 's Female Beauty, but an Air divine,
Thro' which the Mind's all gentle Graces shine?
They, like the Sun, irradiates all between ;
The Body *charms*, because the Soul is *seen*
Hence Men are often Captives to a Face,
They know not why, of no peculiar Grace.
Some Forms tho' bright, no mortal Man can *bear;*
Some none *resist*, tho' not exceeding fair.

Tim and his Handsaw are good in their Place,
Tho' not fit for preaching or shaving a face.

Half Hospitality opens his Door and shuts up his
Countenance.

COURTS.

From Earth to Heav'n when Justice fled
The Laws decided in her Stead
For Heav'n to Earth should she return
Lawyers might beg, and Law books burn.

POOR RICHARD FOR 1747.

PREFACE.

Courteous Reader,

This is the 15th Time I have entertain'd thee with my annual Productions; I hope to thy profit as well as mine. For besides the astronomical Calculations, and other Things usually contain'd in Almanacks, which have their daily Use indeed while the Year continues, but then become of no Value, I have constantly interspers'd *moral* Sentences, *prudent* Maxims, and *wise* Sayings, many of them containing *much good Sense* in *very few* Words, and therefore apt to leave *strong* and *lasting* Impressions on the Memory of young Persons, whereby they may receive Benefit as long as they live, when both Almanack and Almanac-maker have been long thrown by and forgotten. If I now and then insert a Joke or two, that seem to have little in them, my Apology is, that such may have their Use, since perhaps for their Sake light airy Minds peruse the rest, and so are struck by somewhat of more Weight and Moment. The Verses on the Heads of the Months are also design'd to have the same Tendency. I need not tell thee that many of them are of my own Making. If thou hast any Judgement in Poetry, thou wilt easily discern the Workman from the Bungler. I know as well as thee, that I am no *Poet born*, and it is a Trade I never learnt, nor indeed could learn. *If I make Verses* 't is in Spight—Of Nature and my Stars, I write. Why then should I give my Readers *bad Lines* of my own, when *good Ones* of other Peoples are so plenty? 'T is methinks a poor Excuse for the bad Entertainment of Guests that the Food we set before them, tho' coarse and ordinary, is *of one's own raising, off ones own Plantation*, &c when there is Plenty of what is ten times better, to be had in the Market.—On the contrary, I assure ye, my Friends, that I have procur'd the best I could for ye, and *much good may 't do ye.*

I cannot omit this Opportunity of making honourable Mention of the late deceased Ornament and Head of our Profession, Mr. Jacob Taylor, who for upwards of 40 Years (with some

few Intermissions only) supply'd the good people of this and the neighboring Colonies with
the most compleat Ephemeris and most accurate Calculations that have hitherto appear'd in
America. - - - - he was an ingenious Mathe-
matician, as well as an expert and skilful Astronomer, and moreover, no mean Philosopher,
but what is more than all, He was a PIOUS and
HONEST Man.   Requiescat in pace.

I am thy poor Friend, to serve thee,
R. SAUNDERS.

JANUARY.

To show the Strength, and Infamy of Pride,
By all 't is follow'd and by all deny'd.
What Members are there, which at once pursue
Praise, and Glory to contemn it too?
To praise himself *Vincenna* knows a Shame,
And therefore lays a Strategem for Fame;
Makes his Approach in Modesty's Disguise,
To win Applause, and takes it by Surprise.

Strive to be the greatest Man in your Country, and
you may be disappointed; Strive to be the best and you
may succeed: He may well win the race that runs by
himself.

FEBRUARY.

See *Wealth* and *Pow'r!*   Say, what can be more great?
Nothing - - - - but Merit in a low Estate.
To Virtue's humblest Son let none prefer.
Vice, tho' a Crœsus or a Conquerer

Shall Men, like Figures, pass for high, or base
Slight, or important, only by their *Place ?*
Titles are Marks of honest Men, and Wise ;
The Fool, or Knave that wears a Title, lies.

'T is a strange Forest that has no rotten Wood in 't.
And a strange Kindred that all are good in 't.

None know the unfortunate, and the fortunate do not know themselves.

MARCH.

Celestial PATIENCE ! How dost thou defeat
The Foes proud Menace, and elude his Hate?
While *Passion* takes his Part, betrays our Peace ;
To Death and Torture swells each slight Disgrace ;
By not opposing, Thou dust Ill destroy,
And wear thy conquer'd Sorrows into Joy.

There 's a time to Wink as well as to see.

Honest Tom ! you may trust him with a house full of untold Milstones.

There is no Man so bad but he secretly respects the Good.

APRIL.

RELIGIOUS Force divine is best display'd,
In a Desertion of all human Aid :
To succour in Extreams is her Delight,
And cheer the Heart when Terror strikes the Sight.
We, disbelieving our own Senses, gaze
And wonder what a Mortals Heart can raise,
To smile in Anguish, triumph in his Grief,
And comfort those who come to bring Relief.

When there 's more Malice shown than Matter :
On the Writer falls the Satyr.

MAY.

Girls, mark my Words; and know, for Men of Sense,
Your strongest Charms are native Innocence.
Shun all deceiving Arts ; the Heart that 's gain'd
By Craft alone, can ne'er be long retain'd.
Arts on the Mind, like paint upon the Face,
Fright him, thats worth your Love, from your Embrace
In simple Manners all the Secret lies
Be kind and virtuous, you 'll be blest and wise.

Courage would fight, but Discretion won't let him.

Delicate Dick ! whispered the Proclamation.

Cornelious ought to be Tacitus.

JUNE.

O, form'd Heav'n's Dictates nobly to rehearse,
PREACHER DIVINE ! accept the grateful Verse.
Thou hast the Power, the harden'd Heart to warm,
To grieve, to raise, to terrify, to charm ;
To fix the Soul on God, to teach the Mind
To know the Dignity of Human Kind ;
By stricter Rules well-govern'd Life to scan,
And practise o'er the Angel in the Man.

Pride and the Gout are seldom cur'd throughout.

We are not so sensible of the greatest Health as of the
least Sickness.

A good Example is the best Sermon.

JULY.

Men drop so fast, ere Life's mid Stage we tread,
Few know so many Friends *alive* as *dead*
Yet, as *immortal*, in our uphill Chace,
We press coy Fortune with slacken'd Pace.

Our ardent Labours for the Toy we seek,
Join Night to Day, and Sunday to the Week
Between Satiety and fierce Desire.

A Father 's a Treasure ; a Brother 's a Comfort ; a
Friend is both.

Despair ruins some, Presumption many.

A quiet Conscience sleeps in Thunder, but Rest and
Guilt live far asunder.

AUGUST.

A *decent Competence* we fully taste ;
It strikes our *Sense*, and gives a constant Feast :
More, we perceive by Dint of *Thought* alone ;
The Rich must *labour* to possess *their own*,
To feel their great Abundance ; and request
Their humble Friends to *help* them to be blest ;
To *see* their Treasures, *hear* their Glory told,
And *aid* the wretched Impotence of Gold.

He that won't be counsell'd, can't be help'd.

Craft must be at charge for clothes, but Truth can go
naked.

Write Injuries in Dust, Benefits in Marble.

SEPTEMBER.

But some, good Souls, and touch'd with Warmth divine,
Give *Gold* a *Price* and teach its *Beams* to *Shine*
All hoarded Treasures they repute a Load
Nor think their Wealth *their own* till well bestow'd.
Grand Reservoirs of public Happiness,
Thro *secret* Streams diffusively they bless ;
And while their Bounties glide conceal'd from View,
Relieve our *Wants*, and *spare* our *Blushes* too.

What is Serving God ? 'T is doing Good to Man.

What maintains one Vice would bring up two children.

Many have been ruin'd by buying good pennyworths.

OCTOBER

One to destroy, is Murder by the Law,
And Gibbers keep the uplifted Hand in Awe
To murder Thousands, takes a specious Name
War's glorious Art, and gives immortal Fame.
O great Alliance ! O divine Renown !
With Death and Pestilence to share the Crown !
When Men extol a wild Destroyer's Name
Earth's Builder and Preserver they blaspheme.

Better is a little with content than much with contention.

A Slip of the Foot you may soon recover,
But a Slip of the Tongue you may never get over.

What signifies your Patience, if you can't find it when
you want it.

NOVEMBER.

I envy none their Pageantry and Show ;
I envy none the Gilding of their Woe.
Give me, indulgent Heav'n, with Mind serene
And guiltless Heart, to range the Sylvan Scene.
No splendid Poverty, no smiling Care,
No well-bred Hate, or servile Grandeur there.
There pleasing Objects useful Thought suggest,
The Sense is ravish'd and the Soul is blest ;
On every Thorn delightful Wisdom grows,
In every Rill a sweet Instruction flows.

Time enough always proves little enough.

It is wise not to seek a Secret and Honest not to reveal it.

A Mob 's a Monster ; Heads enough but no Brains.

The Devil sweetens Poison with Honey.

DECEMBER.

Old Age *will* come, Disease may come before,
Fifteen is full as mortal as *Threescore*.
Thy Fortune and thy Charms may soon decay ;
But grant these Fugitives prolong their Stay
Their basis totters, their Foundation shakes,
Life that supports them, in a Moment breaks :
Then *wrought* into the Soul, let Virtue shine,
The *Ground* eternal, as the work divine.

He that cannot bear with other Peoples Passions, cannot govern his own.

He that by the Plough would thrive, himself must either hold or drive.

POOR RICHARD FOR 1748.

PREFACE.

KIND READER,

The favourable Reception my annual Labours have met with from the Publick these 15 Years past, has engaged me in Gratitude to endeavour some Improvement of my Almanack. And since my Friend *Taylor* is no more whose *Ephemerides* so long and so agreeably serv'd and entertained these Provinces, I have taken the liberty to imitate his well-known Method, and have given two Pages for each Month; which affords me Room for several valuable Additions, as will best appear on Inspection and Comparison with former Almanacks. Yet I have not so far followed his Method, as not to continue my own where I thought it preferable; and thus my Book is increased to a Size beyond his, and contains much more Matter.

Hail Night serene ! thro' Thee where'er we turn
Our wondering Eyes, Heav'n's Lamps profusely burn ;
And Stars unnumbered all the Sky adorn.
> *But lo !—what 's that I see appear ?*
> *It seems far off a pointed flame ;*
From Earthwards too the shining Meteor came :
> *How swift it climbs th' etherial Space !*
> *And now it traverses each Sphere,*
And seems some knowing Mind, familiar to the place.
Dame, hand my Glass, the longest, strait prepare ;—
'T is he—'t is TAYLOR'S *Soul that travels there.*
O stay ! thou happy Spirit, stay,
And lead me on thro' all the unbeat'n Wilds of Day ;
Where Planets in pure Streams of Ether driven,
> *Swim thro' the blue expanse of Heav'n.*
There let me, thy Companion, stray
> *From Orb to Orb, and now behold*
> *Unnumbered Suns, all Seas of molten Gold,*
And trace each Comet's wandering Way.——

Souse down into Prose again, my Muse ; for Poetry is no more thy element, than Air is of the Flying-Fish ; whose Flights, like thine, are therefore always short and heavy.—

We complain sometimes of hard Winters in this Country ; but our Winters will appear as Summers, when compared with those that some of our Countrymen undergo in the most Northern *British* Colony on this Continent, which is that upon *Churchill* River, in *Hudson's* Bay, Lat. 58d. 56m. Long. from *London* 94d. 50m. West. Captain *Middleton*, a member of the *Royal Society*, who had made many Voyages

thither, and winter'd there 1741-2, when he
was in search of the *North-West* Passage to
the South-Sea, gives an account of it to that
Society, from which I have extracted these
Particulars, viz.

The Hares, Rabbits, Foxes, and Partridges,
in *September* and the beginning of *October*,
change their Colour to a snowy White, and continue white till the following Spring.

The Lakes and standing Waters, which are
not above 10 or 12 Feet deep, are frozen to the
Ground in Winter, and the Fishes therein all
perish.   Yet in Rivers near the Sea, and Lakes
of a greater depth than 10 or 12 Feet, Fishes
are caught all the Winter, by cutting holes
thro' the Ice, and therein putting Lines and
Hooks.   As soon as the Fish are brought into
the open Air, they instantly freeze stiff.

Beef, Pork, Mutton, and Venison, kill'd in
the beginning of the Winter, are preserved by
the Frost for 6 or 7 Months, entirely free from
Putrefaction.   Likewise Geese, Partridges, and
other Fowls, kill'd at the same Time, and kept
with their Feathers on and Guts in, are preserv'd by the Frost, and prove good Eating. All
kinds of Fish are preserv'd in the same Manner.

In large Lakes and Rivers, the Ice is sometimes broken by imprison'd Vapours ; and the
Rocks, Trees, Joists, and Rafters of our Build-
12

ings, are burst with a Noise not less terrible than the firing of many Guns together. The Rocks which are split by the Frost, are heaved up in great Heaps, leaving large Cavities behind. If Beer or Water be left even in Copper Pots by the Bed-side, the Pots will be split before Morning. Bottles of strong Beer, Brandy, strong Brine, Spirits of Wine, set out in the open Air for 3 or 4 Hours, freeze to solid Ice. The Frost is never out of the Ground, how deep is not certain; but on digging 10 or 12 Feet down in the two Summer Months, it has been found hard frozen.

All the water they use for Cooking, Brewing, &c. is melted Snow and Ice; no Spring is yet found free from freezing, tho' dug ever so deep down.—All Waters inland, are frozen fast by the Beginning of *October*, and continue so to the Middle of *May*.

The Walls of the Houses are of Stone, two Feet thick; the windows very small, with thick wooden Shutters, which are close shut 18 Hours every Day in Winter. In the cellars they put their Wines, Brandies, &c. Four large Fires are made every Day, in greats Stoves to Warm the Rooms. As soon as the Wood is burnt down to a Coal, the Tops of the Chimnies are close stopped, with an Iron Cover; this keeps the Heat in but almost stifles the People. And

notwithstanding this, in 4 or 5 Hours After
the Fire is out, the inside of the Walls and
Bed-places will be 2 or 3 Inches thick with
Ice, which is every Morning cut away with a
Hatchet. Three or Four Times a Day, Iron
Shot, of 24 Pounds Weight, are made red hot,
and hung up in the Windows of their Apart-
ments, to moderate the Air that comes in at the
Crevices ; yet this with a Fire kept burning the
greatest Part of 24 Hours, will not prevent Beer,
Wine, Ink, etc. from Freezing.

For their Winter Dress, a Man makes use of
three Pair of Socks, of coarse Blanketting, or
Duffeld, for the Feet, with a Pair of Deerskin
Shoes over them ; two pair of thick *English*
stockings, and a pair of Cloth Stockings upon
them ; Breeches lined with Flannel ; two or
three *English* Jackets, and a Fur, or Leather
Gown over them ; a large Beaver Cac, double,
to come over the Face and Shoulders, and a
Cloth of Blanketting under the Chin ; with
Yarn Gloves, and a large pair of Beaver Mit-
tins, hanging down from the Shoulders before,
to put the Hands in, reaching up as far as the
Elbows. Yet notwithstanding this warm Clothing, those that stir abroad when any Wind
blows from the Northward, are dreadfully
frozen ; some have their Hands, Arms, and
Face blistered and froze in a dreadful Manner,

the Skin coming off soon after they enter a warm House, and some lose their Toes. And keeping House or lying-in for the cure of these Disorders, brings on the Scurvey, which many die of, and few are free from; nothing preventing it but Exercise and Stirring Abroad.

The Fogs and Mists, brought by northerly Winds in Winter, appear visible to the naked Eye to be Icicles innumerable, as small as fine Hairs and pointed as sharp as Needles. These Icicles lodge in their Clothes, and if their Faces and Hands are uncover'd, presently raise Blisters as white as a Linen Cloth, and as hard as Horn. Yet if they immediately turn their Back to the Weather, and can bear a hand out of the Mitten and with it rub the blister'd Part for a small Time, they sometimes bring the Skin to its former State; if not they make the best of their way to a Fire, bathe the part in hot Water, and thereby dissipate the Humours raised by the frozen Air; otherwise the Skin wou'd be off in a short Time, with much hot, serous, watry Matter, coming from under along with the Skin; and this happens to some almost every time they go Abroad, for 5 or 6 Months in the Winter, so extreme cold is the Air, when the Wind blows anything strong. - - - - - - Thus far Captain *Middleton*. And now, my tender Reader, thou that shudderest when the wind blows a little at N-West, and criest, '*Tis ex-trrrrrream cohohold! 'Tis terrrrrrible cohold!* what dost thou think of removing to that delightful Country! Or dost thou not rather choose to stay in *Pennsylvania*, thanking God that *He has caused thy Lines to fall in pleasant places.*

I am,

Thy Friend to Serve thee,

R. SAUNDERS.

JANUARY.

Luke, on his dying Bed, embraced his Wife,
And begged one Favour : Swear, my dearest Life,
Swear, if you love me, never more to wed,
Nor take a second Husband to your Bed.
Anne dropt a Tear. You know, my dear, says she,
Your least Desires have still been Laws to me ;
But from this Oath, I beg you 'd me excuse ;
For I 'm already promised to *J—n H—s.*

Robbers must exalted be,
Small ones on the Gallow-Tree,
While greater ones ascend to Thrones,
But what is that to thee or me?

Lost time is never found again.

FEBRUARY.

Don't after foreign Food and Clothing roam,
But learn to eat and wear what 's rais'd at Home.
Kind Nature suits each Clime with what it wants,
Sufficient to subsist th' Inhabitants.

Observing this, we less impair our Health,
And by this Rule we more increase our Wealth :
Our Minds a great Advantage also gain,
And more sedate and uncorrupt remain.

To lead a virtuous Life, my Friends,
And get to Heaven in Season,
You 've just so much more Need of Faith,
As you have less of Reason.

MARCH.

The Sun, whose unexhausted Light
Does Life and Heat to Earth convey ;
The Moon, who, Regent of the Night,
Shines with delegated Ray ;
The Stars, which constant seem to Sight,
And Stars that regularly stray :
All these God's plastick Will from Nothing brought,
Assign'd thier Stations, and thier Courses taught.

The Heathens when they dy'd, went to Bed without a
Candle.

Knaves & Nettles are akin ; stroak 'em kindly, yet
they 'll sting.

APRIL.

On Education all our Lives depend ;
And few to that, too few, with Care attend :
Soon as Mamma permits her darling Joy
To quit her Knee, and trusts at School her Boy,
O, touch him not, whate'er he does is right,
His Spirit 's tender, tho' his Parts are bright.
Thus all the Bad he can, he learns at School,
Does what he will, and grows a lusty Fool.

Life with Fools consists in Drinking ; With the wise
Man, Living 's Thinking.
Eilen thut felten gut.

MAY.

Read much ; the Mind, which never can be still,
If not intent on Good, is prone to Ill.
And where bright Thoughts, or Reas'nings just you find,
Repose them careful in your inmost Mind.
To deck his Chloe's bosom thus the Swain
With pleasing toil surveys th' enammel'd Plain,
With Care selects each fragrant flow'r he meets,
And forms one Garland of thier mingled sweets.

Sell-cheap kept Shop on Goodwin Sands, and yet had
Store of Custom.

Liberality is not giving much, but giving wisely.

Finikin Dick, curs'd with nice Taste, Ne'er meets
with good Dinner, half starved at a Feast.

JUNE.

Of all the Charms the Female Sex desire,
That Lovers doat on, and that friends admire,
Those most deserve your Wish that longest last,
Not like the Bloom of Beauty, quickly past ;
VIRTUE the Chief : This Men and Angels prize,
Above the finest Shape and brightest Eyes,
By this alone, untainted Joys we find,
As large and as immortal as the Mind.

Alas ! that Heroes ever were made !
The Plague, and the Hero, are both of a Trade !
Yet the Plague spares our Goods, which the Hero does
    not ;
So the Plague take such Heroes, and let thier Fame
    rot.

                                    Q. P. D.

JULY.

When great Augustus ruled the World and Rome,
The Cloth he wore was spun and wove at Home,
His EMPRESS ply'd the Distaff and the Loom.
Old England's Laws the proudest Beauty name,
When single, Spinster, and when married, Dame,
For Housewifery is Woman's noblest Fame.
The Wisest household Cares to Women yield,
A large, an useful and a grateful Field.

To Friend, Lawyer, Docter, tell plain your whole Case ;
Nor think on Bad Matters to put a good Face :
How can they advise, if they see but a Part?
'T is very ill driving black Hogs in the dark.

AUGUST.

To make the cleanly Kitchen send up Food,
Not costly vain, but plentifully Good.
To bid the Cellar's fountain never fail,
Of sparkling Cyder, or of well-brew'd Ale ;
To buy, to pay, to blame, or to approve.
Within, without, below-stairs, or above ;
To shine in every Corner like the Sun,
Still working every where, or looking on.

Suspicion may be no fault, but showing it may be
a great one.

He that 's secure is not safe.

The second Vice is Lying ; the first is running in Debt.

The Muses love the Morning.

SEPTEMBER.

One glorious Scene of Action still behind,
The Fair that likes it is secure to find ;

Cordials and Medicin's gratis to dispense,
A beauteous Instrument of Providence ;
Plaisters, and Salves, and Sores, to understand,
The Surgeon's Art befits a tender Hand,
To friendless pain unhop'd-for Ease to give,
And bid the Hungry eat, and Sickly live.

Two faults of one a Fool will make ; he half repairs,
that owns does forsake.

Harry Smatter, has a Mouth for every Matter.

When you 're good to others, you are best to yourself.

OCTOBER.

And thus if we may credit Fame's Report,
The best and fairest in the Gallic Court,
An Hour sometimes in Hospitals employ,
To give the dying Wretch a glimpse of Joy ;
T' attend the Crouds that hopeless Pangs endure,
And soothe the Anguish which they cannot cure ;
To clothe the Bare, and give the Empty Food ;
As bright as Guardian Angels, and as good.

Half Wits talk much but say little.

If Jack 's in love, he 's no Judge of Jill's Beauty.

Most fools think they are only ignorant.

NOVEMBER.

Nor be the Husband idle, tho' his Land
Yields plenteous Crops without his lab'ring Hand ;
Tho' his collected Rent his Bags supply,
Or honest, careful Slaves scarce need his Eye.
Let him whom Choice allures, or Fortunes yields,
To live amidst his own extended Fields,
Diffuse those Blessings which from Heav'n he found,
In copious Streams to bless the World around.

Pardoning the Bad, is injuring the Good.

He is not well bred, that cannot bear Ill-Breeding in others.

DECEMBER.

Open to all his hospitable door,
His Tenants Patron, Parent to the Poor :
In Friendships dear, discording Neighbours bind,
Aid the distress'd, and humanize Mankind :
Wipe off the sorrowing Tear from Virtue's Eyes,
Bid Honesty oppress'd, again arise :
Protect the Widow, give the Aged Rest,
And blessing live, and die for ever blest.

In Christmas feasting pray take care ;
Let not your table be a Snare ;
But with the Poor God's Bounty share.
Adieu, my Friends, till the next year.

POOR RICHARD FOR 1749.

[PREFACE OMITTED.]

JANUARY.

Advice to Youth.

First, Let the Fear of HIM who form'd thy Frame,
Whose Hand sustain'd thee e'er thou hadst a Name,
Who brought thee into Birth, with Pow'r of Thought
Receptive of immortal Good, be wrought
Deep in thy Soul.   His, not thy own, thou art ;
To him resign the Empire of thy Heart.
His Will, thy Law ; His Service, thy Employ ;
His Frown, thy Dread, his Smile be all thy Joy.

Wealth and Content are not always Bed-fellows.

Wise Men learn by others harms ; Fools by their own.

FEBRUARY.

Wak'd by the Call of Morn, on early Knee,
Ere the World thrust between thy God and thee,
Let thy pure Oraisons, ascending, gain
His Ear, and Succour of his Grace obtain,
In Wants, in Toils, in Perils of the Day,
And strong Temptations that beset thy Way.
Thy best Resolves then in his Strength renew
To walk in Virtue's Paths, and Vice eschew.

The end of Passion is the beginning of Repentance.

Words may shew a man's Wit, but Actions his Meaning.

MARCH.

To HIM intrust thy Slumbers, and prepare
The fragrant Incense of thy Ev'ning Prayer.
But first tread back the Day, with Search severe,
And *Conscience*, chiding or applauding, hear.
Review each Step ; *Where, acting, did I err ?*
Omitting, where ? Guilt either Way infer.
Labour this Point, and while thy Frailties last,
Still let each following Day correct the last.

'T is a well spent penny that saves a groat.

Many Foxes grow grey, but few grow good.

Presumption first blinds a Man, then sets him a running.

APRIL.

LIFE is a shelvy Sea, the Passage fear,
And not without a skilful Pilot steer.
Distrust thy Youth, experienc'd Age implore,
And borrow all the Wisdom of Threescore.
But chief a Father's, Mother's Voice revere ;
'T is Love that chides, 't is Love that counsels here.
Thrice happy is the Youth, whose pliant Mind
To all a Parent's Culture is resign'd.

A cold April, The Barn will fill.

Content makes poor men rich ; Discontent makes rich Men poor.

Too much plenty makes Mouth dainty.

MAY.

O, well begun, Virtue's great Work pursue,
Passions at first we may with Ease subdue ;

But if neglected, unrestrain'd too long,
Prevailing in their Growth, by Habit Strong,
They 've wrapp'd the Mind, have fix'd the stubborn
    Bent,
And Force of Custom to wild Nature lent ;
Who then would set the crooked Tree aright,
As soon may wash the tawny Indian white.

If Passion drives, let Reason hold the Reins.

Neither trust, nor contend, nor lay wagers, nor lend ;
And you 'll have peace to your Lives end.

Drink does not drown Care, but waters it, and makes
it grow faster.

Who dainties love, shall Beggars prove.

JUNE.

Industry's bounteous Hand may *Plenty* bring,
But wanting *frugal Care*, 't will soon take wing.
Small thy Supplies, and scanty in their Source,
'Twixt *Av'rice* and Profusion steer thy Course.
Av'rice is deaf to Want's Heart-bursting Groan,
Profusion makes the Beggar's Rags thy own :
Close Fraud and Wrong from griping Av'rice grow,
From rash *Profusion* desp'rate Acts and Woe.

A Man has no more Goods than he gets Good by.

Welcome, Mischief, if thou comest alone.

Different Sects like different clocks, may be all near
the matter, 'tho they don't quite agree.

JULY.

Honour the softer Sex ; with courteous Style,
And Gentleness of Manners, win their Smile ;
Nor shun their virtuous Converse ; but when Age
And Circumstance consent, thy Faith engage

To some discreet, well-natur'd, chearful Fair,
One not too stately for the Household Care,
One form'd in Person and in Mind to please,
To season Life, and all its Labours ease.

If your head is wax, don't walk in the Sun.

Pretty & Witty will wound if they hit ye.

Having been poor is no shame, but being ashamed of
it, is.

AUGUST.

Gaming, the Vice of Knaves and Fools, detest,
Miner of Time, of Substance and of Rest ;
Which, in the Winning or the Losing Part,
Undoing or undone, will wring the Heart :
Undone, self-curs'd, thy Madness thou wilt rue ;
Undoing, Curse of others will pursue
Thy hated Head.   A Parent's, Household's Tear,
A Neighbour's Groan, and *Heav'n's* displeasure fear.

'T is a laudable Ambition, that aims at being better
than his Neighbours.

The wise Man draws more Advantage from his Enemies, than the Fool from his Friends.

SEPTEMBER.

Wouldst thou extract the purest Sweet of Life,
Be nor Ally nor Principal in Strife.
A Mediator there, thy Balsam bring,
And lenify the Wound, and draw the Sting ;
On *Hate* let *Kindness* her warm Embers throw,
And mould into a Friend the melting Foe.
The weakest Foe boasts some revenging Pow'r ;
The weakest Friend some serviceable Hour.

All would live long, but none would be old.

Declaiming against Pride, is not always a Sign of Humility.

Neglect kills Injuries, Revenge increases them.

OCTOBER.

In Converse be reserv'd, yet not morose,
In Season grave, in Season, too, jocose.
Shun Party-Wranglings, mix not in Debate
With Bigots in Religion or the State.
No Arms to Scandal or Detraction lend,
Abhor to wound, be fervent to defend.
Aspiring still to know, a Babbler scorn,
But watch where Wisdom opes her golden Horn.

9 Men in 10 are suicides.

Doing an Injury puts you below your Enemy; Revenging one makes you but even with him; Forgiving it sets you above him.

NOVEMBER.

In quest of Gain be just : A Conscience clear
Is Lucre, more than Thousands in a Year ;
Treasure no Moth can touch, no Rust consume ;
Safe from the Knave, the Robber, and the Tomb.
Unrighteous Gain is the curs'd Seed of Woe,
Predestin'd to be reap'd by them who sow ;
A dreadful Harvest ! when th' avenging Day
Shall like a Tempest, sweep the Unjust away.

Most of the Learning in use, is of no great Use.

Great Good-nature, without Prudence, is a great Misfortune.

Keep Conscience clear, Then never fear.

DECEMBER.

But not from Wrong alone thy Hand restrain,
The *Appetite* of Gold demands the Rein.

What Nature asks, what Decency requires,
Be this the Bound that limits thy Desires :
This, and the gen'rous godlike Pow'r to feed
The Hungry, and to warm the Loins of *Need :*
To dry Misfortune's Tear, and scatter wide
Thy Blessings, like the Nile's o'erflowing Tide.

A man in a Passion rides a mad Horse.

Reader farewel, all Happiness attend thee ; May each New-Year, better and richer find thee.

HOW TO GET RICHES.

The Art of getting Riches consists very much in THRIFT. All Men are not equally qualified for getting Money, but it is in the Power of every one alike to practise this Virtue.

He that would be beforehand in the World, must be beforehand with his Business : It is not only ill Management, but discovers a slothful Disposition, to do that in the Afternoon, which should have been done in the Morning.

Useful Attainments in your Minority will procure Riches in Maturity, of which Writing and Accounts are not the meanest.

Learning, whether Speculative or Practical, is, in Popular or Mixt Governments, the Natural Source of Wealth and Honour.

PRECEPT I.

In Things of moment, on thy self depend,
Nor trust too far thy Servant or thy Friend :
With private Views, thy Friend may promise fair,
And Servants very seldom prove sincere.

PRECEPT II.

What can be done, with Care perform to Day,
Dangers unthought-of will attend Delay ;
Your distant Prospects all precarious are,
And Fortune is as fickle as she 's fair.

PRECEPT III.

Nor trivial Loss, nor trivial Gain despise ;
Molehills, if often heap'd, to Mountains rise :
Weigh every small Expence, and nothing waste,
Farthings long sav'd, amount to Pounds at last.

13

POOR RICHARD FOR 1750.

PREFACE.

To the Reader :

The Hope of acquiring lasting Fame, is, with many Authors, a most powerful Motive to Writing. Some, tho' few, have succeeded ; and others, tho' perhaps fewer, may succeed hereafter, and be as well known to Posterity by their Works, as the Antients are to us. We *Philomaths*, as ambitious of Fame as any other Writers whatever, after all our painful Watchings, and laborious Calculations, have the constant Mortification to see our Works thrown by at the End of the Year, and treated as mere waste Paper. Our only Calculation is, that short-lived as they are, they outlive those of most of our Cotemporaries.

Yet, condemned to renew the *Sisyphean* Toil, we every Year heave another heavy Mass up the

Muses Hill, which never can the Summit reach,
and soon comes tumbling down again.

This, Kind Reader, is my seventeenth Labour
of the kind. Thro' thy continued Good-will,
they have procur'd me, if no *Bays*, at least
Pence ; and the latter is perhaps the better of
the two ; since 't is not improbable, that a Man
may receive more solid Satisfaction from *Pud-ding*, while he is *living*, than from *Praise*, after
he is *dead*.

In my last, a few Faults escap'd ; some belong
to the Author, but most to the Printer : Let
each take his Share of the Blame, confess, and
amend for the future. In the second Page of
August, I mention'd 120 as the next perfect
number to 28 ; it was wrong, 120 being no
perfect number ; the next to 28 I find to be 496.
The first is 6 ; let the curious Reader, fond of
mathematical Questions, find the fourth. In
the 2d Page of *March*, in some Copies, the
Earth's Circumference was said to be nigh
4000, instead of 24000 Miles, the figure 2 being
omitted at the Begining. This was Mr. Print-er's Fault ; who being also somewhat niggardly
of his Vowels, as well as profuse of his Con-sonants, put in one Place, among the Poetry,
mad, instead of *made*, and in another wrapp'd,
instead of *warp'd* ; to the utter demolishing
of all Sense in those Lines, leaving nothing

standing but the Rhime. These, and some others, of a like kind, let the Readers forgive, or rebuke him for, as to their Wisdom and Goodness shall seem meet : For in such Cases the Loss and Damage is chiefly to the Reader, who, if he does not take my Sense at first Reading, 't is odds he never gets it ; for ten to one he does not read my Works a second Time.

Printers indeed should be very careful how they omit a Figure or a Letter : For by such means sometimes a terrible Alteration is made in the Sense. I have heard, that once, in a new Edition of the *Common Prayer*, the following Sentence, *We shall all be changed in a Moment in the Twinkling of an Eye ;* by the Omission of a single Letter, became *We shall all be hanged in a Moment*, &c. to the no small Surprize of the first Congregation it was read to.

May this Year prove a Happy One to Thee and Thine, is the hearty wish of, Kind Reader,

Thy obliged Friend,

R. SAUNDERS.

JANUARY.

So weak are human Kind by Nature made,
Or to such Weakness by their Vice betray'd,
Almighty *Vanity !* to thee they owe
Their Zest of Pleasure, and their Balm of Woe
Thou, like the Sun, all Colours dost contain,
Varying like Rays of Light on Drops of Rain ;

For every Soul finds Reason to be Proud,
Tho' hiss'd and hooted by the pointing Croud.

There are three Things extreamly hard, Steel, a Diamond and to know one's self.

Hunger is the best Pickle.

He is a Governor that governs his Passions, and he a Servant that serves them.

FEBRUARY.

We smile at Florists, we despise their Joy,
And think their Hearts enamour'd of a Toy ;
But are those wiser, whom we most admire,
Survey with Envy, and pursue with Fire ?
What 's he, who fights for Wealth, or Fame, or Power?
Another *Florio*, doating on a Flower,
A short-liv'd Flower, and which has often sprung,
From sordid Arts, as *Florio's* out of Dung.

A Cypher and Humility make the other Figures & Virtues of tenfold Value.

If it were not for the Belly, the Back might wear Gold.

MARCH.

What 's the bent Brow, or Neck in Thought reclin'd ?
The Body's Wisdom, to conceal the Mind.
A Man of Sense can Artifice disdain,
As Men of Wealth may venture to go plain ;
And he this Truth eternal ne'er forgot,
Solemnity 's a Cover for a Sot ;
I find the Fool, when I behold the Screen :
For 't is the Wise Man's Interest to be seen.

Wouldst thou confound thine Enemy, be good thy self.

Pride is as loud a Beggar as Want, and a great deal more saucy.

Pay what you owe, and what you 're worth you'll know

APRIL.   —

When e'er by seeming Chance, *Fop* throws his Eye
On Mirrors flashing with his Finery,
With how sublime a Transport leaps his Heart ;
Pity such Friends sincere should ever part.
So have I seen on some bright Summer's Day,
A spotted *Calf*, sleek, frolicksome and gay ;
Gaze from the Bank, and much delighted seem,
Fond of the pretty Fellow in the Stream.

Sorrow is good for nothing but Sin.

Many a Man thinks he is buying Pleasure, when he is
really selling himself a Slave to it.

Graft good Fruit all, Or graft not at all.

MAY.

Content let all your Virtues lie unknown,
If there 's no Tongue to praise them, but your own,
Of Boasting more than of a Bomb afraid,
Merit should be as modest as a Maid.
Fame is a Bubble the Reserv'd enjoy,
Who strive to grasp it, as they touch, destroy ;
'T is the World's Debt to Deeds of high Degree ;
But if you pay yourself, the World is free.

'T is hard (but glorious) to be poor and honest : An
empty Sack can hardly stand upright ; but if it does, 't is
a stout one !

He that can bear a Reproof, and mend by it, if he is
not wise, is in a fair way of being so.

Beatus esse sine Virtute nemo potest.*

JUNE.

Daphnis, says *Clio*, has a charming Eye ;
What Pity 't is her Shoulder is awry?

* No one can be happy without virtue.

Aspasia's Shape indeed ---- *but* then her Air,
'T would ask a Conj'rer to find Beauty there.
Without a *But*, *Hortensia* she commends,
The first of Women, and the best of Friends ;
Owns her in Person, Wit, Fame, Virtue, bright ;
But how comes this to pass? ---- She dy'd last Night.

Sound, &c. sound Doctrine, may pass through a Ram's Horn, and a Preacher, without straightening the one, or amending the other.

Clean your Finger, before you point at my Spots.

JULY.
On Time.

See TIME launch'd forth, in solemn Form proceed,
And Man on Man advance, and Deed on Deed !
No Pause, no Rest in all the World appears,
Ev'n live long Patriarchs waste their 1000 Years.
Some Periods void of Science and of Fame,
Scarce e'er exist, or leave behind a Name ;
Meer sluggish Rounds, to let Succession climb,
Obscure, and idle Expletives of Time.

He that spills the Rum loses that only ; He that drinks it, often loses both that and himself.

That Ignorance makes devout, if right the Notion, Troth, Rufus, thou 'rt a Man of great Devotion.

AUGUST.

Others behold each nobler Genius thrive,
And in their generous Labours long survive ;
By Learning grac'd, extend a distant Light ;
Thus circling Science has her Day and Night.
Rise, rise, ye dear Cotemporaries, rise ;
On whom devolve these Seasons and these Skies !
Assert the Portion destin'd to your Share,
And make the Honour of the Times your Care.

Those that have much Business must have much Pardon.

Discontented Minds, and Fevers of the Body are not to be cured by changing Beds or Businesses.

Little Strokes, Fell great Oaks.

SEPTEMBER.

Still be your darling Study Nature's Laws;
And to its Fountain trace up every Cause.
Explore, for such it is, this high Abode,
And tread the Paths which *Boyle* and *Newton* trod.
Lo, Earth smiles wide, and radiant Heav'n looks down,
All fair, all gay, and urgent to be known!
Attend, and here are sown Delights immense,
For every Intellect, and every Sense.

You may be too cunning for One, but not for All.

Genius without Education is like Silver in the Mine.

Many would live by their Wits, but break for want of stock.

Poor Plain dealing! dead without Issue.

OCTOBER.

With Adoration think, with Rapture gaze,
And hear all Nature chant her Maker's Praise;
With Reason stor'd, by Love of Knowledge fir'd,
By Dread awaken'd, and by Love inspir'd,
Can We, the Product of another's Hand,
Nor whence, nor how, nor why we are, demand?
And, not at all, or not aright employ'd,
Behold a Length of Years, and all a Void?

You can bear your own Faults, and why not a Fault in your Wife.

Tho' Modesty is a Virtue, Bashfulness is a Vice.

Hide not your Talents, they for Use were made. —
Vhat 's a Sun-Dial in the Shade?

NOVEMBER.

Happy, thrice happy he! whose conscious Heart,
Enquires his Purpose, and discerns his Part;
Who runs with Heed, th' involuntary Race,
Nor lets his hours reproach him as they pass;
Weighs how they steal away, how sure, how fast,
And as he weighs them, apprehends the last.
Or vacant, or engag'd, our Minutes fly;
We may be negligent, but we must die.

What signifies knowing the Names, if you know not
the Natures of Things.

Tim was so learned, that he could name a Horse in
nine Languages. So ignorant, that he bought a Cow to
ride on.

The Golden Age never was the present Age.

DECEMBER.

And thou *supreme of Beings* and of Things!
Who breath'st all Life, and giv'st Duration Wings;
Intense, O let me for thy Glory burn,
Nor fruitless view my Days and Nights return;
Give me with Wonder at thy Works to glow;
To grasp thy Vision, and thy Truths to know;
To reach at length thy everlasting Shore,
And live and sing 'till Time shall be no more.

'T is a Shame that your Family is an Honour to you!
You ought to be an Honour to your Family.

Glass, China, and Reputation, are easily crack'd, and
never well mended.

Adieu, my Task 's ended.

OF COURTS.

If any Rogue vexatious Suits advance
Against you for your known Inheritance :
Enter by Violence your fruitful Grounds,
Or take the sacred Land-mark from your Bounds,
Or if your Debtors do not keep their Day,
Deny their Hands, and then refuse to pay :
You must with Patience all the Terms attend,
Among the common Causes that depend,
Till yours is call'd : - - - And that long look'd-for Day,
Is still encumber'd with some new Delay :
Your Proofs and Deeds all on the Table spread,
Some of the B - - - - ch perhaps are sick a-bed ;
That J - - - ge steps out to light his Pipe, while this
O'er night was boozy, and goes out to p - - ss.
Some Witness miss'd ; some Lawyer not in Town, ⎫
So many Rubs appear, the Time is gone, ⎬
For Hearing, and the tedious Suit goes on. ⎭
Then rather let two Neighbours end your Cause,
And split the Difference ; tho' you lose one Half;
Than spend the Whole, entangled in the Laws,
While merry Lawyers sly, at both Sides laugh.

POOR RICHARD FOR 1751.

PREFACE.

COURTEOUS READER,

Astrology is one of the most ancient Sciences, had in high Esteem of old, by the Wise and Great. Formerly, no Prince could make War or Peace, nor any General fight a Battle, in short, no important Affair was undertaken without first consulting an *Astrologer*, who examined the Aspects and Configurations of the heavenly Bodies, and mark'd the *lucky Hour*. Now the noble Art (more Shame to the Age we live in!) is dwindled into Contempt; the Great neglect us, Empires make Leagues, and Parliaments Laws, without advising with us; and scarce any other Use is made of our learned Labours, than to find the best Time of cutting Corns, or gelding Pigs. - - - This Mischief we owe in a great

Measure to ourselves: The Ignorant Herd of Mankind, had they not been encourag'd to it by some of us, would never have dared to depreciate our sacred Dictates; but *Urania* has been betray'd by her own Sons; those whom she had favour'd with the greatest Skill in her divine Art, the most eminent Astronomers among the Moderns, the *Newtons*, *Halleys*, and Whistons, have wantonly contemn'd and abus'd her, contrary to the Light of their own Consciences. Of these, only the last nam'd, Whiston, has liv'd to repent, and speak his Mind honestly. In his former Works he had treated *Judiciary Astrology* as a Chimera, and asserted, That not only the fixed Stars, but the Planets (Sun and Moon excepted) were at so immense a Distance, as to be incapable of any Influence on this Earth, and consequently nothing could be foretold from their Positions, but now in the Memoirs of his Life, publish'd 1749, in the 82d Year of his Age, he foretels, Page 607, the sudden Destruction of the *Turkish* Empire, and of the House of *Austria*, German Emperors, &c. and *Popes* of *Rome*; the Restoration of the *Jews*, and Commencement of the Millennium; all by Year 1766; and this not only from Scripture Prophecies; but (take his own Words) - - - - "From the remarkable *astronomical* Signals "that are to alarm Mankind of what is coming,

" *viz.* The *Northern Lights* since 1715 ; the six
" Comets at the Protestant Reformation in four
" Years, 1530, 1531, 1533, 1534, compar'd with
" the seven Comets already seen in these last
"eleven Years 1737, 1739, 1742, 1743, 1744, 1746,
" and 1748. - - - - From the great Annular
" Eclipse of the Sun, *July* 14, 1748, whose Cen-
" ter pass'd through all the four Monarchies,
" from *Scotland* to the East Indies. - - - - From
" the Occultation of the *Pleiades* by the Moon
" each periodical Month, after the Eclipse last
" July, for above three Years, visible to the
" whole *Roman* Empire ; as there was a like
" Occultation of the *Hyades* from *A.* 590, to *A.*
" 595, for six Years foretold by Isaiah. - - - - -
" From the Transit of *Mercury* over the *Sun*,
" *April* 25, 1753, which will be visible thro' that
" Empire. - - - From the Comet of *A. D.* 1456,
" 1531, 1607, and 1682, which will appear again
" about 1757 ending, or 1758 beginning, and
" will also be visible thro' that Empire. - - - -
" From the Transit of *Venus* over the *Sun*, *May*
" 26, 1761, which will be visible over the same
" Empire : And lastly, from the annular Eclipse
" of the *Sun*, *March*, 11, 1764, which will be
" visible over the same Empire." - - - From
these *Astronomical Signs*, he foretels those
great Events, That within 16 Years from this
Time, "the *Millennium* or 1000 Years Reign of

"Christ shall begin, there shall be a *new Heav-*
"*ens*, and a *new Earth ;* there shall be no more
"an Infidel in Christendom, Page 398, nor a
"Gaming-Table at Tunbridge!" - - - - - - When
these Predictions are accomplished, what glorious Proofs they will be of the Truth of our Art?
- - - - And if they happen to fail, there is no
doubt that so profound an Astronomer as Mr.
Whiston, will be able to see *other* Signs in the
Heavens, foreshowing that the Conversion of
Infidels was to be postponed, and the *Millen-*
nium adjourn'd. - - - After these great Things
can any Man doubt our being capable of predicting a little Rain or Sun-shine? - - - Reader,
Farewell, and make the best Use of your Years
and your Almanacks, for you see, that according to *Whiston*, you may have at most, but
sixteen more of them.

Patowmack, July 30, 1750. - - R. SAUNDERS.

JANUARY.

Who rise to *Glory*, must by VIRTUE rise,
'T is *in the Mind* all *genuine Greatness lies :*
On that eternal Base, on that alone,
The World's Esteem you build, and more—your own.
For what avails Birth, Beauty, Fortune's Store,
The Plume of Title, and the Pride of Pow'r,
If, deaf to *Virtue*, deaf to Honour's Call,
To Tyrant *Vice* a wretched Slave you fall?

Pray don't burn my House to roast your Eggs.

Some Worth it argues, a Friend's Worth to know ;
Virtue to own the Virtue of a Foe.

Prosperity discovers Vice, Adversity Virtue.

FEBRUARY.

Affect not that vain Levity of Thought,
Which sets Religion, Virtue, all at nought.
For true Religion like the Sun's blest Beam,
Darts thro' the conscious Mind a heav'nly Gleam,
Irradiates all the Soul, no Care allows,
Calms the best Heart, and smooths the easy Brows.
Yet think it not enough what 's right to know,
But let your Practice that right Knowledge show.
To *Christians* bad rude *Indians* we prefer ;
'T is better not to know, than knowing err.

Many a Man would have been worse, if his Estate had
been better.

We may give Advice, but we cannot give Conduct.

MARCH.

Some sweet Employ for leisure Minutes chuse.
And let your very Pleasures have their Use.
But if you read, your Books with Prudence chuse.
Or Time mis-spent is worse than what you lose.
Be fully e'er you speak your Subject known,
And let e'en then some Diffidence be shown.
Keep something silent, and we think you wise,
But when we see the Bottom, we despise.

He that is conscious of a stink in his Breeches, is jeal-
ous of every Wrinkle in another's Nose.

Love and Tooth-ach have many Cures, but none infallible, except Possession and Dispossession.

APRIL.

O barb'rous Waggoners, your Wrath asswage,
Why vent you on the generous Steed your Rage?
Does not his Service earn you daily Bread?
Your Wives, your Children by his Labour fed?
If, as the *Samian* taught, the Soul revives,
And, shifting Seats, in other Bodies lives,
Severe shall be the brutal Carter's Change,
Doom'd in a Thill-horse o'er rough Roads to range;
And while transform'd the groaning Load he draws,
Some Horse turn'd Carter shall avenge the Cause.

There are lazy Minds as well as lazy Bodies.

Most People return small Favours, acknowledge middling ones, and repay great ones with Ingratitude.

MAY.

With ceaseless Streams a well-plac'd Treasure flows,
When spent increases, and by lessening grows.
Sarepta's Widow, hoping no Supply,
Thought, on her little Store, to eat and die:
Soon as she welcom'd her prophetic Guest,
The Cruse flow'd liberal, and the Corn increas'd,
Th' Almighty Pow'r unfailing Plenty sent,
The Oil unwasted, and the Meal unspent.

Fond Pride of Dress is sure an empty Curse;
E're Fancy you consult, consult your Purse.

Youth is pert and positive, Age modest and doubting:
So Ears of Corn when young and light, stand bold upright, but hang their Heads when weighty, full, and ripe.

JUNE.

What will not *Lux'ry* taste? Earth, Sea, and Air,
Are daily ransack'd for the Bill of Fare.

Blood stuff'd in Guts is *British* Christian's Food,
And *France* robs Marshes of the croaking Brood ;
But he had sure a Palate cover'd o'er
With Brass or Steel, that on the rocky Shore,
First broke the oozy Oister's pearly Coat,
And risk'd the living Morsel down his Throat.

'T is easier to suppress the first Desire, than to satisfy all that follow it.

Don't judge of Men's Wealth or Piety, by their Sunday Appearances.

Friendship increases by visiting Friends, but by visiting seldom.

JULY.

Vice luring, in the Way of *Virtue* lies,
God suffers this ; but tempts not ; tho' He tries.
Go wrong, go right, 't is your own Action still ;
He leaves you to your Choice, of Good, or Ill.
Then chuse the Good ! the Ill submisly bear !
The Man of Virtue is above Despair.
Safe on this Maxim with the Writer rest,
That all that happens, happens for the best.

If your Riches are yours, why don't you take them witn you to the t'other World ?

What more valuable than Gold ? Diamond. Than Diamonds ? Virtue.

To-day is Yesterday's Pupil.

AUGUST.

Ye Party Zealots, thus it fares with you,
When Party Rage too warmly you pursue ;
Both Sides club Nonsense and impetuous Pride,
And *Folly* joins whom *Sentiments* divide.

Vol I—14

You vent your Spleen as Monkeys when they pass,
Scratch at the mimic Monkey in the Glass,
While both are *one ;* and henceforth be it known,
Fools of both Sides shall stand as Fools alone.

If worldly Goods cannot save me from Death, they ought not to hinder me of eternal Life.

'T is great Confidence in a Friend to tell him your Faults, greater to tell him his.

SEPTEMBER.

Ah ! what is Life ?   With Ills encompass'd round,
Amidst our Hopes, Fate strikes the sudden Wound ;
To-day the Statesman of new Honour dreams,
To-morrow Death destroys his airy Schemes.
Is mouldy Treasure in thy Chest confin'd ;
Think, all that Treasure thou must leave behind ;
Thy Heir with Smiles shall view thy blazon'd Hearse,
And all thy Hoards, with lavish Hand disperse.

Talking against Religion is unchaining a Tyger ; The Beast let loose may worry his Deliverer.

Ambition often spends foolishly what Avarice had wickedly collected.

OCTOBER.

Should certain Fate th' impending Blow delay,
Thy Mirth will sicken, and thy Bloom decay ;
Then feeble Age will all thy Nerves disarm,
No more thy Blood its narrow Channels warm ;
Who then would wish to stretch this narrow Span,
To suffer Life beyond the Date of Man ?
The virtuous Soul pursues a nobler Aim,
And Life regards but as a fleeting Dream.

Pillgarlic was in the Accusative Case, and bespoke a Lawyer in the Vocative, who could not understand him till he made use of the Dative.

Great Estates may venture more ; Little Boats must keep near Shore.

Nice Eaters seldom meet with a good Dinner.

NOVEMBER.

She longs to wake, and wishes to get free,
To launch from Earth into ETERNITY,
For while the boundless Theme extends our Thought,
Ten thousand thousand rolling Years are nought.
O endless thought ! divine *Eternity !*
Th' immortal Soul shares but a Part of thee ;
For thou wert present when our Life began,
When the warm Dust shot up in breathing Man.

Not to oversee Workmen, is to leave them your Purse open.

The Wise and Brave dares own that he was wrong.

Cunning proceeds from Want of Capacity.

DECEMBER.

Ere the Foundations of the World were laid,
Ere kindling Light th' Almighty Word obey'd,
Thou wert ; and when the subterraneous Flame,
Shall burst its Prison, and devour this Frame,
From angry Heav'n when the keen Lightning flies,
When fervent Heat dissolves the melting Skies,
Thou still shalt be ; still as thou wert before,
And know no Change when *Time* shall be no more.

The Proud hate Pride—in others.

Who judges best of a Man, his Enemies or himself?

Drunkenness, that worst of Evils, makes some men Fools, some Beasts, some Devils.

'T is not a Holiday that 's not kept holy.

POOR RICHARD FOR 1752.

[PREFACE OMITTED.]

JANUARY.

On Publick Spirit.

Where never Science beam'd a friendly Ray,
Where one vast Blank neglected Nature lay;
From PUBLICK SPIRIT there, by Arts employ'd,
Creation, varying, glads the chearless Void.
By Arts, which Safety, Treasure and Delight,
On Land, on Wave, in woudrous Works unite!
Myriads made happy, *Publick Spirit* bless;
Parent of Trade, Wealth, Liberty and Peace.

Observe old Vellum; he praises former times, as if
he'd a mind to sell 'em.

Kings have long Arms, but misfortune longer: Let
none think themselves out of her Reach.

FEBRUARY.

Unlike where Tyranny, the Rod maintains
O'er turfless, leafless and uncultur'd Plains,
Here Herbs of Food and Physic, Plenty showers,
Gives Fruits to blush, and colours various Flowers.

Where Sands or Stony Wilds once starv'd the Year,
Laughs the green Lawn, and nods the golden Ear.
White shine the fleecy Race, which Fate shall doom,
The Feast of Life, the Treasure of the Loom.

For want of a Nail the Shoe is lost ; for want of a Shoe
the Horse is lost ; for want of a Horse the Rider is lost.

MARCH.

What tho' no *Arch* of *Triumph* is assign'd
To laurel'd Pride, whose Sword has thinn'd Mankind ;
Tho' no vast Wall extends from Coast to Coast,
No Pyramid aspires sublimely lost.
Lo ! stately Streets, lo ! ample Squares invite
The salutary Gale that breathes Delight.
Lo ! Structures mark the hospitable Strand,
Where *Charity* extends her tender Hand ;

The busy Man has few idle Visitors ; to the boiling Pot
the Flies come not.

Calamity and Prosperity are the Touchstones of In-
tegrity.

APRIL.

Where the sick Stranger joys to find a Home,
Where casual Ill, maim'd Labour, freely come ;
Those worn with Age, Infirmity or Care,
Find Rest, Relief, and Health returning fair.
There too the Walls of rising Schools ascend,
For PUBLICK SPIRIT still is *Learning's* Friend,
Where Science, Virtue, sown with liberal Hand,
In future Patriots shall inspire the Land.

The Prodigal generally does more Injustice than the
Covetous.

Generous Minds are all of kin.

MAY.

And when too populous at length confess'd,
From confluent Strangers refug'd and redress'd :
When War so long withdraws his barb'rous Train,
That Peace o'erstocks us with the Sons of Men :
So long Health breathes thro' the pure ambient Air,
That Want must prey on those Disease would spare ;
Then will be all the *gen'rous Godless* seen,
Then most diffus'd she shines, and most benign.

'T is more noble to forgive, and more manly to despise, than to revenge an Injury.

A Brother may not be a Friend, but a Friend will always be a Brother.

Meanness is the Parent of Insolence.

JUNE.

Her Eye far piercing, round extends its Beams,
To *Erie's* Banks, or smooth *Ohio's* Streams,
It fixes where kind Rays till then have smil'd,
(Vain Smile !) on some luxuriant houseless Wild ;
How many Sons of Want might here enjoy
What Nature gives for Age but to destroy ?
' Blush, blush, O *Sun* (she cries) here vainly found
' To rise, to set, to roll the Seasons round !

Mankind are very odd Creatures : One Half censure what they practise, the other half practise what they censure ; the rest always say and do as they ought.

Severity is often Clemency ; Clemency Severity.

JULY.

' Shall Heav'n distil in Dews, descend in Rain,
' From Earth gush Fountains, Rivers flow in vain ?
' There shall the *watry Lives* in Myriads stray,
' And be, to be alone each other's Prey ?

' Unsought shall here the teeming Quarries own
' The various Species of mechanic Stone ?
' From Structure This, from Sculpture That confine ?
' Shall Rocks forbid the latent Gem to shine ?

Bis dat qui cito dat : He gives twice that gives soon ;
i. e. he will soon be called upon to give again.

A Temper to bear much, will have much to bear.

Pride dines upon Vanity, sups on Contempt.

AUGUST.

' Shall Mines obedient aid no Artist's Care,
' Nor give the martial Sword and peaceful Share ?
' Ah ! shall they never precious Ore unfold.
' To smile in Silver, or to flame in Gold ?
' Shall here the vegetable World alone,
' For Joys, for various Virtues rest unknown ?
' While Food and Physic, Plants and Herbs supply,
' Here must they shoot alone to bloom and die ?

Great Merit is coy, as well as great Pride.

An undutiful Daughter, will prove an unmanageable
Wife.

Old Boys have their Playthings as well as young Ones ;
the Difference is only in the Price.

SEPTEMBER.

' Shall Fruits, which none, but brutal Eyes survey
' Untouch'd grow ripe, untasted drop away ?
' Shall here th' irrational, the salvage Kind
' Lord it o'er Stores by Heav'n for Man design'd,
' And trample what mild Suns benignly raise,
' While Man must lose the Use, and Heav'n the Praise ?
' Shall it then be ? '   (Indignant here she rose,
Indignant, yet humane, her Bosom glows.)

The too obliging Temper is evermore disobliging itself.

Hold your Council before Dinner ; the full Belly hates Thinking as well as Acting.

OCTOBER.

' No ! By each honour'd *Grecian Roman* Name,
' By Men for Virtue Deified by Fame,
' Who peopled Lands, who model'd infant State,
' And then bad Empire be maturely great,
' By These I swear (be witness Earth and Skies !)
' Fair Order here shall from Confusion rise,
' Rapt I a future Colony survey !
' Come then, ye Sons of Mis'ry ! come away !

The Brave and the Wise can both pity and excuse when Cowards and Fools shew no Mercy.

Ceremony is not Civility ; nor Civility Ceremony.

If man could have Half his Wishes, he would double his Troubles.

NOVEMBER.

' Let Those, whose Sorrows from Neglect are known,
' (Here taught compell'd empower'd) Neglect attone !
' Let Those enjoy (who never merit Woes)
' In Youth th' industrious Wish, in Age Repose !
' Allotted Acres (no reluctant Soil)
' Shall prompt their Industry, and pay their Toil.
' Let Families, long Strangers to Delight,
' Whom wayward Fate dispers'd, by Me unite ;

It is ill Jesting with the Joiner's Tools, worse with the Doctor's.

Children and Princes will quarrel for Trifles.

Praise to the undeserving, is severe Satyr.

DECEMBER.

' Here live enjoying Life, see Plenty, Peace ;
' Their Lands encreasing as their Sons increase !
' As Nature yet is found in leafy Glades
' To intermix the Walks with Lights and Shades ;
' Or as with Good and Ill, in chequer'd Strife,
' Various the Goddess colours human Life ;
' So in this fertile Clime if yet are seen
' Moors, Marshes, Cliffs, by Turns to intervene :

Success has ruin'd many a Man.

Great Pride and Meanness sure are near ally'd ; Or their Partitions do their Bounds divide.

POOR RICHARD FOR 1753.

––

PREFACE.

Courteous Reader,

This is the twentieth Time of my address-
ing thee in this Manner, and I have reason
to flatter myself my Labours have not been
unacceptable to the Publick. I am particularly
pleas'd to understand that my Predictions of
the Weather give such general Satisfaction; and
indeed such Care is taken in the Calculations,
on which those Predictions are founded, that I
could almost venture to say, there 's not a
single One of them, promising Snow, Rain,
Hail, Heat, Frost, Fogs, Wind, or Thunder,
but what comes to pass punctually and precisely on the very Day, in some Place or other
on this little diminutive Globe of Ours; (and
when you consider the vast Distance of the
Stars from which we take Aim, you must allow
it no small Degree of Exactness to hit any Part
of it). I say on this Globe; for though in other

Matters I confine the Usefulness of my Ephemeris to the Northern Colonies, yet in that important Matter of the Weather, which is of such general Concern, I would have it more extensively useful, and therefore take in both Hemispheres, and all the Latitudes from Hudson's Bay to Cape Horn.

You will find this Almanack in my former Method, only conformable to the New-Stile established by the Act of Parliament, which I gave you in my last at length; the new Act since made for Amendment of that first Act, not affecting us in the least, being intended only to regulate some Corporation matters in England, being unprovided for. I have only added a Column in the second Page of each Month, containing the Days of the Old Stile opposite to their corresponding Days in the New, which may in many Cases, be of Use; and so conclude, (believing you will excuse a short Preface, when it is to make Room for something better).

Thy Friend and Servant,

R. SAUNDERS.

HYMN TO THE CREATOR, FROM PSALM CIV.

AWAKE, my Soul! with Joy thy God adore;
Declare his Greatness; celebrate his Pow'r;
Who, cloth'd with Honour, and with Glory crown'd,
Shines forth, and cheers his Universe around,

Who with a radient Veil of heavenly Light
Himself conceals from all created Sight.
Who rais'd the spacious Firmament on high,
And spread the azure Curtain of the Sky.
Whose awful Throne Heav'n's starry Arch sustains,
Whose Presence not Heav'n's vast Expanse retains.
Whose Ways unsearchable no Eye can find,
The Clouds his Chariot, and his Wings the Wind.
Whom Hosts of mighty Angels own their Lord,
And flaming Seraphim fulfil his Word.
Whose Pow'r of old the solid Earth did found,
Self-pois'd, self-center'd, and with Strength girt round;
From her appointed Sphere forbid to fly,
Or rush unbalenced thro' the trackless Sky.
To reas'ning Man the sov'reign Rule assign'd,
His Delegate o'er each inferior Kind;
Too soon to fall from that distinguish'd Place,
His Honours stain'd with Guilt and foul Disgrace.
  He saw the Pride of Earth's aspiring Lord,
And in his Fury gave the dreadful Word:
Straight o'er her peopled Plains his Floods were pour'd,
And o'er her Mountains the proud Billows roar'd.
Athwart the Face of Earth the Deluge sweeps,
And whelms the impious Nations in the Deeps.
Again God spake - - - - - and at his pow'rful Call
The raging Floods asswage, the Waters fall,
The Tempests hear his Voice, and straight obey,
And at his Thunder's Roar they haste away:
From off the lofty Mountains they subside,
And gently thro' the winding Valleys glide,
Till in the spacious Caverns of the Deep
They sink together, and in Silence sleep.
There he hath stretched abroad thier liquid Plains,
And there Omnipotence their Rage restrains,
That Earth no more her Ruins may deplore,
And guilty Mortals dread thier Wrath no more.

He bids the living Fountains burst the Ground,
And bounteous spread their Silver Streams around :
Down from the Hills they draw thier shining Train,
Diffusing Health and Bounty o'er the Plain.
There the fair Flocks allay the Summer's Rage,
And panting Savages their Flame asswage,
On their sweet winding Banks th' aerial Race
In artless Numbers warble forth his Praise,
Or chant the harmless Raptures of their Loves,
And cheer the Plains, and wake the vocal Groves.
Forth from his Treasures in the Skies he pours
His precious Blessings in refreshing Show'rs,
Each dying Plant with Joy new Life receives,
And thankful Nature smiles, and Earth revives.
The fruitful Fields with Verdure he bespreads,
The Table of the Race that haunts the Meads,
And bids each Forest, and each flow'ry Plain
Send forth their native Physic for the Swain,
Thus doth the various Bounty of the Earth
Support each Species crowding into Birth.
In purple Streams she bids her Vintage flow.
And Olives on her Hills luxuriant grow,
One with its generous Juice to cheer the Heart,
And one illustrious Beauty to impart ;
And Bread of all Heav'n's precious gifts the chief
From desolating Want the sure Relief.
Which with new Life the feeble Limbs inspires,
And all the Man with Health and Courage fires.
The Cloud-topt Hills with waving Woods are crown'd,
Which wide extend thier sacred Shades around,
There Lebanon's proud Cedars nod their Heads ;
There Bashan's lofty Oaks extend thier Shades :
The pointed Firs rise tow'ring to the Clouds,
And Life and warbling Numbers fill the Woods.
  Nor gentle Shades alone, nor verdant Plains,
Nor fair enamell'd Meads, nor flow'ry Lawns,

But e'n rude Rocks and dreary Desarts yield
Retreats for the wild Wand'rers of the Field.
The Pow'r with Life and Sense all Nature fills,
Each Element with varied Being swells,
Race after Race arising view the Light,
Then silent pass away, and sink in Night.
The Gift of Life thus boundlessly bestowed,
Proclaims th' exhaustless Hand, the Hand of God.
Nor less thy Glory in th' etherial Spheres,
  Nor less thy ruling Providence appears.
There from on high the gentle Moon by Night
In solemn Silence sheds her Silver Light,
And thence the glorious Sun pours forth his Beams.
Thence copious spreads around his quick'ning Streams
Each various Orb enjoys the golden Day,
And Worlds of Life hang on his chearful Ray.
Thus Light and Darkness their fix'd Course maintain,
And still the kind Viccisitudes remain :
For when pale Night her sable Curtain spreads,
And wraps all Nature in her awful Shades,
Soft Slumbers gently seal each mortal Eye,
Stretch'd at their Ease the weary Lab'rers lie.
The restless Soul 'midst Life's vain Tumults tost,
Forgets her Woes and ev'ry Care is lost.

JANUARY.

Then from their Dens the rav'nous Monsters creep,
Whilst in their Folds the harmless Bestial sleeps.
The furious Lion roams in quest of Prey,
To gorge his Hunger till the Dawn of Day ;
His hideous Roar with Terror shakes the Wood,
As from his Maker's Hand he asks his Food.
Again the Sun his Morning Beams displays,
And fires the eastern Mountain with his Rays.

'T is against some Mens Principle to pay Interest, and
seems against others Interest to pay the Principal.

Philosophy as well as Foppery often changes Fashion.

FEBRUARY.

Before him fly the Horrors of the Night ;
He looks upon the World—and all is Light.
Then the lone Wand'rers of the dreary Waste
Affrighted to their Holes return in Haste,
To Man give up the World, his native Reign,
Who then resumes his Pow'r, and rules the Plain.
How various are thy Works, Creator wise !
How to the Sight Beauties on Beauties rise !

Setting too Good an Example is a kind of Slander seldom forgiven ; 't is Scandalum Magnatum.

A great Talker may be no Fool, but he is one that
relies on him.

MARCH.

Where Goodness worthy of a God bestows
His Gifts on all, and without Bounds o'erflows ;
Where Wisdom bright appears, and Pow'r divine,
And where Infinitude itself doth shine ;
Where Excellence invisible 's exprest,
And in his glorious Works the God appears confest.
With Life thy Hand hath stocked this Earthly Plain
Nor less the spacious Empire of the Main.

When Reason preaches, if you don't hear her she 'll
box your Ears.

It is not Leisure that is not used.

APRIL.

There the tall Ships the rolling Billows sweep,
And bound triumphant o'er the unfathom'd Deep.
There great Leviathan in regal Pride,
The scaly Nations crouding by his Side,

Far in the deep Recesses of the Main
O'er Nature's Wastes extends his boundless Reign.
Round the dark Bottoms of the Mountains roves,
The hoary Deep swells dreadful as he moves.

The Good-will of the Govern'd will be starved, if not
fed by the good Deeds of the Governors.

Paintings and Fightings are best seen at a distance.

MAY.

Now views the awful Throne of antient Night,
Then mounts exulting to the Realms of Light :
Now launches to the Deep, now stems the Shore,
An Ocean scarce contains the wild Uproar.
Whate'er of Life replenishes the Flood,
Or walks the Earth, or warbles thro' the Wood,
In Nature's various Wants to thee complains.
The Hand, which gave the Life, the Life sustains.

If you would reap Praise you must sow the Seeds,
gentle Words and useful Deeds.

Ignorance leads Men into a party, and Shame keeps
them from getting out again.

Haste makes Waste.

JUNE.

To each th' appointed Sustenance bestows,
To each the noxious and the healthful shows.
Thou spread'st thy Bounty—meagre Famine flies :
Thou hid'st thy Face—their vital Vigour dies.
Thy pow'rful Word again restores their Breath ;
Renew'd Creation triumphs over Death.
Th' Almighty o'er his Works casts down his Eye,
And views their various Excellence with Joy ;

Many have quarrel'd about Religion, that never practised it.

Sudden Pow'r is apt to be insolent, Sudden Liberty saucy ; that behaves best which has grown gradually.

He that best understands the World, least likes it.

JULY.

His Works with Reverence own his pow'rful Hand,
And humble Nature waits his dread Command,
He looks upon the Earth—her Pillars shake,
And from her Centre her Foundations quake.
The Hills he touches—Clouds of Smoke arise,
And sulph'rous Streams mount heavy to the Skies.
   Whilst Life informs this Frame, that Life shall be
(O First and Greatest !) sacred all to Thee.

Anger is never without a Reason, but seldom with a good One.

He that is of Opinion Money will do every Thing may well be suspected of doing every Thing for Money.

An ill Wound, but not an ill Name, may be healed.

AUGUST.*

When out of Favour, none know thee ; when in, thou dost not know thyself.

A lean Award is better than a fat Judgement.

God, Parents, and Instructors, can never be requited.

SEPTEMBER.

When Nature sinks, when Death's dark Shades arise,
And this World's Glories vanish from these Eyes ;
Then may the Thought of Thee be ever near,
To calm the Tumult, and compose the Fear.

    *August poetry wanting in copy.

15

In all my Woes thy Favour my Defence ;
Safe in thy Mercy, not my Innocence,
And through what future Scenes thy Hand may guide
My wond'ring Soul, and thro' what States untry'd.

He that builds before he counts the Cost, acts foolishly ;
and he that counts before he builds, finds that he did not
count wisely.

Patience in Market, is worth Pounds in a year.

Danger is Sauce for Prayers.

OCTOBER.

What distant Seats soe'ver I may explore,
When frail Mortality shall be no more ;
If aught of meek or contrite in thy Sight
Shall fit me for the Realms of Bliss and Light,
Be this the Bliss of all my future Days,
To view thy Glories, and to sing thy Praise.
When the dread Hour, ordain'd of old, shall come,
Which brings on stubborn Guilt its righteous Doom.

If you have no Honey in your Pot, have some in your
Mouth.

A Pair of good Ears will drain dry an hundred
Tongues.

NOVEMBER.

When Storms of Fire on Sinners shall be pour'd,
And all th' Obdurate in thy Wrath devour'd ;
May I then hope to find a lowly Place
To stand the meanest of th' etherial Race ;
Swift at thy Word to wing the liquid Sky,
And on thy humblest Messages to fly.
Howe'er thy blissful Sight may raise my Soul,
While vast Eternitie's long Ages roll.

Serving God is doing good to Man, but praying is thought an easier Service, and therefore more generally chosen.

Nothing humbler than Ambition, when it is about to climb.

DECEMBER.

Perfection on Perfection tow'ring high,
Glory on Glory rais'd, and Joy on Joy,
Each Pow'r improving in the bright'ning Mind,
To humble Virtues, lofty Knowledge join'd ;
Be this my highest Aim, howe'er I soar,
Before thy Footstool prostrate to adore,
My brightest Crown before thy Feet to lay,
My Pride to serve, my Glory to obey.

The discontented Man finds no easy Chair.

Virtue and a Trade, are a Child's best Portion.

Gifts much expected, are paid, not given.

HOW TO SECURE HOUSES, &C. FROM LIGHTNING

It has pleased God in his Goodness to Mankind, at length to discover to them the Mean of securing their Habitations and other Buildings from Mischief by thunder and Lightning. The Method is this : Provide a small Iron Rod (it may be of the Rod-iron used by the Nailors but of such a length, that one End being thre or four Feet in the moist Ground, the other may be six or eight Feet above the highest Part of the Building. To the upper end of the Ro fasten about a Foot of Brass Wire, the size of

common Knitting-needle, sharpened to a fine
Point; the Rod may be secured to the House
by a few small Staples. If the House or Barn,
be long, there may be a Rod and Point at each
End, and a middling Wire along the Ridge
from one to the other. A house thus furnished
will not be damaged by Lightning, it being at-
tracted by the Points, and passing thro' the
Metal into the Ground without hurting anything. Vessels also, having a sharp pointed
Rod fix'd on the Top of their Masts, with a
Wire from the Foot of the Rod reaching down,
round one of the Shrouds, to the Water, will
not be hurt by Lightning.

POOR RICHARD FOR 1754.

PREFACE.

KIND READER,

I have now serv'd you three Apprenticeships, yet, old as I am, I have no Inclination to
quit your Service, but should be glad to be able to
continue in it three times three Apprenticeships
longer.

The first Astrologers, I think, were honest
Husbandmen; and so it seems are the last;
for my brethren Jerman and Moore, and myself,
the only remaining Almanack makers of this
Country, are all of that Class: Tho' in inter-
mediate Times our Art has been cultivated in
great Cities, and even in the Courts of Princes;
Witness History from the Days of King NEBU-
CHADNEZZAR I. of Babylon, to those of
Queen JAMES I. of England. - - - - - But you
will ask perhaps, how I prove that the first

Astrologers were Countrymen? - - - I own this
is a Matter beyond the Memory of History, for
Astrology was before Letters; but I prove it
from the Book of the Heavens, from the Names
of the twelve Signs, which were mostly given
to remark some Circumstance relative to rural
Affairs, in the several successive Months of the
Year, and by that Means to supply the Want
of Almanacks. - - - - - - Thus, as the Year of the
Ancients began most naturally with the Spring,
Aries and Taurus, that is, the Ram and the Bull,
represented the successive Addition to their
Flocks of Sheep and Kine, by their Produce in
that Season, Lambs and Calves. - - - - - Gemini
were originally the Kids, but called the Twins,
as Goats more commonly bring forth two than
one : These followed the Calves. - - - - Cancer,
the Crab came next, when that Kind of Fish
were in Season. - - - - Then follow'd Leo, the
Lion, and Virgo, the Wench, to mark the Summer Months, and Dog-Days, when those Creatures were most mischievous.   In Autumn
comes first Libra, the Ballance, to point out the
Time for selling the Summer's Produce; or
rather, a Time of Leisure for holding Courts of
Justice in which they might plague themselves
and Neighbours ; I know some suppose this Sign
to signify the equal Poise, at that Time of Day
and Night; but the other Signification is the

truer, as plainly appears by the following Sign
Scorpio, or the Scorpion, with the Sting in his
Tail, which certainly denotes the Paying of
Costs. - - - - Then follows Sagittary, the Archer,
to show the season of Hunting; for now the
Leaves being off the Trees and Bushes, the
Game might be more easily seen and struck
with their Arrows. - - - - The Goat accompanys
the short Days and long Nights of Winter, to
show the Season of Mirth, Feasting and Jollity;
for what can Capricorn mean, but Dancing or
Cutting of Capers? - - - - At length comes Aqua-
rius, or the Water-bearer, to show the Season
of Snows, Rains and Floods; and lastly Pisces,
or the two Shads, to denote the approaching
Return of those Fish up the Rivers: Make
your Wears, hawl your Seins; Catch 'em and
pickle 'em, my Friends; they are excellent Rel-
ishers of old Cyder. - - - - But if you can't get
Shad, Mackerell may do better.

I know, gentle Readers, that many of you
always expect a Preface and think yourselves
slighted if that 's omitted. So here you have it,
and much good may 't do ye. As little as it is to
the Purpose, there are many less so, now-a-days.
- - - - - I have left out, you see, all the usual
Stuff about the Importunity of Friends, and
the like, or I might have made it much bigger.
You think, however, that 't is big enough for

Conscience, for any Matter of Good that's in it;
- - - I think so too, if it fills the Page, which is
the Needful, at present, from
Your loving Friend to serve.
R. SAUNDERS.

JANUARY.

Hail, infinite CREATOR ! with thy Praise
The Muse began, with thee shall end my Lays,
These are thy Works, blest Architect divine !
This Earth, and all this beauteous Offspring thine
Thy Breath first bid inactive Matter move,
And strait with Life the genial Atoms strove
Producing Animal, and Plant, and Flow'r,
Concurrent proof of Wisdom and of Pow'r.

The first Degree of Folly, is to conceit one's self wise ;
the second to profess it ; the third to despise Counsel.

Take heed of the Vinegar of sweet Wine, and the
Anger of Good-nature.

FEBRUARY.

Thy potent Word infus'd the solar Light,
And spread the Curtain of refreshing Night ;
With splendid Orbs enrich'd the Void profound,
Rang'd the bright Worlds, and roll'd their Courses round.
O sing his Praises then ! How justly due,
Created Kinds, the Strains of Praise from You ?
How grateful the deserv'd Returns of Love !
Praise him thou Earth, ye Worlds that roll above,
Each Pow'r, whole Nature, all his Works, conspire
In Songs of Praise, an Universal Choir.

The Bell calls others to Church, but itself never minds
the Sermon.

Cut the Wings of your Hens and Hopes, lest they lead you a weary Dance after them.

MARCH.

Thou SUN, Creation's pure resplendent Eye ;
And all ye solar Orbs that deck the Sky,
Round whose vast System, peopled Planéts move.
Ye central Suns of numerous Earths above.
Praise the dread Pow'r, whose Goodness ye proclaim,
And let your warbling Spheres attune his Name.
Thou Moon, who with thy Rays of silver Light,
Dost gild the shapeless Gloom of awful Night ;

In Rivers and bad Governments, the lightest Things swim at top.

The Cat in Gloves catches no Mice.

APRIL.

And you satillary Orbs on high,
Who kindly Beams to distant Worlds supply,
Hymn your Creator's Praise, whose Skill divine
Impower'd your Mass to roll, your Globes to shine.
Ye Comets ! that in long Ellipses stray,
Whole Ages finishing your annual Way ;
Thou Darkness ! Nature's emblematic Tomb,
Yield him your Reverence of impressive Gloom,
In silent Praise - - - - - - And thou dread Space profound,
Thro' all thy waste interminable Bound.

If you 'd know the Value of Money, go and borrow some.

The Horse thinks one thing, and he that saddles him another.

Love your Neighbour; yet don't pull down your Hedge.

MAY.

Winds ! who in troubled Air your Voices raise,
Sweet with loud Accents in your Maker's Praise ;
And you, soft Breezes, that perfume the Spring,
Bear him a Tribute on your gentle Wing.
Spread it, ye pealing Thunders, round the Sky,
Wide as your Vollies roll, or Lightnings fly.
Ye Meteors ! your Creator's Praises show :
The spangled Dew, the Cloud-reflected Bow,

When Prosperity was well mounted, she let go the Bridle, and soon came tumbling out of the Saddle.

Some make Conscience of wearing a Hat in the Church, who make none of robbing the Altar.

JUNE.

And moist'ning Show'r,—ye Frosts ! his Praise proclaim ;
The pendant Icicle's clear native Gem :
Hoar Mists congeal'd, that dress the Meadow pale :
Blue Vapour, whitening Snows, and pearly Hail.
Praise him, ye Seasons ! Spring with youthful Face,
And Summer blooming with maturer Grace ;
Ripe Autumn clad in Vines, with Harvests crown'd,
And Winter old—his solemn Praise resound.

In the Affairs of this World Men are saved, not by Faith, but by the Want of it.

Friendship cannot live with Ceremony, nor without Civility.

Praise little, dispraise less.

JULY.

The Flow'ry Tribes, in all their bright Array,
Thier lovely Forms and dazzling Hues display.
Ye fruitful Branches ! white with vernal Bloom,
In rich Oblations breathe your fresh Perfume.

Praise him, ye Plants ! with all your sweet Supplies ;
Ye od'rous Herbs, in grateful Incense rise.
Insects ! that creep on Earth, or spread the Wing,
In Troops your tributary Homage bring.

The learned Fool writes his Nonsense in better Language than the unlearned ; but still 't is Nonsense.

A Child thinks 20 Shillings and 20 Years can scarce ever be spent.

AUGUST.

Fowls of the upper Air ! and Brutes supine !
And Fish ! that swim the Floods, or Ocean Brine.
Ye Seraphims, bright flames ! ye Angel Choirs !
To the lov'd Theme tune all your sounding Lyres.
Saints ! thron'd in Bliss, who once convers'd below,
In noblest Strains your loftiest Praise bestow.
Man ! Image of thy Maker's moral Pow'r,
Last, labour'd Work of Heav'n's creating Hour ;

Don't think so much of your own Cunning, as to forget other Men's : A Cunning Man is overmatched by a cunning Man and a Half.

Willows are weak, but they bind the Faggot.

You may give a Man an Office, but you cannot give him Discretion.

SEPTEMBER.

O shall his Goodness, his Indulgence move
No warm Returns, nor swell the Breath of Love ?
Priest of the mute Creation, He demands
Thier Offerings from thy consecrated Hands,
Deputed Lord ; - - - - from thy dead Slumber part ;
Let Nature wake, awake the Pow'rs of Art,
And with exerted Force attune his Praise,
In Notes may emulate cælestial Lays.
Let Music her divinest Succours bring,
The breathing Flute, the Viols warbling String,

He that doth what he should not, shall feel what he would not.

To be intimate with a foolish Friend, is like going to Bed to a Razor.

Little Rogues easily become great Ones.

OCTOBER.

And dulcit Voice - - - - - Ye Concerts louder grow !
Let the shrill Trump, the deep'ning Organ blow,
While with the Notes, the tremulating Ground,
And echoing Roofs, strike awful Rapture round.
Praise him each Creature, Plenitude and Space ;
Inanimate, and Things of living Race.
From the terrestrial to the Starry Pole,
Praise him his Works, and thou my prostrate Soul !

You may sometimes be much in the wrong, in owning your being in the right.

Friends are the true Scepters of Princes.

Where Sense is wanting, everything is wanting.

NOVEMBER.

Thus while in vain the wretched human Brood,
Pursue on Earth a false, imagin'd Good ;
That Good, which Creatures never can bestow,
With him still only found from whom they flow ;
While Gold or Lust, with a deceitful Bribe,
Tempt to sure Woes the easy list'ning Tribe ;
While Faction leads th' unsteady Herd aside,
And Vanity perverts the Son of Pride ;

Many Princes sin with David, but few repent with him.

He that hath no Ill-Fortune will be troubled with good.

For Age and Want save while you may ;
No morning Sun lasts a whole Day.

DECEMBER.

Would I from Vice, from Luxury remove,
Conversing with the Themes of heav'nly Love.
These shall my Hours of Virtuous Life amuse,
Cheer its dull Glooms, and brighter Hopes iufuse ;
Pleas'd the lov'd Visit frequeut to rcnew,
While certain Bliss my rais'd Desires pursue,
To meditate my Maker, aud my Lays
Tune to his Pow'r who gave me Breath to praise.

Learning to the Studious ; Riches to the Careful ;
Power to the Bold ; Heaven to the Virtuous.

Now glad the Poor with Christmas Cheer ;
Thank God you 're able so to end the Year.

POOR RICHARD FOR 1755.

PREFACE.

Courteous Reader,

It is a common saying, that *One Half of the World does not know how the other Half lives.* To add somewhat to your knowledge in that Particular, I gave you in a former Almanack, an Account of the manner of living at *Hudson's-Bay,* and the Effects produced by the excessive Cold of that Climate, which seem'd so strange to some of you, that it was taken for a Romance, tho' really authentick. - - - In this, I shall give you some idea of a Country under the Torrid Zone, which for the Variety of its Weather (where one would naturally expect the greatest Uniformity) is extreamly remarkable. The Account is extracted from the Journal of Monsieur *Bouguer,* one of the *French* Academicians, sent by their King to measure a Degree of Latitude under

238

the Equinoctial, in order to settle a Dispute between the *English* and *French* Philosophers concerning the Shape of the Earth, others being at the same Time sent for the same Purpose to *Lapland*, under the Polar Circle. - - - The Mountains in that Country are so lofty, that the highest we have, being compared to them, are mere Mole-hills. This Extract relates chiefly to the Country among those Mountains.

The Method of this Almanack is the same I have observed for some Years past ; only in the third Column the names of some of the principal fixed Stars are put down against those Days on which they come to the Meridian at nine a Clock in the Evening, whereby those unacquainted, may learn to know them.   I am,

Your obliged Friend and Servant,
R. SAUNDERS.

THE HAPPY MAN.

Sure Peace is his : A solid Life, estrang'd
To Disappointment and fallacious Hope,
Rich in Content.   THOMSON.

Happy the man, who free from noisy Sports,
And all the Pomp and Pageantry of Courts :
Far from the venal World can live secure,
Be moral, honest, virtuous - - - tho' but poor,
Who walking still by Equity's just Rules,
Detesting sordid knaves, and flattering Fools :
Regarding neither Fortune, Pow'r, nor State
Nor ever wishing to be vainly great.

Without Malevolence and Spleen can live,
And what his neighbour wants, with Joy would give ;
A Foe to Pride, no Passion's guilty Friend,
Obeying Nature, faithful to her End ;
Severe in Manners, as in Truth severe,
Just to himself, and to his Friends sincere ;
His temper even, and his steady Mind
Refin'd by Friendship, and by Books refin'd.
Some low roof'd Cottage holds the happy Swain,
Unknown to Lux'ry, or her servile Train ;
He studying Nature grows serenely wise,
Like *Socrates* he lives, or like him dies.
He asks no Glory gain'd by hostile Arms,
Nor sighs for Grandeur with her pointed Charms.
With calm Indiff'rence views the shifting Scene,
Thro' all magnanimous, resign'd, serene.
On Hope sustain'd he treads Life's devious Road,
And knows no Fear, except the Fear of GOD.
Would Heav'n indulgent grant my fond Desire,
Thus would I live, and thus should Life expire.

EPITAPH ON A WORTHY CLERGYMAN.

Still like his Master, known by breaking Bread,
The Good he entertained, the needy fed ;
Of Humour easy, and of Life unblam'd,
The Friend delighted, while the Priest reclaim'd,
The Friend, the Father, and the Husband gone,
The Priest still lives in this recording Stone ;
Where pious Eyes may read his Praises o'er,
And learn each Grace his Pulpit taught before.

EPITAPH ON ANOTHER CLERGYMAN.

Here lies, who need not here be nam'd,
For Theologic Knowledge fam'd ;
Who all the Bible had by rote,
With all the Comments Calvin wrote ;

Parsons and Jesuits could confute,
Talk Infidels and Quakers mute,
To every Heretick a foe;
Was he an honest man? - - - - *So, so.*

JANUARY.

The Farmer.

O happy he! happiest of mortal men!
Who far remov'd from Slavery, as from Pride,
Fears no Man's Frown, nor cringing waits to catch
The gracious nothing of a great Man's Nod;
Where the lac'd Beggar bustles for a Bride,
The Purchase of his Honour; where Deceit,
And Fraud, and Circumvention, drest in Smiles.

A Man without a Wife, is but half a Man.

Speak little, do much.

He that would travel much, should eat little.

FEBRUARY.

Hold shameful Commerce, and beneath the Mask
Of Friendship and Sincerity, betray.
Him, nor the stately Mansion's gilded Pride,
Rich with whate'er the imitative Arts,
Painting or Sculpture, yield to charm the Eye;
Nor shining Heaps of massy Plate, enwrought
With curious, costly Workmanship, allure.
Tempted nor with the Pride nor Pomp of Power,

When the Wine enters, out goes the Truth.

If you would be loved, love and be loveable.

MARCH.

Nor Pageants of Ambition, nor the Mines
Of grasping Av'rice, nor the poison'd Sweets
Of pamper'd Luxury, he plants his Foot
With Firmness on his old paternal Fields,
16

And stands unshaken. There sweet Prospects rise
Of Meadows smiling in their flow'ry Pride,
Green Hills and Dales, and Cottages embower'd,
The Scenes of Innocence, and calm Delight.

Ask and have, is sometimes dear buying.

The hasty Bitch brings forth blind Puppies.

APRIL.

There the wild Melody of warbling Birds,
And cool refreshing Groves, and murmuring Springs,
Invite to sacred Thought, and lift the Mind
From low Pursuits, to meditate the God !

RURAL LIFE IN AN HIGHER CLASS.

But sing, O Muse ! the Swain, the happy Swain,
Whom Taste and Nature leading o'er his Fields,

Where there is Hunger, Law is not regarded ; and
where Law is not regarded, there will be Hunger.

Two dry Sticks will burn a green One.

MAY.

Conduct to every rural Beauty. See !
Before his Footsteps winds the waving Walk,
Here gently rising, there descending flow
Thro' the tall Grove, or near the Water's Brink,
Where Flow'rs besprinkled paint the shelving Bank
And weeping Willows bend to kiss the Stream.
Now wand'ring o'er the Lawn he roves, and now
Beneath the Hawthorn's secret Shade reclines ;

The honest Man takes Pains, and then enjoys Pleasures ; the knave takes Pleasure, and then suffers Pains.

Think of three Things, whence you came, where you
are going, and to whom you must account.

JUNE.

Where purple Violets hang their bashful Heads,
Where yellow Cowslips, and the blushing Pink,
Their mingled Sweets, and lovely Hues combine.
Here, shelter'd from the North, his ripening Fruits
Display their sweet Temptations from the Wall,
Or from the gay Espalier ; while below,
His various Esculence, from glowing Beds,
Give the Fair Promise of delicious Feasts.

Necessity has no Law ; Why? Because 't is not to be had without Money.

There was never a good knife made of bad Steel.

The Wolf sheds his Coat once a Year, his Disposition never.

JULY.

There from his forming Hand new Scenes arise,
The fair Creation of his Fancy's Eye.
Lo ! bosom'd in the solemn shady Grove,
Whose rev'rend Branches wave on yonder Hill,
He views the Moss-grown Temple's ruin'd Tower,
Cover'd with creeping Ivy's cluster'd Leaves,
The Mansion seeming of some rural God,
Whom Nature's Chorister's, in untaught Hymns

Who is wise? He that learns from every One.
Who is powerful? He that governs his Passions.
Who is rich? He that is content.
Who is that? Nobody.

AUGUST.

Of wild yet sweetest Harmony, adore.
From the bold Brow of that aspiring Steep,
Where hang the nibbling Flocks, and view below,
Their downward Shadows in the glassy Wave,
What pleasing Landscapes spread before his Eye.
Of scatter'd Villages, and winding Streams,

And meadows green, and Woods, and distant Spires,
Seeming, above the blue Horizon's Bound,

A full Belly brings forth every Evil.

The Day is short, the Work great, the Workman lazy, the Wages high, the Master urgeth ; Up, then, and be doing.

The doors of Wisdom are never shut.

SEPTEMBER.

To prop the Canopy of Heaven.   Now lost
Amidst a blooming Wilderness of Shrubs,
The golden Orange, Arbute ever green,
The early blooming Almond, feathery Pine,
Fair Opulus,* to Spring, to Autumn dear,
And the sweet Shades of varying Verdure, caught.

Much Virtue in Herbs, little in Men.

The Master's Eye will do more Work than both his Hands.

When you taste Honey, remember Gall.

OCTOBER.

From soft *Acacia's* gently waving Branch,
Heedless he wanders ; while the grateful Scents
Of Sweet-briar, Roses, Honeysuckles wild,
Regale the Smell ; and to th' enchanted Eye
Mezareon's purple *Laurustinus'* white,
And pale Laburnum's pendent Flow'rs display
Their diff'rent Beauties. O'er the smooth shorn Grass
His lingering Footsteps leisurely proceed,

Being ignorant is not so much a Shame, as being unwilling to learn.

God gives all Things to Industry.

An hundred Thieves cannot strip one naked Man, especially if his Skin's off.

* The Gelder Rose.

NOVEMBER.

Iu Meditation deep :—When, hark ! the Sound
Of Distant Water steals upon his Ear ;
And sudden opens to his pausing Eye
The rapid rough Cascade, from the rude Rock
Down dashing in a Stream of lucid Foam :
Then glides away, meand'ring o'er the Lawn,
A liquid Surface ; shining seen afar,
At Intervals, beneath the shadowy Trees ;

Diligence overcomes Difficulties, Sloth makes them.

Neglect mending a small Fault, and 't will soon be a great One.

Bad Gains are truly Losses.

DECEMBER.

Till lost and bury'd in the distant Grove.
Wrapt into sacred Musing, he reclines
Beneath the Covert of embow'ring Shades ;
And, painting to his Mind the bustling Scenes
Of Pride and bold Ambition, pities Kings.

A long Life may not be good enough, but a good Life is long enough.

Be at War with your Vices, at Peace with your Neighbours, and let every New-Year find you a better Man.

POOR RICHARD FOR 1756.

—

PREFACE.

Courteous Reader,

I suppose my Almanack may be worth the Money thou hadst paid for it, hadst thou no other Advantage from it, than to find the *Day of the Month*, the *remarkable Days*, the *Changes of the Moon*, the *Sun and Moons Rising and Setting*, and to foreknow the *Tides* and the *Weather;* these, with other Astronomical Curiosities, I have yearly and constantly prepared for thy Use and Entertainment, during now near two Revolutions of the Planet *Jupiter*. But I hope this is not all the Advantage thou hast reaped ; for with a View to the Improvement of thy Mind and thy Estate, I have constantly interspers'd in every little Vacancy, *Moral Hints, Wise Sayings, and Maxims of*

Thrift, tending to impress the Benefits arising from *Honesty, Sobriety, Industry* and *Frugality;* which if those hast duly observed, it is
highly probable thou art *wiser* and *richer* many
fold more than the Fence my Labours have cost
thee. Howbeit, I shall not therefore raise my
Price because thou art better able to pay ; but
being thankful for past Favours, shall endeavor
to make my little Book more worthy thy Regard, by adding to those *Recipes* which were
intended to *Cure the Mind*, some valuable
Ones regarding the *Health of the Body*. They
are recommended by the skilful, and by successful Practice. I wish a Blessing may attend
the Use of them, and to thee all Happiness,
being

    Thy obliged Friend,

        R. SAUNDERS.

JANUARY.

Astronomy, hail, Science heavenly born !
Thy Schemes, the Life assist, the Mind adorn.
To changing Seasons give determin'd Space,
And fix to Hours and Years their measur'd Race
The point'ng *Dial*, on whose figur'd Plane,
Of Times still Flight we Notices obtain ;
The *Pendulum*, dividing lesser Parts,
Their Rise acquire from thy inventive Arts.

A Change of Fortune hurts a wise Man no more than
a Change of the Moon.

FEBRUARY.

Th' acute *Geographer*, th' *Historian* sage
By thy Discov'ries clear the doubtful Page
From marked Eclipses, *Longitude* perceive,
Can settle *Distances*, and Æra's give.
From his known Shore the Seaman distant far,
Steers safely guided by thy *Polar Star ;*
Nor errs, when Clouds and Storms obscure its Ray,
His Compass marks him as exact a Way.

Does Mischief, Misconduct, and Warning displease ye ;
Think there 's a Providence ' t will make ye easy.

Mine is better than Ours.

MARCH.

When frequent Travels had th' instructive Chart
Supply'd the Prize of Philosophic Art !
Two curious mimic Globes, to Crown the Plan,
Were form'd ; by his CREATOR'S Image, Man.
The First, with Heav'ns bright Constellation vast,
Rang'd on the Surface, with th' Earth's Climes the last
Copy of this by human Race possest
Which Lands indent, and spacious Seas invest.

Love your Enemies, for they tell you your Faults.

He that has a Trade has an Office of Profit and Honour.

The Wit of Conversation consists more in finding it in others, than shewing a great deal yourself. He who goes out of your Company pleased with his own Facetiousness and Ingenuity, will the sooner come into it again. Most men had rather *please* than *admire* you, and seek less to be *instructed* and *diverted*, than *approved* and *applauded*, and it is certainly the most delicate Sort of Pleasure, to *please another*.

But that sort of *Wit*, which employs itself insolently in Criticizing and Censuring the Words and Sentiments of others in Conversation, is absolute *Folly;* for it answers none of the Ends of Conversation. He who uses it neither *improves others*, is *improved* himself, or pleases any one.

APRIL.

Fram'd on imaginary Poles to move,
With Lines and different Circles mark'd above,
The pleasur'd Sense, by this Machine can tell,
In what Position various Nations dwell :
Round the wide Orb's exterior Surface spread ;
How side-ways some the solid Convex tread :
While a more sever'd Race of busy Pow'rs
Project, with strange Reverse, their Feet to ours.

Be civil to all; sociable to many ; familiar with few; Friend to one ; enemy to none.

Vain-glory flowereth, but beareth no Fruit.

As I spent some Weeks last Winter, in visiting my old Acquaintance in the *Jerseys*, great Complaints I heard for Want of money, and that leave to make more Paper Bills could not be obtained. *Friends and Countrymen*, my Advice on this Head shall cost you nothing, and if you will not be angry with me for giving it, I promise you not to be offended if you do not take it.

You spend yearly at least *two hundred thousand pounds*, it is said, in European, East-Indian and West-Indian commodities. Supposing one half of this expense to be in *things absolutely necessary*, the other half may be called *superfluities*, or, at best, conveniences, which, however, you might live without for one little year, and not suffer exceedingly. Now to save this half, observe these few directions ;

1. When you incline to have new clothes, look first well over the old ones, and see if you cannot shift with them another year, either by scouring, mending, or even patching if necessary. Remember, a patch on your coat, and money in your pocket, is better and more creditable, than a writ on your back, and no money to take it off.

2. When you incline to buy China ware, Chinces, India silks, or any other of their flimsy, slight manufactures, I would not be so hard with you, as to insist on your absolutely *resolving against it ;* all I advise is, to *put it off* (as you do your repentance) *till another year*, and this, in some respects, may prevent an occasion for repentance.

3. If you are now a drinker of punch, wine or tea, twice a day, for the ensuing year drink them but once a day. If you now drink them but once a day, do it but every other day. If you now do it but once a week, reduce the practice to once a fortnight. And, if you do not exceed in quantity as you lessen the times, half your expense in these articles will be saved.

4. When you incline to drink rum, fill the glass *half* with water.

Thus at the year's end, there will be a *hundred thousand pounds* more money in your country.

If paper money in ever so great a quantity could be made, no man could get any of it without giving something for it. But all he saves in this way, will be *his own for nothing*, and his country actually so much richer. Then the merchant's old and doubtful debts may be honestly paid off, and trading become surer thereafter, if not so extensive.

MAY.

So on the Apple's smooth suspended Ball,
(If greater we may represent by small)

The swarming Flies their reptile Tribes divide,
And cling Antipodal on every side.
Hence pleasant Problems may the mind discern
Of ev'ry Soil their Length of Days to learn ;
Can tell when round, to each fix'd Place, shall come
Faint Dawn, Meridian Light, or Midnight Gloom.

Laws too gentle are seldom obeyed ; too severe, seldom executed.

Trouble springs from Idleness ; Toil from Ease.

Love and be loved.

JUNE.

These gifts to astronomic Art we owe,
Its Use extensive, yet its Growth by slow.
If back we look on ancient Sages Schemes,
They seem ridiculous as Childrens Dreams ;
How shall the Church, that boasts unerring Truth,
Blush as the Raillery of each modern Youth.
When told her Pope, of Heresy arraign'd
The Sage, who Earth's Rotation once maintain'd?

A wise Man will desire no more than what he may get justly, use soberly, distribute chearfully and leave contentedly.

The diligent Spinner has a large Shift.

JULY.

Vain *Epicurus*, and his frantic Class,
Misdeem'd our Globe a plane quadrangle Mass ;
A fine romantic Terras, spread in Slate,
On central Pillars that support its Weight
Like *Indian Sophs*, who this terrestrial Mould
Affirm, four sturdy Elephants uphold.
The Sun, new every morn, flat, small of Size,
Just what it measures to the naked Eyes.

A false Friend and a Shadow attend only while the Sun shines.

To-morrow every Fault is to be amended ; but that To-morrow never comes.

It is observable that God has often called Men to Places of Dignity and Honour, when they have been busy in the honest Employment of their Vocation. *Saul* was seeking his Father's Asses, and *David* keeping his Father's Sheep, when called to the kingdom. The Shepherds were feeding their Flocks, when they had their glorious Revelation. God called the four Apostles from their Fishery, and *Matthew* from the Receipt of Custom ; *Amos* from among the Horsemen of *Tekoah*, *Moses* from keeping *Jethro's* Sheep, *Gideon* from the Threshing Floor, etc. God never encourages Idleness, and despises not Persons in the meanest Employments.

AUGUST.

As pos'd the *Stagyrite's* dark School appears,
Perplex'd with Tales devis'd of *Chrystal Spheres*
Strange *solid Orbs*, and *Circles* oddly fram'd
Who with Philosophy their Reveries nam'd.
How long did *Ptolmy's* dark Riddle spread
With Doubts deep puzzling each scholastic Head
Till, like the *Theban* wise in story fam'd,
COPERNICUS that *Sphynxian* Monster sham'd.

Plough deep while Sluggard sleep ;
And you shall have Corn to sell and to keep.

He that sows Thorns should never go barefoot.

SEPTEMBER.

He the true Planetary system taught,
Which the learn'd Samian first from Egypt brought;

Long from the World conceal'd, in Error lost,
Whose rich Recovery latest Times shall boast.
Then TYCHO rose, who with incessant Pains,
In their due Ranks replac'd the stony Trains
His Labours by a fresh Industry mov'd,
Helvelius, Flamstead, Halley, since improv'd.

Laziness travels so slowly that Poverty soon overtakes him.

Sampson with his strong Body, had a weak Head, or he would not have laid it in a Harlot's lap.

OCTOBER.

The *Lyncean* GALILEO then aspires
Thro' the rais'd Tube to mark the Stellar fires !
The *Gallaxy* with clustering Lights overspread,
The new-nam'd Stars in bright *Orions* Head,
The varying *Phases* circling Planets show
The *Solar Spots*, his Fame was first to know.
Of *Joves Attendants*, Orbs till then unknown,
Himself the big discovery claims alone.

When a Friend deals with a Friend, Let the bargain be clear and well penn'd, That they may continue Friends to the End.

He that never eats too much, will never be lazy.

NOVEMBER.

Cassini next, and Huygens, like renown'd,
The *moons* and wondrous *Ring* of *Saturn* found
Sagacious KEPLER, still advancing saw
The *elliptic motion*, Natures plainest Law,
That Universal acts thro' every Part.
This laid the Basis of *Newtonian* Art.
NEWTON ! vast mind ! whose piercing Pow'rs apply'd

The secret Cause of Motion first descry'd ;
Found Gravitation was the primal Spring
That wheel'd the Planets round their central King.

To be proud of Knowledge, is to be blind with Light ;
To be proud of Virtue, is to poison yourself with the
Antidote.

Get what you can, and what you get, hold ;
Tis the Stone that will turn all your Lead into Gold.

There is really a great Difference in Things sometimes
where there seems to be but little Distinction in
Names. The *Man* of Honour is an internal, the *Person*
of Honour an external, the one a real, the other a fic-
titious, Charactor. A *Person* of Honour may be a profane
Libertine, penurious, proud, may insult his inferiors,
and defraud his Creditors ; but it is impossible for a
Man of Honour to be guilty of any of these. The *Person*
of Honour may flatter for Court Favours, or cringe for
Popularity ; he may be *for* or *against* his Country's
Good, as it suits his private Views. But the *Man* of
Honour can do none of these.

DECEMBER.

Mysterious Impulse ! that more clear to know
Exceeds the finite Reach of Art below.
Forbear, bold mortal ! 't is an impious Aim
Own God immediate acting thro' the frame.
Tis He, unsearchable, in all resides ;
He the FIRST CAUSE their Operations guides
Fear on his awful Privacy to press
But, honouring HIM, thy Ignorance confess.

An honest Man will receive neither Money nor Praise
that is not his due.

Saying and Doing have quarrel'd and parted.

Tell me my Faults, and mend your own.

Well, my friend, thou art just entering the last Month of another year. If thou art a Man of Business, and of prudent Care, be like thou wilt now settle thy accounts, to satisfy thyself whether thou has gain'd or lost in the Year past, and how much of either, the better to regulate thy future Industry or thy common Expenses. This is commendable—But it is not all.—Wilt thou not examine also thy *moral* Accompts, and see what improvements thou hast made in the Conduct of Life, what Vice subdued, what Virtue acquired ; how much *better*, and how much wiser, as well as how much richer thou art grown ? What shall it *profit* a Man, if he *gain* the whole World, but *lose* his own Soul. Without some Care in this Matter, tho' thou may'st come to count thy thousands, thou wilt possibly still appear poor in the Eyes of the Discerning, even *here*, and be really so for ever *hereafter*.

POOR RICHARD FOR 1757.

PREFACE.

COURTEOUS READER,

As no temporal Concern is of more Importance to us than Health, and that depends so much on the Air we every Moment breathe, the Choice of a good wholesome Situation to fix a Dwelling in, is a very serious Affair to every Countryman about to begin the World, and well worth his Consideration, especially as not only the Comfort of Living, but even the Necessaries of Life, depend in a great Measure upon it; since a Family frequently sick can rarely if ever thrive. - - - - The following Extracts therefore from a late Medical Writer, Dr. Pringle, on that Subject, will, I hope, be acceptable and useful to some of my Readers.

I hear that some have already, to their great Advantage, put in Practice the Use of Oxen recommended in my last. - - - - 'T is a Pleasure to me to be in any way serviceable in communicating useful Hints to the Publick ; and I shall be obliged to others for affording me the Opportunity of enjoying that Pleasure more frequently, by sending me from time to time such of their own Observations, as may be advantageous if published in the Almanack.

I am thy obliged Friend,

RICHARD SAUNDERS.

How to make a STRIKING SUNDIAL, by which not only a Man's own Family, but all his Neighbours for ten Miles round, may know what a Clock it is, when the Sun shines, without seeing the Dial.

Chuse an open Place in your Yard or Garden, on which the Sun may shine all Day without any Impediment from Trees or Buildings. On the Ground mark out your Hour Lines, as for a horizontal Dial, according to Art, taking Room enough for the Guns. On the Line for One o'Clock, place one Gun ; on the Two o'Clock Line two Guns, and so of the rest. The Guns must all be charged with Powder, but Ball is unnecessary. Your Gnomon or Style must have twelve burning Glasses annex't to it, and be so placed that the Sun shining through the Glasses, one after the other, shall cause the Focus or burning Spot to fall on the Hour Line of One, for Example, at One a Clock, and there kindle a Train of Gunpowder that shall fire one Gun. At Two a Clock, a Focus shall fall on the Hour Line of Two, and kindle another Train that shall discharge two Guns successively : and so of the rest.

Note, There must be 78 Guns in all. Thirty-two Pounders will be best for this Use ; but 18 Pounders may do, and will cost less, as well as use less Powder, for nine Pounds of Powder will do for one Charge of each eighteen Pounder, whereas the Thirty-two Pounders would require for each Gun 16 Pounds.

Note also, That the chief Expense will be the Powder, for the Cannon once bought, will, with Care, last 100 Years.

Note moreover, that there will be a great Saving of Powder in Cloudy Days.

Kind Reader, Methinks I hear thee say, That is indeed a good Thing to know how the Time passes, but this Kind of Dial, notwithstanding the mentioned Savings, would be very Expensive ; and the Cost greater than the Advantage, Thou art wise, my Friend, to be so considerate beforehand ; some Fools would not have found out so much, till they had made the Dial and try'd it. - - - - Let all such learn that many a private and many a publick Project, are like this Striking Dial, great Cost for little Profit.

JANUARY.

CONVERSATION HINTS.

Good Sense and Learning may Esteem obtain.
Humor and Wit a Laugh, if rightly ta'en;
Fair Virtue Admiration may impart;
But 't is GOOD-NATURE only wins the Heart;
It moulds the Body to an easy Grace,
And brightens every Feature of the Face;
It smooths th' unpolished Tongue with Eloquence,
And adds Persuasion to the finest Sense.

He that would rise at Court, must begin by creeping.

Many a Man's own Tongue gives Evidence against his Understanding.

Nothing dries sooner than a Tear.

FEBRUARY.

Would you both please, and be instructed too,
The pride of shewing forth yourself subdue.
Hear every Man upon his fav'rite Theme,
And ever be more knowing than you seem.
The lowest Genius will afford some Light,
Or give a Hint that had escaped your Sight.
Doubt, till he thinks you on Conviction yield,
And with fit Questions let each Pause be fill'd.
And the most knowing will with Pleasure grant,
You 're rather much reserv'd than ignorant.

'T is easier to build two Chimneys than maintain on in Fuel.

Anger warms the Invention, but overheats the Oven.

RULES OF LAW FIT TO BE OBSERVED IN PURCHASING
From an old Book.

First, see the Land which thou intend'st to buy
Within the Sellers title clear doth lie.

And that no Woman to it doth lay claim
By Dowry, Jointure, or some other Name.
That it may cumber.   Know if bound or free
The Tenure stand, and that from each Feoffee
It be released : That the Seller be so old
That he may lawful sell, thou lawful hold.
Have special Care that it not mortgag'd lie,
Nor be entailed on Posterity.
Then if it stand in Statute bound or no :
Be well advised what Quit Rent out must go ;
What Custom, Service hath been done of old,
By those who formerly the same did hold,
And if a wedded Woman put to Sale,
Deal not with her, unless she bring her Male.
For she doth under Covert-Baron go,
Altho' sometimes some also traffick so.
Thy Bargain being made, and all this done,
Have special Care to make thy Charter run
To thee, thine Heirs, Executors, Assigns,
For that beyond thy Life securely binds.
These Things foreknown and done, you may prevent
Those Things rash Buyers many times repent.
And yet, when as you have done all you can
If you 'd be sure, deal with an honest Man.

Very good Rules, these, and sweetly sung.   If they are
learnt by heart, and repeated often to keep them in
Memory, they may happen to save the Purchaser more
Pence than the Price of my Almanack.   In Imitation of
this old Writer, I have thoughts of turning Coke's Insti-
tutes, and all our Province Laws into Metre, hoping
thereby to engage some of our young Lawyers and old
Justices to read a little.

It is generally agreed to be Folly, to hazard the loss of
a Friend, rather than to lose a Jest.   But few consider how
easily a Friend may be thus lost.   Depending on the

known Regard their Friends have for them, Jesters take
more Freedom with Friends than they would dare to do
with others, little thinking how much deeper we are
wounded by an Affront from one we love. But the
strictest Intimacy can never warrant Freedoms of this
Sort ; and it is indeed preposterous to think they should ;
unless we can suppose Injuries are less Evils when they
are done to us by Friends, than when they come from
other Hands.

MARCH.

The Rays of Wit gild wheresoe'er they strike,
But are not therefore fit for all alike
They charm the lively, but the grave offend
And raise a Foe as often as a Friend ;
Like the resistless Beams of blazing Light,
That cheer the strong, and pain the weekly sight
If a bright Fancy therefore be your Share
Let Judgment watch it with a Guardian's care.

It is Ill-manners to silence a Fool, and Cruelty to let
him go on.

Scarlet, Silk and Velvet have put out the Kitchen Fire.

APRIL.

'T is like a Torrent, apt to overflow,
Unless by constant Government kept low ;
And ne'er inefficacious passes by,
But overturns or gladdens all that 's nigh.
Or else, like Trees, when suffer'd wild to shoot,
That put forth much, but all unripen'd Fruit ;
It turns to Affection and Grimace,
As like to Wit as Gravity to Grace.

He that would catch Fish, must venture his Bait.

Men take more pains to mask than mend.

One To-day is worth two To-morrows.

MAY.

How hard soe'er it be to bridle Wit,
Yet Mem'ry oft no less requires the Bit :
How many, hurried by its Force away,
For ever in the Land of Gossips stay !
Usurp the Province of the Nurse, to lull,
Without her Privilege for being dull !
Tales upon Tales they raise, ten Stories high,
Without Regard to Use or Symmetry.

The way to be safe, is never to be secure.

Dally not with other Folks Women or Money.

Work as if you were to live 100 years, Pray as if you were to die To-morrow.

JUNE.

A Story should, to please, at least seem true,
Be apropos, well told, concise, and new ;
And whensoe'er it deviates from these Rules,
The Wise will sleep, and leave Applause to Fools.
But others, more intolerable yet,
The Waggeries that they 've said, or heard, repeat
Heavy by Mem'ry made, and what 's the worst,
At second-hand as often as at first.

Pride breakfasted with Plenty, dined with Poverty, supped with Infamy.

Retirement does not always secure Virtue ; Lot was upright in the City ; wicked in the Mountain.

Excess of Wit may oftentimes beguile :
Jests are not always pardon'd - - - by a Smile.
Men may disguise their Malice at the Heart,
And seem at Ease - - - - tho' pain'd with inward Smart.

Mistaken, we - - - - think all such Wounds of course
Reflection cures ; - - alas ! it makes them worse.
Like Scratches they with double Anguish seize.
Rankle with Time, and fester by Degrees.

But sarcastical Jests on a Man's Person or his Manners,
tho' hard to bear, are perhaps more easily borne than
those that touch his Religion.   Men are generally warm
in what regards their religious Tenets, either from a
Tenderness of Conscience, or a high Sense of their own
Judgements.   People of plain Parts and honest Dispositions, look on Salvation as too serious a Thing to be
jested with ; and Men of speculative Religion, who
profess from the Conviction rather of their Heads than
Hearts, are not a bit less vehement than the real Devo-
tees.   He who says a slight or a severe Thing of their
Faith, seems to them to have thereby undervalued their
Understanding, and will consequently incur their Aver-
sion, which no Man of common Sense would hazard, for
a lively Expression ; much less a person of good Breeding, who should make it his chief Aim to be well with all.

Like some grave Matron of a noble Line,
With awful Beauty does Religion shine.
Just Sense should teach us to revere the Dame,
Nor, by imprudent Jests, to spot her Fame.
In common Life you 'll own this Reas'ning right,
That none but Fools in gross Abuse delight :
Then use it here - - - nor think the Caution vain,
To be polite, Men need not be profane.

JULY.

But above all Things, raillery decline,
Nature but few does for that Talk design ;
'T is in the ablest Hand a dangerous Tool,
But never fails to wound the meddling Fool ;

For all must grant it needs no common Art
To keep Men patient while we make them smart.
Not Wit alone, nor Humour's self, will do,
Without Good-nature, and much Prudence too.

Idleness is the Dead Sea, that swallows all Virtues : Be active in Business, that Temptation may miss her Aim ; The Bird that sits, is easily shot.

Shame and the Dry-belly-ach were Diseases of the last Age, this seems to be cured of them.

AUGUST.

Of all the Qualities that help to raise
In Men, the Universal Voice of Praise,
Whether in Pleasure or in Use they end,
There 's none that can with MODESTY contend.
Yet 't is but little that its Form be caught,
Unless its Origin be first in Thought ;
Else rebel Nature will reveal the Cheat,
And the whole Work of Art at once defeat.

Tho' the Mastiff be gentle, yet bite him not by the Lip.

Great Alms giving, lessen no Man's living.

The Royal Crown cures not the Head-ach.

ON THE FREEDOM OF THE PRESS.

While free from Force the Press remains,
Virtue and Freedom chear our Plains,
And Learning Largesses bestows,
And keeps unlicens'd open House.
We to the Nation's publick Mart
Our Works of Wit, and Schemes of Art,
And philosophic Goods, this Way,
Like Water carriage, cheap convey.
This Tree which Knowledge so affords,
Inquisitors with flaming Swords

From Lay-Approach with Zeal defend,
Lest their own Paradise should end.

The Press from her fecundous Womb
Brought forth the Arts of Greece and Rome ;
Her offspring, skill'd in Logic War,
Truth's Banner wav'd in open Air ;
The Monster Superstition fled,
And hid in Shades her Gorgon Head ;
And awless Pow'r, the long kept Field,
By Reason quell'd, was forc'd to yield.

This Nurse of Arts, and Freedom's Fence,
To chain, is Treason against Sense :
And Liberty, thy thousand Tongues
None silence who design no Wrongs ;
For those who use the Gag's Restraint,
First Rob, before they stop Complaint.

SEPTEMBER.

Hold forth upon yourself on no Pretence,
Unless invited, or in Self-Defence ;
The Praise you take, altho' it be your Due,
Will be suspected if it come from you,
If to seem modest, you some faults confess,
The World suspect yet more, and never less :
For each Man, by Experience taught, can tell
How strong a Flatterer does within him dwell.

Act uprightly and despise Calumny ; Dirt may stick to
a Mud Wall, but not to polish'd Marble.

OCTOBER.

No part of Conduct asks for Skill more nice,
Tho' none more common, than to give Advice :
Misers themselves, in this will not be saving,
Unless their Knowledge makes it worth the having.

And Where 's the Wonder, when we will intrude,
An useless Gift, it meets Ingratitude ?
Shun then, unask'd, this arduous Task to try ;
But, if consulted, use Sincerity.

The Borrower is a Slave to the Lender ; the Security to both.

Singularity in the right, hath ruined many : Happy those who are convinced of the general Opinion.

NOVEMBER.

Be rarely warm in Censure or in Praise ;
Few Men deserve our Passion either ways :
For half the World but floats 'twixt Good and Ill,
As Chance disposes Objects, these the Will ;
'T is but a see-saw Game, where Virtue now
Mounts above Vice, and then sinks down as low.
Besides, the Wise still hold it for a Rule,
To trust that Judgment most, that seems most cool.

Proportion your Charity to the strength of your Estate, or God will Proportion your Estate to the Weakness of your Charity.

The Tongue offends, and the Ears get the Cuffing.

Some antient Philosophers have said, that Happiness depends more on the inward Disposition of Mind than on outward Circumstances ; and that he who cannot be happy in any State, can be so in no State. To be happy, they tell us we must be content. Right. But they do not teach us how we may become content. Poor Richard shall give you a short good Rule for that. To be content look backward on those who possess less than yourself, not forward on those who possess more. If this does not make you content, you don't deserve to be happy.

CONTENTMENT ! Parent of Delight,
So much a stranger to our Sight.
Say, Goddess, in what happy Place
Mortals behold thy blooming Face ;
Thy gracious Auspices impart,
And for thy Temple chuse my Heart.
They whom thou deignest to inspire,
Thy Science learn, to bound Desire ;
By happy Alchymy of Mind
They turn to Pleasure all they find.
Unmov'd when the rude Tempest blows,
Without an Opiate they repose ;
And, cover'd by your Shield, defy
The whizzing Shafts that round them fly ;
Nor, meddling with the Gods Affairs,
Concern themselves with distant Cares ;
But place their Bliss in mental Rest,
And feast upon the Good possest.

DECEMBER.

Would you be well receiv'd where'er you go,
Remember each Man vanquish'd is a Foe :
Resist not therefore to your utmost Might,
But let the Weakest think he 's sometimes right .
He, for each Triumph you shall thus decline,
Shall give ten Opportunities to shine ;
He sees, since once you owned him to excel,
That 't is his Interest you should reason well.

Sleep without Supping, and you 'll rise without owing for it.

When other Sins grow old by Time,
Then Avarice is in its prime,
Yet feed the Poor at Christmas time.

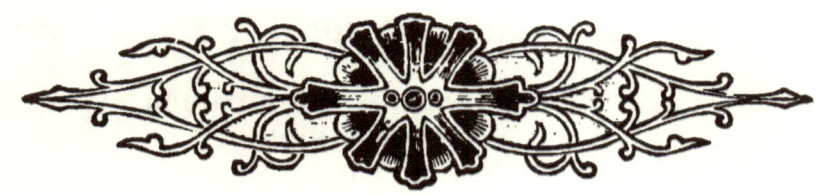

POOR RICHARD FOR 1758.

PREFACE.

COURTEOUS READER,

I have heard that nothing gives an Author so great Pleasure, as to find his Works respectfully quoted by other learned Authors. This pleasure I have seldom enjoyed, for tho' I have been, if I may say it without Vanity, an *eminent Author* of Almanacks annually now a full quarter of a Century, my Brother Authors in the same Way, for what Reason I know not, have ever been very sparing in their Applauses; and no other Author has taken the least notice of me, so that did not my Writings produce me some solid *Pudding*, the great Deficiency of *Praise* would have quite discouraged me.

I concluded at length, that the People were the best Judges of my Merit; for they buy my Works; and besides, in my Rambles, where I am not personally known, I have frequently heard one or other of my Adages re-

peated, with, *as Poor Richard says*, at the End
on 't ; this gave me some Satisfaction, as it
showed not only that my Instructions were regarded, but discovered likewise some Respect
for my Authority ; and I own that to encourage
the practice of remembering and repeating
those wise Sentences, I have sometimes *quoted
myself* with great gravity.

Judge then how much I must have been grati-
fied by an Incident I am going to relate to you.
I stopt my Horse lately where a great Number
of people were collected at a Vendue of Merchant Goods. The Hour of Sale not being
come, they were conversing on the Badness of
the Times, and one of the Company call'd to a
plain clean old Man, with white Locks, *Pray
Father* Abraham, *what think you of the Times ?
Won't these heavy Taxes quite ruin the Country ? How shall we* BE EVER *able to pay them ?
What would you advise us to ?* —— Father
Abraham stood up, and reply'd, If you 'd have
my Advice, I 'll give it you in short, *for a
Word to the Wise is enough, and many Words
won't fill a Bushel, as Poor Richard says.*
They join'd in desiring him to speak his Mind,
and gathering round him, he proceeded as fol-
lows ;

" Friends, says he, and Neighbours, the Taxes
are indeed very heavy, and if those laid on by

the Government were the only Ones we had to pay, we might more easily discharge them ; but we have many others, and much more grievous to some of us. We are taxed twice as much by our *Idleness*, three times as much by our *Pride*, and four times as much by our *Folly*, and from these Taxes the Commissioners cannot ease or deliver us by allowing an Abatement. However let us hearken to good Advice, and something may be done for us ; *God helps them that help themselves*, as *Poor Richard* says in his Almanac of 1733.

It would be thought a hard Government that should tax its People one tenth Part of their *Time*, to be employed in its Service. But *Idleness* taxes many of us much more, if we reckon all that is spent in absolute *Sloth*, or doing of nothing, with that which is spent in idle Employments or Amusements, that amount to nothing. *Sloth*, by bringing on Diseases absolutely shortens Life. *Sloth, like Rust, consumes faster than Labour wears, while the used Key is always bright*, as *Poor Richard* says. But *dost thou love Life, then do not squander Time, for that 's the Stuff Life is made of*, as *Poor Richard* says.—How much more than is necessary do we spend in Sleep ! forgetting that *The Sleeping Fox catches no Poultry*, and that *there will be sleeping enough in the Grave*, as

Poor Richard says. If Time be of all Things the most precious, *wasting of Time* must be, as *Poor Richard* says, *the greatest Prodigality*, since, as he elsewhere tells us, *Lost Time is never found again;* and what we call *Time-enough, always proves little enough.* Let us then be up and doing, and doing to the Purpose ; so by Diligence shall we do more with less Perplexity. *Sloth makes all things difficult, but Industry all Things easy*, as *Poor Richard* says ; and *He that riseth late, must trot all Day, and shall scarce overtake his Business at night.* While *Laziness travels so slowly, that Poverty soon overtakes him*, as we read in *Poor Richard*, who adds, *Drive thy Business, let not that drive thee; and Early to Bed, and early to rise, makes a Man healthy, wealthy, and wise.*

So what signifies *wishing* and *hoping* for better times. We may make these Times better if we bestir ourselves. *Industry need not wish* as *Poor Richard* says, and *He that lives upon Hope will die fasting. There are no Gains, without Pains;* then *Help Hands, for I have no Lands*, or if I have, they are smartly taxed. And as *Poor Richard* likewise observes, *He that hath a Trade hath an Estate*, and *He that hath a Calling hath an Office of Profit and Honour;* but then the *Trade* must be worked at, and the *Calling* well followed, or neither the *Estate*, nor the *Office*, will enable us to pay our Taxes.—If we are industrious we shall never starve; for as *Poor Richard* says, *At the working Man's House Hunger looks in, but dares not enter.* Nor will the Bailiff or the Constable enter, for *Industry pays Debts while Despair encreaseth them*, says *Poor Richard.*——What though you have found no Treasure, nor has any rich Relation left you a Legacy, *Diligence is the Mother of Good-luck*, as *Poor Richard* says, *and God gives all things to Industry.* Then *plough deep, while Sluggards sleep, and you shall have Corn to sell and to keep*, says *Poor Dick.* Work while it it is called To-day, for you know not how much you may be hindered To-morrow, which makes *Poor Richard* say, *One To-day is worth two To-morrows;* and farther, *Have you somewhat to do To-morrow, do it to To-day.* If you were a Servant would you not be ashamed that a good Master should catch you idle? Are you then your own Master, *be ashamed to catch yourself idle*, as *Poor Dick* says. When there is so much to be done for yourself, your Family, your Country, and your gracious King, be up by Peep of Day; *Let not the Sun look down and say, Inglorious here he lies.* Handle your Tools without Mittens; remember that *the Cat in Gloves catches no Mice*, as *Poor Richard* says. 'T is true there is much to be done, and perhaps

you are weak-handed, but stick to it steadily,
and you will see great Effects, for *constant
Dropping wears away Stones*, and by *Diligence
and Patience, the Mouse ate in two the Cable;*
and *little Strokes fell great Oaks*, as *Poor Richard* says in his Almanack, the Year I cannot
just now remember.

Methinks I hear some of you say, *Must a
Man afford himself no Leisure?*—I will tell
thee My Friend, what *Poor Richard* says, *Employ thy Time well if thou meanest to gain
Leisure; and, since thou art not sure of a Minute, throw not away an Hour.* Leisure is Time
for doing something useful; this Leisure the
diligent man will obtain, but the lazy man
never; so that, as *Poor Richard* says, *a Life of
Leisure and a Life of Laziness are two Things.*
Do you imagine that Sloth will afford you more
Comfort than Labour? No, for as *Poor Richard* says, *Trouble springs from Idleness, and
grievous Toil from needless Ease. Many without Labour, would live by their* WITS *only, but
they break for want of stock.* Whereas Industry gives Comfort, and Plenty and Respect:
*Fly Pleasures and they'll follow you. The dili-
gent Spinner has a large Shift; and now I have
a Sheep and a Cow, every Body bids me Good
morrow*, all which is well said by *Poor Richard.*

But with our Industry, we must likewise be
18

steady, settled, and *careful*, and oversee our own
Affairs *with our own Eyes*, and not trust too
much to others ; for, as *Poor Richard* says,

> *I never saw an oft removed Tree,*
> *Nor yet an oft removed Family,*
> *That throve so well as those that settled be.*

And again, *Three Removes is as bad as a Fire ;*
and again, *Keep thy Shop, and thy Shop will
keep thee ;* and again, *If you would have your
Business done, go ; if not, send.* And again,

> *He that by the Plough must thrive,*
> *Himself must either hold or drive.*

And again, *The Eye of a Master will do more
Work than both his Hands ;* and again, *Want
of Care does us more Damage than Want of
Knowledge ;* and again, *Not to oversee Workmen, is to leave them your Purse open.* Trust-
ing too much to others Care is the Ruin of
many ; for, as the *Almanack* says, *In the Affairs of this World, Men are saved, not by
Faith, but by the Want of it ;* but a Man's own
Care is profitable ; for, saith *Poor Dick, Learning is to the Studious,* and *Riches to the Careful,* as well as *Power to the Bold,* and *Heaven
to the Virtuous.* And, farther, *If you would
have a faithful Servant, and one that you like,
serve yourself.* And again, he adviseth to Cir-

cumspection and Care, even in the smallest
Matters, because sometimes *a little Neglect
may breed great Mischief,* adding, *for want of
a Nail, the Shoe was lost; for want of a Shoe
the Horse was lost; and for want of a Horse
the Rider was lost,* being overtaken and slain
by the Enemy, all for want of Care about a
Horse-shoe Nail.

So much for Industry, my Friends, and Atten-
tion to one's own Business; but to these we
must add *Frugality,* if we would make our *Industry* more certainly successful. A man may,
if he knows not how to save as he gets, *Keep
his Nose all his Life to the Grindstone,* and die
not worth *a Groat* at last. *A fat Kitchen
makes a lean Will,* as Poor Richard says; and

*Many Estates are spent in the Getting,
Since Women for Tea forsook Spinning and Knitting,
And Men for Punch forsook Hewing and Splitting.*

If you would be wealthy, says he, in another Almanack, *think of Saving, as well as of Getting:
The* Indies *have not made Spain rich, because
her* Outgoes *are greater than her* Incomes.
Away then with your expensive Follies, you
will not have so much cause to complain of
hard Times, heavy Taxes, and chargeable
Families; for as *Poor Dick* says,

Women and Wine, Game and Deceit,
Make the Wealth small and the Wants great.

And farther, *What maintains one Vice would
bring up two Children.* You may think perhaps that a *little* Tea or a *little* Punch now and
then, Diet a *little* more costly, Clothes a *little*
finer, and a *little* Entertainment now and then,
can be no *great* Matter; but remember what
Poor Richard says, *Many* a Little *makes a
Mickle;* and farther, *Beware of* little *Expences; a small Leak will sink a great Ship;*
and again, *Who Dainties love shall Beggars
prove;* and moreover, *Fools make Feasts and
wise Men eat them.*

Here you are all got together at this Vendue
of *Fineries* and *Knicknacks.* You call them
Goods, but if you do not take Care, they will
prove *Evils* to some of you. You expect they
will be sold *cheap,* and perhaps they may for
less than they cost; but if you have no Occasion
for them, they must be *dear* to you. Remember
what *Poor Richard* says, *Buy what thou hast
no Need of, and ere long thou shalt sell thy
Necessaries.* And again, *At a great Pennyworth pause a while:* He means, that perhaps
the Cheapness is *apparent* only, and not *real;* or
the Bargain, by straitning thee in thy Business,
may do thee more Harm than Good. For in
another Place he says, *Many have been ruined*

by buying good *Pennyworths*. Again *Poor
Richard* says, *'T is foolish to lay out Money in
a Purchase of Repentance;* and yet this Folly
is practised every Day at Vendues, for want
of minding the Almanack. *Wise Men*, as *Poor
Dick* says, *learn by others Harms, Fools scarcely
by their own;* but *Felix quem faciunt aliena
Pericula cautum*. Many a one, for the Sake
of Finery on the Back, have gone with a hungry Belly, and half starved their Families;
Silks and Sattins, Scarlet and Velvets, as *Poor
Richard* says, *put out the Kitchen Fire.*
These are not the *Necessaries* of Life; they
can scarcely be called the *Conveniences*, and
yet only because they look pretty how many
want to *have* them. The *artificial* Wants of
Mankind thus become more numerous than the
natural; and as *Poor Dick* says, *For one* poor
Person there are an hundred indigent. By
these, and other Extravagancies, the Genteel
are reduced to Poverty, and forced to borrow
of those whom they formerly despised, but who
through *Industry* and *Frugality* have main-
tained their Standing; in which case it appears
plainly, that a *Ploughman on his Legs is higher
than a Gentleman on his Knees*, as *Poor Richard* says. Perhaps they have had a small Estate left them, which they knew not the Getting
of,—they think *'t is Day and will never be*

Night; that a little to be spent out of *so much,* is not worth minding; (*a Child and a Fool,* as *Poor Richard* says, *imagine Twenty Shillings and Twenty Years can never be spent*) but, *always taking out of the Meat-tub, and never putting in, soon comes to the Bottom ;* then, as *Poor Dick* says, *When the Well 's dry, they know the Worth of Water.* But this they might have known before, if they had taken his Advice; *If you would know the Value of Money, go and try to borrow some ; for he that goes a borrowing goes a sorrowing;* and indeed so does he that lends to such People, when he goes *to get it in again.*—*Poor Dick* farther advises, and says,

> *Fond* Pride of Dress, *is sure a very Curse;*
> *E'er* Fancy *you consult, consult your Purse.*

And again, *Pride is as loud a Beggar as Want, and a great deal more saucy.* When you have bought one fine Thing you must buy ten more, that your appearance may be all of a Piece ; but *Poor Dick* says, *'Tis easier to* suppress *the first Desire, than to* satisfy *all that follow it.* And 't is as truly Folly for the Poor to ape the Rich, as for the Frog to swell, in order to equal the Ox.

> *Great Estates may venture more,*
> *But little Boats should keep near Shore.*

'T is however a Folly soon punished ; for *Pride that dines on Vanity sups on Contempt,* as *Poor Richard* says. And in another Place, *Pride breakfasted with Plenty, dined with Poverty, and supped with Infamy.* And after all, of what Use is this *Pride of Appearance,* for which so much is risked, so much is suffered ! It cannot promote Health, or ease Pain ; it makes no Increase of Merit in the Person, creates Envy, it hastens Misfortune.

> *What is a Butterfly ? At best*
> *He 's but a Caterpillar drest.*
> *The gaudy Fop 's his Picture just.*

as *Poor Richard* says.

But what Madness must it be to *run in Debt* for these Superfluities ! We are offered by the Terms of this Vendue, *Six Months Credit ;* and that perhaps has induced some of us to attend it, because we cannot spare the ready Money, and hope now to be fine without it. But, ah, think what you do when you run in Debt ; *You give to another Power over your Liberty.* If you cannot pay at the Time, you will be ashamed to see your Creditor ; you will be in Fear when you speak to him ; you will make poor pitiful sneaking Excuses, and by Degrees come to lose your Veracity, and sink into base downright lying ; for as *Poor Richard* says, *The second Vice is Lying, the first is running in Debt.* And again, to the same Purpose, *Lying rides upon Debt's Back.* Whereas a freeborn *Englishman* ought not to be ashamed or afraid to see or speak to any Man living. But Poverty often deprives a Man of all Spirit and Virtue; *'T is hard for an empty Bag to stand upright*, as *Poor Richard* truly says. What would you think of that Prince, or that Government, who should issue an Edict forbidding you to dress like a Gentleman, or a Gentlewoman, on Pain of Imprisonment or Servitude! Would you not say, that you are free, have a Right to dress as you please, and that such an Edict would be a Breach of your Privileges, and such a Government tyrannical! And yet you are about to put yourself under that Tyranny when you run in Debt for such Dress! Your Creditor has Authority at his Pleasure to deprive you of your Liberty, by confining you in Goal for Life, or to sell you for a Servant, if you should not be able to pay him! When you have got your Bargain, you may, perhaps, think little of Payment! but *Creditors, Poor Richard*, tells us, *have better Memories than Debtors;* and in another Place says, *Creditors are a superstitious Sect, great Observers of set Days and Times.* The Day comes round before you are aware, and the Demand is made before you are prepared to satisfy it, Or if you bear your Debt in Mind, the Term which at first seemed so long, will, as it lessens, appear extreamly short. *Time* will seem to have added Wings to his Heels as well as Shoulders. *Those have a short Lent,* saith *Poor Richard, who owe Money to be paid at Easter.* Then, since as he says, *The Borrower is a Slave to the Lender, and the Debtor is the Creditor,* disdain the Chain, preserve your Freedom ; and maintain your Independency ; Be *industrious* and *free ;* be *frugal* and *free.* At present, perhaps, you may think yourself in thriving Circumstances, and that you can bear a little Extravagance without Injury ; but,

For Age and Want save while you may ;
No Morning Sun lasts a whole Day,

as *Poor Richard* says.—Gain may be temporary and uncertain, but ever while you live Experience is constant and certain ; and *'t is easier to build two Chimnies than to keep one in Fuel,* as *Poor Richard* says. *So rather go to Bed supperless than rise in Debt.*

Get what you can, and what you get hold.
' T is the stone that will turn all your Lead into Gold,

as *Poor Richard* says. And when you have got the Philosopher's Stone, sure you will no longer complain of the bad Times, or the Difficulty of paying Taxes.

This Doctrine, my Friends, is *Reason* and *Wisdom;* but after all, do not depend too much on your own *Industry*, and *Frugality*, and *Prudence*, though excellent Things; for they may all be blasted without the Blessing of Heaven; and therefore ask that Blessing humbly, and be not uncharitable to those that at present seem to want it, but comfort and help them. Remember *Job* suffered and was afterwards prosperous.

And now to conclude, *Experience keeps a dear School, but Fools will learn in no other, and scarce in that;* for it is true, *we may give Advice, but we cannot give Conduct*, as *Poor Richard* says: However, remember this, *They that won't be counselled, can't be helped*, as *Poor Richard* says: and farther, That *if you will not hear Reason, she 'll surely wrap your Knuckles.*

Thus the old Gentleman ended his Harangue. The People heard it, and approved the Doctrine, and immediately practised the contrary, just as if it had been a common Sermon; for the Vendue opened, and they began to buy extravagantly, notwithstanding all his Cautions, and their own Fear of Taxes.—I found the good Man had thoroughly studied my Almanacks, and digested all I had dropt on those Topicks during the Course of Five-and-Twenty Years. The frequent mention he made of me must have tired any one else, but my Vanity was wonderfully delighted with it, though I was conscious that not a tenth Part of this Wisdom was my own which he ascribed to me, but rather the *Gleanings* I had made of the Sense of all Ages and Nations. However, I resolved to be the better for the Echo of it ; and though I had at first determined to buy Stuff for a new Coat, I went away resolved to wear my old one a little longer. *Reader*, if thou wilt do the same, thy Profit will be as great as mine.

> *I am, as ever,*
> *Thine to serve thee,*
> RICHARD SAUNDERS.

July 7, 1757.

JANUARY.
On Ambition.

I know, young Friend, Ambition fills your Mind,
And in Life's Voyage is th' impelling Wind ;
But at the Helm let sober Reason stand
And steer the Bark with Heav'n-directed Hand :
So shall you safe *Ambitions* Gale receive,
And ride securely, tho' the Billows heave ;
So shall you shun the giddy Hero's Fate,
And by her Influence be both good and great.

One Nestor is worth two Ajaxes.

When you 're an Anvil, hold you still ;
When you 're a Hammer, strike your fill.

FEBRUARY.

She bids you first, in Life's soft Vernal Hours,
With active Industry wake Natures Powers;
With rising Years, still rising Arts display,
With new-born Graces mark each new-born Day,
'T is now the Time young Passion to command
While yet the pliant Stem obeys the Hand;
Guide now the Courser with a steady rein
E'er yet he bounds o'er Pleasures flow'ry Plane;
In Passion's Strife, no Medium you can have;
You rule a Master, or submit a Slave.

When Knaves betray each other, one can scarce be blamed or the other pitied.

He that carries a small Crime easily, will carry it on when it comes to be an Ox.

MARCH.

For whom these Toils, you may perhaps enquire;
First for *yourself*, next Nature will inspire,
The filial Thought, fond Wish, and Kindred Tear
Which makes the Parent and the Sister dear:
To these, in closest Bands of Love, ally'd,
Their Joy and Grief you live, their Shame or Pride;
Hence timely learn to make their Bliss your own,
And scorn to think or act for Self *alone*.

Happy Tom Crump ne'er sees his own Hump.

Fools need Advice most, but wise Men only are the better for it.

APRIL.

Hence bravely strive upon your own to raise
Their Honour, Grandeur, Dignity and Praise.
But wider far, beyond the narrow Bound
Of Family, *Ambition* searches round:

Searches to find the Friend's delightful Face,
The Friend at last demands the second place,
And yet beware ; for most desire a Friend
From meaner Motives, not for Virtue's End.
There are, who with fond Favour's fickle Gale
Now sudden swell, and now contract their Sail.

Silence is not always a Sign of Wisdom, but Babbling
is ever a Folly.

Great Modesty often hides great Merit.

You may delay, but Time will not.

MAY.

This Week devour, the next with sickening Eye
Avoid, and cast the sully'd Plaything by ;
There are, who tossing in the Bed of Vice,
For Flattery's Opiate give the highest Price ;
Yet from the saving Hand of Friendship turn,
Her Medicines dread, her generous Offers spurn.
Deserted Greatness ! who but pities thee ?
By crowds encompass'd, thou no friend canst see :

Virtue may always make a Face handsome, but Vice
will certain make it ugly.

Prodigality of Time produces Poverty of Mind as well
as of Estate.

JUNE.

Or should kind Truth invade thy gentle Ear,
We pity still ; for thou no Truth canst hear.
Ne'er grudg'd thy Wealth to swell an useless State,
Yet, frugal, deems th' Expence of Friends too great ;
For Friends ne'er mixing in ambitions Strife,
For Friends, the richest Furniture of Life !
Be yours, my son, a nobler, higher Aim
Your Pride to burn with Friendship's sacred Flame ;

Content is the Philosopher's Stone, that turns all it touches into Gold.

He that 's content hath enough.

He that complains has too much.

Pride gets into the Coach, and Shame mounts behind.

JULY.

By Virtue kindled, by like Manners fed,
By mutual Wishes, mutual Favours spread,
Increas'd with Years, by candid Truth refin'd
Pour all its boundless Ardours thro' your mind
By yours the care a chosen Band to gain ;
With them to Glory's radiant Summit strain,
Aiding and aided each, while all contend
Who best, who bravest, shall assist his Friend.

The first Mistake in public Business, is the going into it.

Half the Truth is often a great Lie.

The Way to see by Faith is to shut the Eye of Reason.

The Morning Daylight appears plainer when you put out your Candle.

AUGUST.

Thus still should private Friendships spread around,
Till in their joint Embrace the Publick's found,
The common Friend !—Then all her Good explore ;
Explor'd, pursue with each unbiass'd Power
But chief the greatest should her Laws revere,
Ennobling Honours, which she bids them wear
Ambition fills with Charity the Mind,
And pants to be the Friend of all Mankind.

A full Belly makes a dull Brain.

The Muses starve in a Cook's Shop.

Spare and have is better than spend and crave.

Good-Will, like the Wind, floweth where it listeth.

SEPTEMBER.

Her Country all beneath one ambient Sky
Whosoe'er beholds you radiant Orb on high,
To whom one Sun impartial gives the Day,
To whom the Silver Moon her milder Ray,
Whom the same Water, Earth, and Air sustain,
O'er whom one Parent-King extends his Reign
Are her compatriots all, by her belov'd,
In Nature near, tho' far by Space remov'd ;
On common Earth, no Foreigner she knows ;
No Foe can find, or none but Virtue's Foes :

The Honey is sweet, but the Bee has a Sting.

In a corrupt Age, the putting the World in order would
breed Confusion ; then e'en mind your own Business.

OCTOBER.

Ready she stands her cheerful Aid to lend ;
To Want and Woe an undemanded Friend.
Nor thus advances others Bliss alone ;
But in the Way to theirs, still finds her own.
Their's is her own. What, should your Taper light
Ten Thousand, burns it to yourself less bright ?
" Men are ungrateful."——Be they so that dare !
Is that the Giver's or Receiver's Care ?

To serve the Publick faithfully, and at the same time
please it entirely is impracticable.

Proud Modern Learning despises the antient : School-
men are now laught at by school-boys.

NOVEMBER.

Oh ! blind to Joys, that from true Bounty flow ;
To think those e'er repent whose *Hearts* bestow !
Man to his Maker thus best Homage pays,
Thus peaceful walks thro' Virtues pleasing Ways

Her gentle Image on the Soul imprest,
Bids each tempestuous Passion leave the Breast
Hence with her livid Self-devouring Snakes
Pale Envy flies ; her quiver Slander breaks :
Thus falls (dire Scourge of a distracted Age !)
The Knave-led, one ey'd Monster, Party Rage.

Men often mistake themselves, seldom forget themselves.

The idle Man is the Devil's Hireling, whose Livery is Rags, whose Diet and Wages are Famine and Diseases.

DECEMBER.

Ambition jostles with her Friends no more ;
Nor thirsts Revenge to drink a Brothers Gore ;
Fiery Remorse no stinging Scorpions rears :
O'er trembling Guilt no falling Sword appears.
Hence Conscience, void of Blame, her Front erects,
Hence just Ambition boundless Splendors crown
And hence she calls Eternity her own.——

Rob not God, nor the Poor, lest thou ruin thyself ; The Eagle snatcht a Coal from the Altar, but it fired her Nest.

With bounteous cheer
Conclude the Year.

FINIS.